Also available from Pegasus Crime:

Plaid and Plagiarism
Scones and Scoundrels
Thistles and Thieves

BOOKS ONE, TWO, AND THREE OF
THE HIGHLAND BOOKSHOP MYSTERY SERIES

Heather *and* Homicide

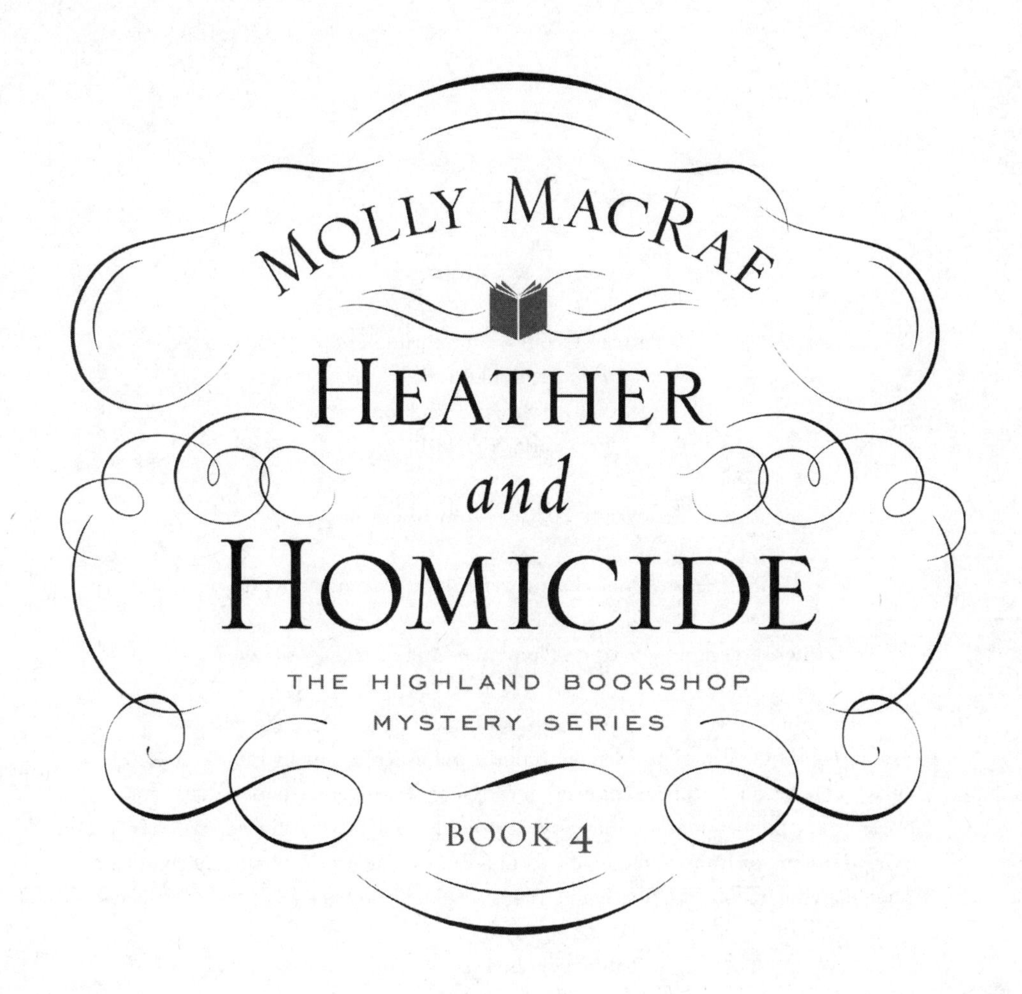

PEGASUS CRIME
NEW YORK LONDON

HEATHER AND HOMICIDE

Pegasus Crime is an imprint of
Pegasus Books, Ltd.
148 W. 37th Street, 13th Floor
New York, NY 10018

First Pegasus Books hardcover edition December 2020

Interior design by Sabrina Plomitallo-González, Pegasus Books

ISBN: 978-1-64313-584-7

10 9 8 7 6 5 4 3 2 1

Printed in the United States of America
Distributed by Simon & Schuster
www.pegasusbooks.com

For libraries and bookshops,
and the people who keep them open

HEATHER
and
HOMICIDE

1

In a lay-by on the B 8044, Heather Kilbride fought to refold the map. No way was there room in the front seat of a Ford Fiesta for a steering wheel, a driver, and the Ordnance Survey's *Road Map 2—Western Scotland and the Western Isles.* The thing was as tall as she was and twice as wide, and the more she flapped it around, the more it beat back like a malevolent paper bat. And this had been her idea—to forgo GPS and follow a route traced in faded pink highlighter on a map left in the glove box ten years ago. Brilliant.

She punched the map's midsection.

A punch isn't progress. Calum's voice in her head. The memory of it.

Heather closed her eyes. Dropped the map. Folded her hands over her heart. Waited through sixty beats. Sixty more.

When she opened her eyes, the map was draped over the steering wheel, as though it had always meant to be helpful, letting her focus on the sign staring at her through the windscreen: *Give your litter a lift—take it home.* Fair enough. She wouldn't stuff malign bits of paper out the window. Not today. She flattened the map across her lap, folded, flattened, repeated, no longer worried about crumples. A shame about the rip separating Lewis and Harris up there in the corner, but no matter. She was heading for the coast, not the isles—certainly not that island—and not that far north.

She pressed one more fold flat and judged her handiwork. A rumpled rhomboid. Gone for good were the smooth surface, compact shape, and crisp lines she'd optimistically unfolded that morning. And Calum was gone for good, too. Did that make the wad in her lap symbolic?

Heather flipped the map over her shoulder into the back seat and started the car. The Fiesta coughed and died. She counted ten heartbeats and blew her nose. "*Dinnae fash*, Cal. I've got this."

She started the car again and pulled onto the B 8044 heading west.

Half an hour later, a gull's-eye view opened before Heather—harbor, headland, lighthouse, sea—with rooftops and chimneys hugging the coast of blues and grays. A scene of purpose and prosperity, and even on a dreich day like this, a scene of comfort.

Her first view of Inversgail disappeared as the road wound down through the hills toward the town. Heather lowered her window and called a question to some sheep in a field. "Don't your bums get cold sitting on a wet hillside?"

She raised the window, but imagined she heard an old ewe bleating back, "You'll care when it's your own *bahookie* you're blathering about."

"Aye, too right," Heather said. That was why she'd packed carefully. And why she didn't trust that idyllic bird's-eye view of Inversgail. That illusion of ease and safety. She'd done her homework. She knew she'd find a decent library and local paper, pubs and coachloads of tourists, and, with luck, she'd also find her bedsit. Then there was the other wee matter—of murder.

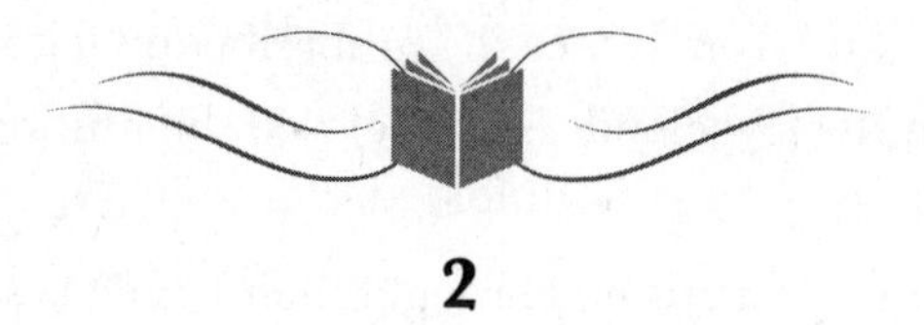

2

Janet Marsh stopped and popped her umbrella open when she reached the statue of Robert Louis Stevenson on Inversgail's High Street. Rain hadn't started in earnest, and might not, but Stevenson's spattered coat and a drip from his moustache gave her a sympathetic shiver despite her own warm and waterproof jacket. November on the west coast of Scotland was proving to be as gray and drippy as the statue.

Though not entirely dour. Business was good. She and her partners felt settled and more confident in their roles as owners of Yon Bonnie Books, with its Cakes and Tales tearoom and Bedtime Stories B&B above. And even on a dreich day, maybe especially on a dreich day, the shops and houses of Inversgail seemed settled and confident, too. On such a day, the deeper colors in the surrounding hills, harbor, and sea gave a sense of longevity. The Stevenson statue wasn't entirely dour, either; the clandestine group that called themselves the Knit Wits had brightened the statue with a pair of scarlet spats.

"Good to see you looking dapper as always, R.L.," Janet said to the statue.

Stevenson, pensive as always, didn't answer. But a car backfired, and Janet turned to see a rust-spotted Fiesta on its way up the hill toward the Inversgail Library and Archives, or perhaps the school.

She held her hand from under the umbrella and felt nothing measurable falling from the low clouds, so she closed the umbrella and climbed the hill to the library.

Years ago, she and Curtis had brought their young family to Inversgail for summers, and Janet had thought nothing of climbing these hills. This past spring, when she, Tallie, Christine, and Summer had bought the bookshop and packed up their Midwestern American lives to live here, it became a different story. Her over-sixty prairie-bred lungs hadn't been prepared, and she'd had to catch her breath halfway up most hills. Plus, her calves whined for rest stops. She'd been surprised that her youthful stamina hadn't lasted.

Of course, she'd also been surprised that her marriage hadn't lasted. Being an optimistic and determined problem solver, she'd tackled both surprises.

"A head-butt straight to his midsection," she'd said to Christine Robertson, her oldest friend. "He's soft. I'll take him down."

"He's a rat," Christine had said. "He's feeling guilty, too. Use it."

Janet had. The divorce settlement included a generous alimony and their house in Inversgail, paid in full. As for her lungs and calves, walking and riding her bike were solving that problem, and now when she passed through the library's automatic doors, she felt almost jaunty. The doors whispered shut behind her.

Immediately, the director's voice broke the library's peace with an announcement over the sound system. "Will the driver of the dark green Mini, number plate SB 48 PGW, please return to the carpark and move their car so that an illegally parked coach may exit? And will the driver of the illegally parked coach, whose number plate I also have, please refrain from parking illegally in future? Parking regs are clearly posted. *Ta* very much."

A man with clenched fists stomped past Janet and out the door. From his fuming mutters about calling the police on librarians and Mini drivers, she assumed he was the coach driver. From his language, he certainly had the bad manners of someone who would park illegally at a library.

Tutting under her breath, Janet went to wait her turn at the circulation desk, stopping at the "wait here" sign requesting privacy for patrons checking out their materials. Sharon Davis, the director, stood behind the desk, leveling the fierce eye of a hunting sea eagle at the departing back of the coach driver. Sharon still held the intercom microphone, and Janet imagined she waited for a reason to crank up the volume and use it to call the police herself.

The woman standing at the desk in front of Sharon cleared her throat.

"So sorry for the interruption." Sharon smiled at the woman and set the microphone down. "Tell me again. How may I help?"

"I asked about a short-term membership. Borrowing privileges for the few weeks I'll be here. Perhaps as long as a month."

As a retired librarian, Janet was interested in the answer to the woman's question. She didn't want to be obvious about listening to the conversation in front of her, though, so she glanced to the right along the counter, pretending to look for something. A brochure or a bookmark.

"It will require a bit of paperwork," Sharon said, "but yes, temporary privileges are available."

Bravo for progress and meeting the public's needs, Janet thought. She wondered what brought the woman to town at this time of year. Inversgail was a tourist town, but spring, summer, and fall were the more popular months. Janet took a step forward, the better to hear, and then felt too nosey. She repeated the pretense of looking for something, this time glancing left.

And there she found Ian Atkinson, propped on one elbow farther along the counter. Ian was a bestselling crime novelist and an expert at languid poses. Janet was sure he thought his presence graced anywhere he chose to lean. She also thought he didn't pretend as well as she did. He was clearly watching Sharon and the other woman, and just as clearly eavesdropping; he was jotting notes. After a moment, he stretched and sauntered over to stand in line behind Janet.

"Oh, hello," he said quietly, doing a double take. "I didn't see you."

Irritating man. Of course he'd seen her. His stretch, saunter, double take, and remark hadn't been any more convincing than if he'd sung "I'm a little teapot" and expected her to believe it. For a man with the talent to drape himself artfully in any doorway, and the gift and perseverance to write a dozen internationally acclaimed novels, he fumbled at many normal human interactions.

"Did your colleagues spring you for good behavior over the lunch hour?" he asked.

"Something like that." Janet gave a perfunctory smile. As annoying as she found him, Ian's Single Malt Mysteries were a boon to Yon Bonnie Books, so she worked hard to tamp down her personal opinion of him. It was a struggle, though, and she would be the first to admit she could tamp harder.

"With Sharon handling the desk, this might take longer than you like," Ian said. "She's a frightful gasbag."

"*Wheesht*, Ian," Janet hissed.

"You're sounding ver-r-r-ry Scottish these days," he said softly.

She didn't. It would take more than adopting vocabulary to disguise her Midwestern twang. Ian didn't sound Scottish, either. He came from Slough, outside London.

"She's arranging to have temporary borrowing privileges." He nodded toward the woman at the desk.

"I heard." *Drat.* Janet wished she hadn't let on she'd been listening, too.

But Ian didn't comment, so maybe he'd missed her slip. "Heather's in the area doing a spot of research," he said.

"You know her?" Janet asked.

"Heather? A lovely name, don't you think? I caught it as she introduced herself, but sadly, no, I don't know her. Mind you, I'd be happy to change that."

Janet narrowed an eye at him, stopping an incipient leer in its tracks.

They watched as the woman—Heather—dug through her bag for identification. Dressed in skinny jeans and a cargo jacket, she looked fit. She'd twisted her hair into a knot at the back of her head. Hair and jacket were a similar shade of brown—both slightly faded, but aging well. Janet thought she might be early to midforties.

"She asked directions to Sutherland Close," Ian continued quietly. "Near Maida's, it sounded like. I gather she's staying in one of those short-term lets. People are mad about them these days, though I don't know why. I prefer the reliability of a name-brand, five-star hotel when I tour. Oh, but I say." He put a disingenuous hand to his forehead. "I've just insulted your own wee B&B, haven't I? So sorry. And sorry, too, that Heather apparently doesn't have the good taste to book one of your rooms."

"We might be full up, Ian," Janet said. "We often are." They just as often weren't. "Besides, we'd be a bit dear for a month's stay. But that's the wonderful thing about a tourist town, isn't it? There are accommodations for all budgets and plenty to choose from."

Janet wondered if the chance to offer his mock sympathy hadn't been Ian's whole reason for coming to stand in line behind her. But if he chose to slither low, she would raise her chin and go high.

Then she lost a bit of altitude. "Don't you believe in personal space, Ian? For Heaven's sake, how long were you listening to catch those details? *Why* were you listening?"

"Occupational hazard," he said, flipping hair from his forehead. His hair length and habit of flipping went along with his languid poses.

"You've used that excuse before. And it really is *no* excuse."

"A reason more than an excuse," Ian said, "And Sharon doesn't mind."

"You're kidding. She knows you eavesdrop and she lets you?"

Ian cocked his head with interest. "That question had no hint of shock, Janet. You *aren't* shocked. You're interested. You're looking for tips."

"Tips? What are you talking about?"

"Tips for better detecting. That sounds like the subtitle for an Alexander McCall Smith novel."

Janet loved McCall Smith and she loathed the smug look on Ian's face. But not as much as she disliked his next suggestion.

"I'm always happy to spread my ways and wisdom, Janet. Call me anytime. Better yet, wander over and I'll put the kettle on."

Janet turned back toward the counter so he wouldn't catch her eyes rolling. At some point after she and Curtis had divorced and stopped coming to Inversgail, Ian had arrived in town and bought the house next to theirs. She was a firm believer in being a good neighbor, but having Ian next door made it that much harder to tamp her opinion of him. When he—too often—looked over the hedge dividing their backyards and offered gardening advice, she found herself "tamping" weeds with amazing energy.

Sharon the librarian looked ready for a good gossip. Elbows on the counter, temporary card apparently issued, she reminded Janet of a bartender on a sleepy afternoon. Except that Ian had been right when he'd guessed this was Janet's lunch hour, and it was ticking away. In case Sharon really was passing the time of day instead of passing along information, Janet took two steps past the "wait here" sign to give her a visual nudge.

"Tip number one—quiet shoes and two steps closer than that," Ian whispered in Janet's ear.

Janet did move two steps closer. *To get away from an irritating pest*, she told herself, *not because I'm taking tips on eavesdropping from one*. On the other hand, she *could* hear better.

"Do you ken a lawyer named William Clark?" the woman named Heather asked.

Janet knew that name. She'd heard it at the bookshop several weeks earlier, after a memorial bike ride honoring Dr. Malcolm Murray, his brother Gerald, and Lachlann Maclennan, all recently deceased. The people speaking Clark's name had exchanged indecipherable looks, and when asked about those looks, had immediately clammed up and left the bookshop. Ian hadn't been there, but his name had come up, too.

She tried, now, to get his attention. She shouldn't have bothered. He was taking notes again.

"Clark?" Sharon said. "It's a common enough name."

"They can't all be lawyers," Heather said. "I have an appointment with this one."

"Here?" Sharon asked. "Now?"

"No, no." Heather took a half-step back. "I just wondered if you know him and ken what he's like. I just thought . . . it's a small town, aye?"

"Not as small as all that," Sharon said.

"Aye, sorry."

"An easy mistake to make. The town looks smaller than it is." For the first time, Sharon looked at the line waiting for her. "So, then. Welcome to Inversgail. Is there anything else I can help you with before you go?"

"A lunch recommendation? Nothing fancy."

Sharon smiled at Janet. "Cakes and Tales. It's a tearoom adjoining Yon Bonnie Books down the other end of the High Street."

"A tearoom?"

Janet heard the wrinkled nose in Heather's question.

"Aye. They do lovely wee sandwiches," Sharon said. "If you're doing research, it's good to know the location of the best bookshop in town, as well as an accommodating library."

"Sounds a bit twee. Is there something less touristy? Anything near the *Inversgail Guardian*'s office?"

"You'll want Nev's, then. Right next door to the *Guardian*. There's no sign and it's as far from twee as haggis from Hogmanay."

"Perfect."

Heather thanked Sharon for her help, and Janet moved up to the desk to collect the book she'd reserved. Sharon went to get it—an autobiography of Barbara Pym in diaries and letters—and Janet wondered if Ian was now taking notes about *her*. What he lacked in subtlety he didn't make up for in charm. She turned to give him a quelling eye, whether he deserved it or not. But Ian was gone and another man stood behind her.

Ian's probably gone to Nev's, Janet thought. *Watch out, Heather.*

"There you are," Sharon said, handing Janet her book. "I'm sorry that last woman didn't like the sound of your tearoom. We can't please them all, can we?"

"We can't. I'm curious about that saying, though—as far from twee as haggis from Hogmanay. It's one I haven't heard. Is it common?"

"Och no, and it hardly makes sense, does it? That's just me having a bit of fun. But if it shows up in her next book, we'll know where she got it. You might like to get some of her books in for the shop. Heather Kilbride is her name. She says she's a true-crime writer here to research the Murray Murder Case. I assume all three words are capitalized when she sees them in her mind; she sounded very earnest. I didn't like to tell her that dragging all that out in the open again, so soon, seems unnecessary."

"Good heavens, yes, and painful for so many."

Angry honking came from the carpark, waning and ebbing as the library doors opened and closed.

"That wee man will have a heart attack if he doesn't learn to be patient," Sharon said. She didn't seem overly concerned for his health.

"The Mini driver hasn't shown up yet?" Janet asked. "The wee man will have a heart attack *and* a stroke."

"He'll be foaming at the mouth by the time Constable Hobbs arrives," Sharon agreed. "I'm sure he made good on his threat to call the police. His kind do. And much good it will do him; the Mini driver will likely turn up any moment." Sharon didn't seem concerned about police arriving, either, whether fast or slow. In fact, she winked at Janet.

The wink jarred something loose from the corner of Janet's mind where she shoved anything to do with Ian Atkinson. "Did Ian hear that she's a writer? Does he know what she's working on?"

"It's so hard to know with Ian. Now, if you don't mind, Janet." Sharon nodded toward the line behind her. "Other people are waiting."

Janet left the library worried about what Heather Kilbride's research might stir up. The memorial bike ride had brought some sense of closure to the tragic deaths of the three men, but it couldn't have laid all the misery to rest so soon. Grief and mourning would go on for months, if not years. Or forever.

Ahead of Janet, the coach driver, with fists looking like bludgeons, breathed fire next to a green Mini.

"Sorry," a voice came from behind her. She'd stopped in the middle of the footpath, and a man exiting the library brushed past her—the man who'd been behind her at the checkout desk.

She started to call after him to apologize, but stopped when she saw him, keys in hand, casually stroll toward the coach driver and the Mini. With a minimal glance for the driver, he unlocked the Mini, got in, and locked the door.

The nearly molten coach driver boiled over. Janet caught some of his words—she was sure she heard *beat*, *pulp*, and *bare hands* several times—but much of what he spewed went past her in a blur of gutturals and rolled *R*s. He stood in front of the Mini, arms raised and roaring. The man in the Mini calmly started the engine.

"He's like the Hulk," a man standing near Janet said. "A Glaswegian Hulk. If he really wanted to do damage, he could. It's possible he has previous experience with the penalties for grievous bodily harm."

"Oh, dear," said the woman next to him. "And here come the *weans* from the Primary. It's their day to visit with the story lady."

Janet recognized the woman. Agnes Black was an infrequent customer at Yon Bonnie Books.

"This is more exciting than anything they'll hear from the story lady," the man said.

The Mini driver let the car slowly roll forward half a foot. The coach driver roared and held his ground. Janet took out her phone.

"Take a video," Agnes said. "It'll go viral."

"I'm calling Constable Hobbs," Janet said.

"The coach driver already did," said Agnes. "I wonder what's taking him so long? Och, well. That's Norman, then, isn't it?"

"He does a fine job, our Norman," said the man. "Here he comes now."

Constable Norman Hobbs stepped from his vehicle and surveyed the scene before him. Then he pointed his nose and peaked cap at the coach driver and marched forward. He said nothing as he covered the distance between them, but the ring of his constabulary boots might as well have barked, "What's all this, then?" When he reached the coach driver, he pointed his right index finger at him. Then he pointed to the sidewalk at the edge of the carpark, making it clear he expected the coach driver to move in that direction. The coach driver did and Hobbs followed.

The Mini driver, his path now clear, drove away.

Hobbs spoke quietly but at no great length to the coach driver. A few choice words from the coach driver reached Janet's ears, but then he appeared to think better of commenting and remained silent. She heard Hobbs caution him not to leave his coach in the library carpark in the future and to mind all other local parking regulations. Janet and the others watched the subdued driver maneuver the coach out of the tight carpark. She thought Hobbs looked satisfied with the outcome and not at all surprised that the Mini was already gone.

"Didn't you want to speak to the Mini driver?" she asked Hobbs. "He wasn't parked legally, either, was he?"

"The Mini driver was doing his civic duty by calling attention to rogue coach drivers," the man beside Agnes said. "A rebel with a carpark cause."

"A calm one with nerves of steel," Janet said. "He didn't look any more ruffled by that ruffian than you did, Norman."

"A *stramash* is all in a day's work, eh, Constable?" said the man. "It calls for an even temperament. That's a plus in both professions."

"Norman's and the Mini driver's?" Janet asked. "Do you know him?" Then she realized that Sharon knew him, too. Sharon hadn't winked at *her.* She'd winked at the Mini driver standing behind her, after telling Janet he'd turn up any minute.

"I can't say I know the chap," the man said, "but I can put a name to him. A lawyer. William Clark." He turned to Agnes. "Can I give you a lift, Nessy?"

Agnes waved goodbye to Janet.

Janet, puzzled, didn't notice. *What is it about William Clark? One minute Sharon won't acknowledge knowing the man, and the next minute she's winking at him. Mention his name and—hey, presto—normal people turn peculiar.* He's *peculiar.*

"Norman," Janet said, "I have questions for you."

But he'd already started back to his vehicle.

"Norman?" Janet rushed to catch up, and then to get in front of him to try pinning him with her eyes. It wasn't an easy thing to do. Pinning eyes a foot above her own required an acute angle in her neck. "Norman, was that Mini driver the same William Clark that you, James Haviland, and Rab were so mysterious about a few weeks back? At the bookshop, after the memorial ride, James said that he, Ian, and a lawyer named William Clark had been named to oversee the trust Gerald Murray set up in his will. Don't pretend you don't know what I'm talking about."

"I wouldn't dream of it, Mrs. Marsh, and I'm happy to answer your question."

"Good, because I have a few more."

Hobbs opened his car door. Janet held it as he climbed in. He closed the door and lowered his window. "William Clark, Mrs. Marsh," he said as he started the engine.

"Yes?"

"William"—he shrugged one shoulder—"and Clark"—he shrugged the other—"they're very common names." He raised his window and drove away.

Janet fumed over cagey constables on her way back to Yon Bonnie Books. Fumed quietly, and not as colorfully as the coach driver, but with feeling. When she came to the Stevenson statue, she felt like shaking her fist, but didn't. R. L. didn't deserve it. Neither did Norman, she knew.

She stopped beside the statue and thought about that. Why *should* Norman tell her anything about William Clark? Norman did his job well. He was trustworthy—ninety-nine percent of the time—and he didn't gossip. And why did she care about William Clark, anyway? Who or what he was or did was none of her business. *Except, tell me there's a secret and I'll tell you no lie; I* will *want to know it.* Janet and the statue stood side by side staring across the harbor toward the Inversgail Light.

Norman wasn't the only one being careful about William Clark, though. There was James and Rab. And now Sharon, who'd played the cagey game with Heather. Heather, who was digging into the Murray murders and had an appointment with William Clark. *Drat, I meant to ask Norman if he knew about Heather and her project.* But if William Clark kept appointments with researchers, then he wasn't a recluse, and that meant other people would know him and know about him. Other people who were less guarded or circumspect. Ian, for instance. *But it would be so much easier and less annoying if Norman would just come clean.*

By now, her lunch hour was almost eaten up. Before rushing on her way, Janet glanced at the statue's face. She got the feeling Stevenson looked more troubled now, and wondered if that was an omen. Then she wondered when she'd become so superstitious. Besides, the sky was beginning to clear, and that was always a good sign. She put her head back, breathed in the sea air, and breathed out, shutting her eyes and opening them again in time to see three seagulls directly above.

An elderly woman rolled her shopping trolley to a stop beside Janet. "A warning," she said. "If you believe in such."

"What's a warning?" Janet asked.

"Three gulls flying together overhead." The woman pointed at the birds as they flapped away over the rooftops. "A warning of death, soon to come."

3

Yon Bonnie Books had only changed hands twice since Colonel Stuart Farquhar opened it in 1919. First, when the Farquhar family sold the business after eighty-three years, and then when Janet, her daughter, Tallie, and their friends Christine Robertson and Summer Jacobs bought it. Farquhar, a colonel in the Black Watch during the Great War, had come home to Inversgail with a need to heal by surrounding himself with books. He'd counted himself lucky that this cure was also profitable.

The bookshop and its new sister businesses occupied a two-story, late-18th-century granite block building. Many of the businesses on Inversgail's High Street benefited from the same construction. The picturesque facades attracted photographers and other tourists from around the world, and the sturdy frameworks had allowed for useful renovations and updates over the years. Yon Bonnie Books, Cakes and Tales Tearoom, and Bedtime Stories B&B were wired and wireless enough to suit any need. The plumbing was modern, too.

Janet returned to the shop still somewhat flustered by the elderly woman's warning, but no longer fuming at Norman Hobbs. She shared the late Colonel Farquhar's belief in the remedy of books.

After helping a customer decide to buy two books in the Porridge the Tartan Cat series rather than choose between them, she felt more herself. Then, during a lull, she told Tallie about the trip to the library, and worked herself up again. Tallie, good daughter that she was, told her mother she'd be right back. She disappeared down an aisle, between tall bookshelves, in the direction of the tearoom.

"There," Tallie said a few minutes later. She set a teapot and a plate of tea sandwiches on the sales counter. "You might be hardly fuming and only slightly flustered, but you're completely famished. I know the signs and they have nothing to do with superstition."

"I don't believe the seagull warning, though," Janet said. "Not for a minute and no more than I believed her story that a cat washing its ears predicts rain. I'm sure it's the same woman. I wonder who she is."

"Rab might know her," Tallie said. "He might be related. We should hire her and they can take turns reading tea leaves for the day-trippers."

"Where is Rab?" Janet set her teacup down.

"It's Monday. That means we don't know where he is."

"Do we know where he is any other day?"

"Only when he's here," Tallie said.

Rab MacGregor was a sandy-haired, loose-limbed man who spent part of each day sitting on the harbor wall with his Cairn Terrier, Ranger, and various harbor cats. He also apparently worked part-time for them in the bookshop and the tearoom. The arrangement and his hours had never been formalized. That wasn't for lack of trying on Janet's part, but Rab showed up often enough and at critical moments, and they'd finally left it at that. Ranger showed up when Rab did, and spent his time being photogenic while napping in a chair near the shop's fireplace. Rab occasionally read tea leaves, to the delight of pensioners on day trips. More recently, he'd been making Chinese thread books—*zhen xian bao*—for the bookshop to sell. These were elegant, complicated, folded paper books based on patterns from Chinese folk art.

"I'll tell you what else I don't believe," Janet said. "Not for even *less* than a minute."

"What are you disbelieving so thoroughly?" Christine asked, sweeping down the aisle from the tearoom. The way Christine moved, through a room and through life, always bolstered Janet's spirits.

Christine was the one native Scot among the four partners. She'd grown up in Inversgail, and then emigrated to the States with her husband, Tony. They'd landed at the University of Illinois, where they'd met Janet and Curtis and become lifelong friends. After Tony died, Christine welcomed the bookshop venture as a way to pull herself back together. It also came at the right time for her to give her aging parents the help they needed and the chance to stay in their own house. She admired them, complained about them, and doted on them.

"Tallie made your situation sound dire, so I thought you could probably use a fresh pot," Christine said, and set the pot on the counter. "I need to get back. We're swamped with tea-swillers, but first I want to hear what's so preposterous that even you don't believe it."

"There are plenty of things I don't believe," Janet said.

"That, in itself, is not believable," Christine said. "You're the rosy-eyed one of our group, whereas I like to disbelieve two or three things every day before breakfast."

"That's not how the quotation goes," Tallie said.

"I don't believe it," said Christine. "There, see? That's how it works. I do it all the time."

"I can tell you two things I don't believe right off the bat," Janet said.

"I only have time for one. Make it the shortest."

"You're absurd," Janet said, "so I'll tell you the most absurd. Three seagulls flying overhead are a warning of death to come." Janet expected Christine to sputter a laugh or call her a cheat for choosing something too obvious. "Christine? What's wrong?"

"It's nothing. I don't believe you knew." Christine's smile flickered and went out.

"Knew what?"

"About the seagulls. Mum believes that, and the frailer she gets, the more she worries over signs of death. I'd best get back."

"Oh, Christine, I'm sorry. I wasn't laughing at your mum."

"I didn't think you were. It's her frailty and her worries that get to me." Christine waved over her shoulder and was gone.

Tallie refilled Janet's teacup and handed it to her. "You know who might know something about William Clark? Christine. She didn't hear that conversation after the memorial ride. She was in the tearoom, and until today we haven't thought of him again."

"There are plenty of people who *must* know him," Janet said. "But you're right. Christine might, or her mum and dad. This probably isn't the time to ask, though. She really does worry."

"It might get her mind off her mum and the seagulls."

"But first she needs time to remember that *she* doesn't believe the seagulls."

❧

The next morning dawned less than bright, but far from dreich, so Janet dressed for a quick bike ride before work. She and Tallie shared the stone cottage on Argyll Terrace where they'd spent so many summers. Built of granite, like the bookshop, the house had four rooms down and two more cozied up under the eaves. As Janet sat at the top of the stairs, tying her shoes, Tallie passed her on the way to the bathroom.

"You know, Mom, there is another explanation for Norman's and Sharon's seemingly odd behavior yesterday."

"Seemingly? It wasn't my imagination, excellent though it is."

"It is excellent, and so are your critical thinking skills. Hear me out."

"My skills and imagination are all ears. Lay it on them."

Janet had been proud of her daughter when she graduated from law school, joined a prestigious firm, and then furthered her career by teaching contract law. She'd been even more proud when Tallie admitted, twenty years on, that she'd burned out and wanted to do something about it. They had both been ecstatic when Tallie found the real estate listing for Yon Bonnie Books.

"We know two police officers named Norman," Tallie said. "What are the odds of that?"

"Odd odds, definitely. So what?"

The other Norman was Inspector Reddick, whom they'd last seen during the investigation into the Murray murders.

"So *our* Norman and Sharon might be right. William Clark might be a common name, in which case there could easily be two William Clarks, even two who are lawyers. The Mini driver might not have been our William Clark."

"Christine would be so proud of me, dear." Janet started down the stairs. "I haven't had my breakfast and I find that explanation absolutely, utterly, and preposterously unbelievable."

Some mornings Janet rode with two or three other women. The group met at the Stevenson statue almost every morning that rain wasn't bucketing down. Janet's overall goal was to join them in the spring for the next Haggis Half Hundred—a fifty-mile ride through the hills above Inversgail. The reward for going the distance was a plate of tatties, neeps, and haggis at the finish. With every labored breath up the steepest hills, Janet pictured herself enjoying every mouthful.

Her shorter goal was to spend time alone. To that end, she went solo most mornings, riding at her own pace and with her own thoughts. She satisfied Tallie by wearing a helmet and making certain she'd charged her phone. She took binoculars along to satisfy herself, hoping someday she'd spot something extraordinary—a golden eagle or one of the rare Scottish wildcats. This morning she only saw two buzzards, gulls (which she refused to count), and unlimited sheep.

She liked sheep. Christine was afraid of them. But Janet would never tease her about it, no more than Christine teased Janet about her fear of heights. Friends didn't. They protected each other.

Janet thought about protection as she puffed up the next long hill. The instinct to provide it. The need to escape from under it when it threatened to smother. When her thoughts turned to threats, she almost missed a pair of blackface lambs having a mock battle with their baby horns. How would Heather Kilbride's murder research threaten the people who'd just been through so much?

Janet let her mantra of *pedal, pedal, pedal, ohhh my* take over until the next downward slope, and then she was almost to the Beaton Bridge. *Pedal, pedal, pedal, ohhh my*, and then she'd reached the middle of that span. She raised her hands in victory. *Unbeaten by the ride to the Beaton Bridge.*

She was still a bit winded, but not like the first time she'd come this far. That awful day, only the side of the bridge had kept her from collapsing, and when she'd looked below the bridge, along the burn, she'd seen Malcolm Murray's damaged bike, and then Malcolm, half-hidden by the rocks, lying dead in the thistles . . .

Janet blinked. She blinked again and rubbed her eyes. She must be seeing things. Hallucinating. Because it couldn't be . . .

She fumbled for her binoculars, brought them to her eyes, and was hit by a nauseating wave of déjà vu. A bicycle, an arm, a hand in the water. How could it be?

She left her bike, as she had that other awful day. There was still no clear path down the terrible slope, but she could do this again. She lost sight of the bicycle and the arm, the catastrophe now sheltered from her view by rocks the size of Highland cattle. As she picked her way down toward the burn, she called Christine.

"Have you phoned the police?" Christine asked. "Janet, answer me. I need to know you're all right. Have you called 9-9-9?"

"No. I . . . no."

"Why not? You're not thinking clearly, Janet."

"Yes I am. I'll call them when you've talked me down from hysteria. This way I'm not alone when I get there."

"Hold on, then. I'll get Dad to phone them. But you stay with me, do you hear?"

Janet nodded, then said yes. She listened to Christine give instructions to her father, pictured his kind face turn serious and his shaky finger press the three nines for the police emergency number.

"Do you have any idea who it is?" Christine asked.

Janet had stopped her careful descent while Christine talked to her father. Christine's voice in her ear jarred her back to movement. "I only saw the arm. The same way I found Malcolm. Christine, how could this happen again? It *can't* be happening again."

"I'm here. Hold it together."

"I will. I'm almost there. There's more water and the rocks are tricky, but I can see—" She stopped again. "I can see her. Facedown, but, yes, a woman. Jeans, cargo jacket. Oh my God, Christine, it's her. It's *her.*"

"*Who,* Janet?" Christine demanded. "Talk to me. Dad's on the phone with the police dispatcher. Start babbling if that helps, but talk to me."

Janet couldn't babble. She couldn't make herself move or go close enough to feel for a pulse. Feel a wrist that would be so cold. She hadn't become paralyzed like this last time. *What is* wrong *with me?*

"Janet!"

"Yes. I'm here. It's Heather Kilbride, Christine, a researcher, a true-crime writer. She only arrived yesterday. I saw her at the library. I need to get closer. The bloody rocks—no! No, I didn't mean that literally. There's no blood, but . . . oh my word."

"Yes, Janet, words. Use them."

"It's a dummy, Christine. It isn't a body. It's a big bloody *rag doll* dressed in Heather's clothes."

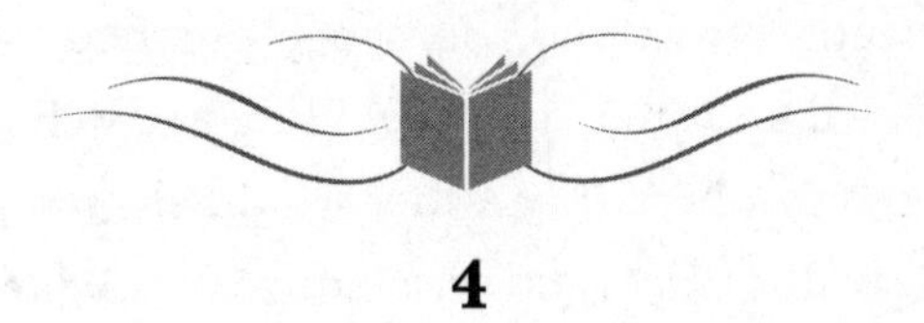

4

Janet peered closer. "She was wearing jeans and this jacket at the library yesterday. What kind of sick—tell your dad to call off the emergency. Apologize for me, too. To him and them. They'll think I'm a stupid, bloody—"

"No they won't," Christine said. "They'll think Dad is. But at this point, you might want to calm down a bit."

"I will when I'm good and ready. After I kick something."

"Get back on your bike. Go home and swear in the shower. It's better than singing and not as painful as kicking."

"I will—no. Not yet. I'll wait to see if Norman shows up. And if he doesn't, I'll call him myself. I want him to see this."

"Don't be long," Christine said. "See you at the shop."

"See you." Janet put her phone away. She changed her mind and took it out again, and now she did go close enough to feel for the "victim's" pulse—or to kick the stuffing out of her—and she started taking pictures.

"Hello," a high, light voice called from a distance. "What are you doing?"

Janet straightened and tried to see who'd hailed her and from where. She didn't want to answer before knowing whom she might offend by the candid words she'd like to use.

"Across the burn," the voice called. "Up the rise."

Janet looked and then stared. Someone perched part way up the opposite bank waved an arm like a signal flag to catch her attention. A *numpty* if she ever saw one. Only a fool would sit in a place like that. A female numpty by the voice, and on a bank so steep Janet would rather jump from a plane than set foot anywhere near it. At least she'd have a parachute if she jumped from a plane.

Then Janet saw a flash of reflection. Binoculars. The numpty must be a birder, a nutcase looking for a nuthatch. But the binoculars were a good idea. She could use her own to get a look at the nutcase. That way she'd know to cross the street if she ever saw her coming. Janet raised her binoculars, and as she worked to get them focused, the woman called again.

"I'm coming down. I'll come across."

"Oh good Lord," Janet muttered. She couldn't bear to watch and turned her back, not daring to look again until she *hadn't* heard a scream and a tumbling, rolling plummet. What she finally heard was the splish-splashing of footsteps crossing the burn. When she did look, Heather, in dripping wellies, stood on the bank smiling at her.

Janet kept her first, blistering thoughts to herself. She wasn't sure about trusting her second, third, or possibly fourth thoughts, either. Not until she knew what was going on and why.

She had to say something, though, and commenting on the measurable and mundane seemed safe. She looked at the whisky-colored water chuckling along behind Heather, and then pointed at her wellies. "The water looks much deeper."

"There's a natural set of stepping stones, just here," Heather said. "Or I suppose someone arranged them. I wonder who and how long ago? Hi, I'm Heather. Heather Kilbride. I see you've found my evil twin."

Something felt evil, but blaming the dummy didn't seem fair. Janet looked between the two. They were close twins, but not identical—cargo jackets, skinny jeans, and hair knotted at their napes, but their taste diverged when it came to footwear. The dummy wore trainers.

Another difference—unlike the jacket Janet had seen at the library, the one Heather wore now didn't match the brown of her hair as closely. It looked older, more faded, and frayed at the cuffs. Not to mention at least two sizes too big.

"Your twin's jacket probably fits you better," she said.

"This is my brother's." Heather looked down at herself, smoothing her hands over the jacket. Then she let the too-long sleeves fall down over her hands and wrapped her arms around herself. "I'm not padded out with wool like a sheep, and that hillside's cold and damp. So, what *are* you doing here? You appeared out of nowhere. Gave me quite a fright."

"Gave *you* a fright?" Janet said, giving in to first thoughts this time. "If you think 'appearing out of nowhere' is a fright, what do you think this horrible display of yours is? Besides being bloody gruesome and inappropriate? Did the possibility that you'd give someone a heart attack from seeing this occur to you? Or trigger traumatic flashbacks? Did you think at all? What kind of bloody game are you playing?"

Heather backed away, shrinking farther into her brother's jacket. "It's no game. That's not how this is meant. It's for myself."

"For you?" Janet said. "What about anyone who came along and saw this?"

"Who? No one going past in a car would see. They'd have to stop. There haven't been many cars along the road since I've been here and not one stopped."

"Hill walkers, then. Bicyclists."

"Look, I'm sorry, but you've misunderstood," Heather said, sounding placatory. "I've not set out to hurt anyone. This is for me, so I can see—"

"You recreated the death of a respected member of the community, of a doctor beloved by his patients. What do you need to *see* if you can't see how that *would* hurt?"

Heather put her hands up as though to fend off another onslaught of anger. The too-long jacket sleeves flapped beyond the ends of her fingertips, though, making the gesture less protective than pathetic. "I'm sorry.

I am so sorry. It honestly was not meant to hurt anyone." She wiped her nose on a sleeve and looked as though she'd like to bolt back across the burn or let the water swallow her.

Now I'm *a numpty,* Janet thought, *and I've reduced* this *tone-deaf numpty to a blubbering bampot.* Janet felt like kicking something again. Starting with herself.

And where was Norman Hobbs? When she'd stood on the bridge, the rocks had blocked her view of all but the dummy's forearm and its hand in the water. They performed their act of concealment from this side, too. It might be nice to hear a pair of constabulary boots crushing dry bracken and thistles as they came down the bank. But she didn't, and this was no longer a "situation." Janet could smooth it over and be on her way.

Heather cut into Janet's thoughts. "You're American."

"Loud and crass?"

Heather shook her head.

"I think I probably was. I usually try not to be."

"On the scale of loud and crass, you were barely a blip. You did better on the scale of angry and hurt. May I ask how you knew Dr. Murray?"

"I didn't. Friends of mine did. They're the ones you'd hurt with this."

"I'm glad your friends didn't come along with you, then," Heather said with a smile as unsteady as a fledgling. It wobbled and didn't fly far. "I would like a chance to explain what I'm doing. If you've a mind to listen."

Janet checked the time. She'd have to pedal fast, but she could still make it home for a shower before she needed to be at the shop. "Go ahead."

"It's my own method." The smile fluttered again.

"Method for doing what?"

"Research. I'm looking into the Murray case. Writing a book. I'm immersing myself in the facts of the crime, but also in the *scene* of the crime, through a recreation of it. I looked at the scene, first from Malcolm Murray's perspective, and then explored it from other points of view. *Literally* other points of view. Right here, close up. The road and the bridge and the wider view all come into it, as well. The method might be unconventional, but it works for me."

"And you must be part mountain goat," Janet said.

"It's not as difficult to climb up there as it looks, and the view is gorgeous. Of the town and the sea, I mean, not the murder scene. Would you like to see?"

"Not just now." Janet suppressed a shudder. The view was just as gorgeous from the safety of her bike on a paved surface.

"I took photos of the murder scene from the bridge, but the rocks are a limiting factor. The wee bit they let you see makes it hard to feel anything more than a tickle of unease. You can't even call it dread, and there isn't much emotional heft in something so vague. So, I'm curious now. With all the wide world to look at from the bridge, what caught your eye? How did you spot my victim?"

"Lucky, I guess."

"*Un*lucky. I am sorry."

Janet could have told Heather she was mistaken; that it wasn't hard to feel more than a tickle of unease from the wee bit the rocks let her see while she'd stood on the bridge. It hadn't been hard the first time, when she'd found Malcolm Murray, and it had been even easier today. Janet found it mildly interesting that Heather didn't seem to know she'd been the one to find Malcolm. Or maybe she did know that a woman named Janet Marsh had found Malcolm, but Janet hadn't reciprocated when Heather introduced herself. She'd been too focused on "something evil."

"Why the evil twin?" Janet nudged the dummy with her toe. "Why not make it look more like Dr. Murray?"

"I never met him, and I don't have any particular feelings about him. Not yet, anyway. That's partly what my method is about. As I gather facts and feelings, I'm developing a connection to Malcolm Murray. But to make this stage of my research more personal, I modeled the dummy on myself. She's a bit of a *tattie-bogle*, isn't she? But I need her for the emotional punch, for the visceral reaction people look for in my writing. A dummy of a random old man wouldn't do anything for me, and down the road, that lack of punch won't do anything for my readers."

"Random old man," Janet said. "What a sad epitaph."

"He wasn't random to the folk who knew and loved him, I do know that, and it's why I feel so awful that you stumbled across this. I'll know it better, too, and know *him* better, as my research goes along. I've made a good start, mind. I stopped by the *Inversgail Guardian* yesterday and spoke with the managing editor, James Haviland. He seemed interested when I told him I'm coming at the case from another angle and suggested we share information."

"The case is solved. What other angle is there?"

"I won't try to dispute the official record," Heather said. "I'll be looking more for the psychological insights that people love to read, and I hope to offer more answers. There's a deeper core to a crime like this. I'll be talking to other people, too, as I look for ways to help readers understand the crime. Talking to the local police—Constable Hobbs, is it? And a lawyer named William Clark."

"What's his connection to the case?"

"I haven't spoken to him yet."

"But you've heard that he has a connection?"

"I've either heard or read his name."

Janet nodded as though that answered her question. "How long does research for a book like this take? Tracking down people for interviews, getting access to records. Keeping your own records straight, too, I should think. What else?"

Heather gave a noncommittal "Mm," and then asked, "Are you superstitious?"

"What? No, not really." Then, hoping her tone left no room for doubt, Janet said, "No. I'm not."

"I am," Heather said. "It's not something I'm proud of, nor do I understand why, but I don't seem to be able to help it. That's by way of saying, if you don't mind, I'd rather not go into details any more than I already have. So I don't jinx anything."

"No worries." *Irritating as I find that,* Janet thought. "You're shivering. How long are you staying out here?"

"I'll be fine once I'm moving again. I want to walk further down the burn and reflect on the spiritual implications of the water after it's washed over the victim's hand."

"Did you come out here on the bike?"

"Aye. The twin's a contortionist and fits in the paniers."

"Well, make sure you get something warm inside you when you're finished. There's a tearoom on the High Street. Cakes and Tales. A bit twee, some say, but the scones are always fresh and the tea is always hot."

Janet watched as Heather waved and walked away down the burn. She'd spent more time with Heather than she should have, and now she'd have to skip her shower or apologize to Tallie and the rest for being late. But a warm shower sounded like a lifesaver.

"Bloody unconventional research methods," she complained as she made her own way back around the rocks. Then, as she tripped over a fist-sized rock, "*Bloody* tattie-bogles."

"All right there, Mrs. Marsh?"

"Good Lord, Norman." *Bloody lurking constables.* "Yes, thank you. My toe is fine and my heart didn't stop. What's a tattie-bogle?"

"Meant to scare the crows."

"Well, then, I'm an old crow, because that woman's tattie-bogle scared the caw out of me. I was sure we'd had another tragedy."

"Is that all it was? May I borrow your binoculars?"

Janet took the binoculars from around her neck and passed them over. He focused them on the steep slope.

"Swing to the left a tad if you want to see where she was sitting," Janet said.

"I don't. There's been a possible wildcat sighting in the area and I thought maybe . . ."

"How did you see something the size of a housecat up there with your naked eye?"

"Wishful thinking, no doubt. If I saw anything, it's long gone."

"*Long* gone? How long have you been standing here?"

Hobbs handed back the binoculars. "I arrived in the midst of your conversation with Ms. Kilbride. Easy enough to hear, and I caught the gist."

"Did you hear her mention William Clark? Is that why you didn't join us?"

"Not at all, Mrs. Marsh," Hobbs said with dignified huff.

"But don't you want to speak with her?"

"If she doesn't leave litter behind when she goes, then she's done nothing illegal. She knows how to reach me, if need arises. Are you coming?" He started back up toward the road.

Janet followed, muttering, "If need arises." Louder, she said, "*She* wants to speak to *you*. You must have heard her say that. I think you don't *want* to talk to her."

"No more than you wanted her to know about your role in the Murray case, as she calls it."

"Well, and I didn't. She also doesn't know my connection to the tearoom. Did you hear how cleverly I tested that?"

"Very clever, but why not tell her?"

"She didn't ask my name and I didn't see any reason to tell her."

"That doesn't sound like your usual open and friendly self, Mrs. Marsh. Nor does it sound like the clear-thinking owner of the local bookshop after meeting a noted true-crime writer."

"*Is* she noted?" Janet asked. "Do you know her books?"

"I don't. That doesn't tell you whether she's noted or not, mind. I've never fancied true crime. With your book expertise, you're better equipped to find that out than I am."

"If I look into it, would you like to know what I find out?"

"That'd be brilliant."

"If you had these questions and ideas running through your head, you really should have joined us on the other side of the rocks, Norman."

"From what I heard, you held your own well enough. Would you like a lift? I can pop your bike into the back."

"No, thank you. I *can*, I *do*, and I *will continue* to hold my own, *perfectly* well."

"I've seen ample evidence of that, Mrs. Marsh. May I share one more idea with you before you go?"

"Of course. And I'm sorry if I sounded testy just now. What's your idea?"

"I wonder if your true-crime writer didn't ask your name, because she already knows it, and knows also that you did not just happen to stumble across her wee drama."

"But I did."

"Aye, from your point of view. But I wonder if, through her research, she's learnt of your bicycling habits. I wonder if she waited there, expecting you."

5

Hypothermia is no joke. Calum's voice in her head. Heather pumped her arms as she walked down the burn.

"Warming my blood, Calum," she said aloud. "Warding off the shivers. No need to natter." She smiled, knowing he would have hated the alliteration. That was another difference between them. He'd not been fanciful, not even when they were kids. He'd liked things plain and straightforward. He'd faced life that way. "My way has merit, too, even if that means not telling every truth. It might be a sin to tell a lie, but not every omission is a sin *or* a lie."

The burn widened ahead, curling and braiding itself around a herd of large, flat rocks. Heather stopped on the bank, gauging distance and depth, and took a chance she'd make it to the closest rock with dry feet.

"Not quite," she said after a splash and a scramble. When she was sitting on the smooth, cool granite, she pulled off her left boot. "A wet sock is no matter. Aren't we made up of some great huge percentage of water?" She tipped the boot and let the water trickle back into the burn. "Water to water and verily to verily, or whatever. Sorry, Cal, I don't mean to make light."

The sun had come out as she'd hiked down the burn. It hadn't gone in again, so she left the boot off and stood it next to her on the rock. Then she took a map and Calum's leather diary from one of the jacket's cargo pockets. She'd found both in the pocket when she'd cleared his flat years ago. The same as she'd found the malevolent *Road Map 2* in the Fiesta's glovebox.

"You were aye prepared, Calum," she said. "Ta for that."

This map showed Inversgail and a bit of the coast, and it also had a line of faded pink highlighter. Heather traced the line with her finger, following it across the harbor toward the headland. "And plain as day, it disappears. That is both straightforward and not. But you didn't mean to leave a puzzle, and I don't mind following trails, even if that makes me a half-blind pilgrim blundering toward your sad destination."

She took her phone from another pocket and tapped a number she'd added after arriving the day before. "Aye, hello, I'd like to rent one of your kayaks."

Janet told the old tom and the kitten, Smirr and Butter, they were in charge of the house while she was gone. Smirr, the color of a soft rain, tucked himself into a neat loaf and then stretched a deft paw and trapped yellow Butter's tail. Back arched, the kitten danced away sideways.

"Do your best with him, Smirr," Janet said. "He couldn't ask for a better role model for learning proper cat behavior. Supper when I get home."

Smirr blinked, as if to say he'd wait patiently.

A cat or two waiting at home—the "well-fed, well-petted, and properly revered" cats Mark Twain had spoken of—was a fine thing. Not at all the same as someone watching and waiting on a hillside.

Janet had pushed aside Norman's suggestion that Heather had organized the scene at the burn and waited for her. After showering, she'd changed into what she thought of as bookseller chic—dark slacks, light blouse, and blazer—and hopped back on her bike. Even running late, it made more sense to walk or pedal between home and Yon Bonnie Books than to drive. They lived barely a mile from the shop, and leaving the car home left one more of the few nearby parking spaces free for customers.

She didn't fly down the hill from Argyll Terrace toward the harbor. Traffic, pedestrians, and uneven pavement gave her ample reasons for a sedate coast and then a slow pedal along the High Street. Slow enough to scan the harbor for seals and the harbor wall for Rab MacGregor. She saw neither. She didn't scan overhead for trios of prophetic seagulls.

Two kayaks sliced through the water on their way out of the harbor, silent and purposeful, making it look easy. And cold. Janet shivered, but not on behalf of the kayakers. She shivered at the memory of a moonless, fog-thick night, when she, Christine, Tallie, and Summer had been set adrift in a sabotaged rowboat. No oars, no protection, and no way of signaling for help.

Janet pushed thoughts of fog and hopelessness aside. Ahead lay comforts of other sorts—their new, old building with books full of fresh stories and ideas, steaming pots of aromatic tea, and soft pillows in warm beds. Janet rode past the windows of the bookshop and tearoom and around the corner to the narrow street behind. The back door opened into their stockroom. She unlocked it, rolled the bike inside and propped it on its kickstand, and hung her helmet from the handlebars.

She heard Tallie, but didn't see her, when she entered through the stockroom door. Talking with a customer, it sounded like, perhaps in the history, art, and architecture aisle. Yon Bonnie's bookcases were an eclectic assemblage of styles, mixed and matched over the century of the shop's life. Most of them were at least a foot taller than Janet or Tallie. They formed aisles, like canyons of books, running from the sales counter toward the tearoom door. That door always stood open for customers—and the smells of buttery shortbread and scones—to come and go.

Janet took her jacket and purse to the office behind the sales counter and stopped to send Christine a text letting her know she'd arrived. She leafed through the morning mail and picked a few cat hairs from the front of her blazer. Neither the cat hairs nor the mail were urgent.

A text came in from Christine: *ok?*

Och aye ttyl, Janet replied, and then went back out into the shop to earn her keep for the day. Tallie and her customer were just coming from the travel, cookbook, and crafts aisle as she did.

"I'm less of an old bat than I thought," Janet said. "My echo location skills are off. I thought I heard you in art and architecture."

"No worries," Tallie said. "You're as batty as ever. We were over there, and opted for a change of scenery on the way back."

The woman with Tallie put two books on the counter—*A Handbook of Scotland's Coasts* and *A Taste of Scotland's Islands.* "Bats are brill and beneficial, and your colleague is a canny bookseller," she said. "I didn't know I needed another cookery book until this lovely thing caught my eye." She stroked the cookbook until lovely things on the counter caught her eye. Adding three of their new recipe postcards to the books, she pushed the stack toward Tallie. "That's me for today, but I promise I'll be back for one of these." She started stroking one of the zhen xian bao. "I've a friend who's difficult to buy for."

"Come back for our party in a fortnight, too," Tallie said. "We're celebrating the one hundred and twenty-fifth birthday of Stuart Farquhar, the founder of Yon Bonnie Books."

"I'll do that. Cheery-bye the *noo.*"

"Isn't it pure brill making people that happy?" Janet said as the door closed behind the woman. "And isn't it nice that I'm hardly late at all? How's the morning so far? Is Rab in?"

"Either no or not yet," Tallie said.

"A normal day, then. Thank goodness."

"So what happened on your ride? Christine said there'd been an 'interesting misunderstanding' with a 'numpty researcher,' and your text only said you'd be late."

"And she and I are both right, as we so often are."

"Are there nuances to 'interesting' and 'misunderstanding' that I should know about?" Tallie asked.

"Plenty. Also to 'numpty' and 'researcher,' but—" Janet put her palms on the counter. "I want time to think them through. I don't want to spill them out all over the shop. There isn't time for the whole story between customers. Later is soon enough."

"There might be time," Tallie said. "There often is. Discreetly. Between customers. Like now."

Janet shook her head.

"Your points make good sense," Tallie said, "but they sound rehearsed."

"They are, and thank you for saying they make not just sense but *good* sense. The bottom line is, if I get all worked up telling you the whole story, as I'm sure you can imagine happening—"

"You're actually pretty good about not getting worked up at work," Tallie said.

"Thank you. However, customers might have an unexpected Jekyll and Hyde experience as I lurch between gnashing my teeth and offering them a bookmark with their purchase. Where are you going?"

Tallie headed for the fiction aisle without answering. She came back with three copies of *The Strange Case of Dr. Jekyll and Mr. Hyde* and set them near the cash register. "Impulse buys, in case you can't help yourself and go all Hyde anyway."

"You're a natural at the book business, dear." Janet sat down on the high stool behind the counter and crossed her legs. "Another bottom line is that nothing really happened, and I'm fine." She smiled at her daughter. Possibly too brightly, judging by the squint of Tallie's left eye.

"I can tell you're fine from seeing two more bottom lines." Tallie tipped her head to look at Janet's ankles. "One black sock. One blue."

"Oh, for—"

"Who is this researcher and what is she researching?" Tallie interrupted.

"Heather Kilbride. She's a writer. But I can fill you in later."

"We've run into some odd writers," Tallie mused.

"We only notice the odd ones. The quiet ones go about their business and blend in. Honestly, there's no need to worry. Norman was there. Sort of." Janet saw the squint in Tallie's eye again and hurried on. "Norman wasn't at all alarmed, and said I held my own well enough. I do that even better when I spend time with books and people looking for books. So—"

The bell over the door jingled, and Janet called good morning to the trio who'd come in. She'd seen two of them the day before outside the library—Agnes Black and the man who'd called her Nessy and given her a lift. The third was another woman Janet occasionally saw in the shop, though not often enough to know her name.

Agnes twiddled her fingers at Janet and then directed the other two toward the fireplace and its comfortable, overstuffed armchairs. She appeared to be in charge, which didn't surprise Janet. Agnes, a bit older than she, looked like the capable sort of grandmother who dug the garden, baked cookies, and stood no nonsense. She looked now as though she'd brought the others on a field trip to Yon Bonnie Books.

Tallie watched the three troop past and then turned back to Janet. "At least give me a hint. What's the writer like?"

"You can see for yourself. She might stop in for tea."

"Lovely!" Agnes, who moved as quietly as a grandmother cat, put an elbow on the counter across from Tallie.

Tallie didn't jump as dramatically as Butter the kitten had that morning, but she startled enough to make her laugh and apologize to Agnes.

"It's the shoes," Agnes said. "Good for my bunions. Did I hear right, that you're offering tea to wandering writers? Because *we're* writers. Derek? Sheila?" Agnes waved the other two back to the counter. They'd sunk into a couple of the armchairs, but levered themselves out again.

"Now," Agnes said to Janet and Tallie, "I feel as though I know you through this wonderful shop and our conversations about books, but this morning calls for proper introductions. I'm Agnes Black, retired primary teacher. Sheila?"

"Aye," the other woman said. "Sheila. That's me. Not retired. I do freelance graphic design."

"Nairn," Agnes said. "She's Sheila Nairn."

"Aye. That's me," Sheila said. "You're up, Derek."

"Derek Spiers, Inversgail Church of Scotland. I'm happy to meet you, and I'm embarrassed to say I've not been in the shop in several years." He bowed slightly as he apologized.

"How nice to meet you, Agnes, Sheila, Derek," Janet said, wondering if the shop was going to be hit up for a donation of some kind. "We're Janet and Tallie Marsh. How may we help you?"

Sheila and Derek, each a decade or two younger than Agnes, continued to let her take the lead.

"We've a proposition for you," Agnes said, and then paused.

How much *are they hitting us up for?* Janet wondered. She felt her eyebrows rise at the possibilities and hoped that Agnes interpreted their rise as an invitation to carry on.

Apparently, she did. "We're members of a small writing group, and we're looking for a new place to hold our meetings."

"As a way to shake things up," Derek added, and then, at a look from Agnes, "Sorry, Nessy. Carry on."

"Derek's right," Agnes added. "We think that new surroundings will give us new perspectives and give new vigor to our prose."

"Wonderful," Janet said with relief. "We might know some of your other members."

"Oh, right," said Tallie. "But, if your group stops meeting at the pub, will you still call it Pub Scrawl?"

"We're not that group," Agnes said.

"Those snobs," Sheila said. She waved off the look her comment earned from Agnes. "I'm not apologizing. Their pretentious noses are so high in the air it's a wonder they don't drown when it rains."

"We tried to join them," Agnes said, "but were met with some resistance. Since then, we've been meeting at the library. Sharon has been very accommodating."

"But we like the look of your meeting area there at the fireplace," Derek put in. "Sorry to hurry things along, Nessy, but I've other appointments this morning."

"Och aye, you're right, Derek," Agnes said. "What do you think, Janet? Tallie, would we be a nuisance?"

"We can't guarantee there'd be more than three of the four chairs available on any given day," Janet said, thinking of Ranger and his preferred seat.

"We work well the way we are," Agnes said. "We've no plans to expand."

"Not with la-di-dah literary gits, anyway," Sheila said.

"And you should know that one of those gits works here," Janet said. "Except that we don't think of him that way at all."

"If you're talking about Rab, you needn't worry," Derek said. "Sound as they come."

"Logistics, then," Tallie said. "When do you meet?"

"We like to say it's when the muse strikes us," Agnes said. "The truth is we're all busy and we meet whenever we're able to fit it in. We can give a week's notice, though. Sometimes two."

"And what's a typical meeting like?" Tallie asked. "I'm thinking of other customers. Do you read aloud?"

"We do, and that's where the library's meeting room has been helpful," Agnes said. "But I think we can agree to keep our voices down." Sheila and Derek nodded.

"As well, we'll not read aloud any of the more graphic portions of our works in progress," Agnes said.

Janet's ears pricked at the word *graphic*. She glanced at Tallie. Her daughter had an admirable poker face.

"What kind of writing do you do?" Janet asked.

Derek glanced left, then right, and leaned toward them. "We write murder."

"We're crime fiction writers," Agnes said, giving Derek a playful slap on the arm.

"Does *your* group have a name?" Tallie asked.

"Due to lack of consensus," Sheila said, "no."

"Tell you what." Agnes put a business card on the counter. "We'll give you time to talk it over, and you can ring me with the verdict."

Derek and Sheila cast last looks toward the chairs by the fireplace, and then they followed a pleased-looking Agnes out the door.

When they'd gone, Tallie mimicked Derek's left and right glances and leaned toward Janet. "'We write steamy romance.' That's what you thought he was going to say, isn't it? I know it was, because I thought so, too."

"Did I hear someone mention *ssssteamy* romance?" Ian Atkinson appeared from the fiction aisle. He came only as far as the end of the bookcase, then leaned his shoulders against its corner. With a flip of his hair and one ankle crossed over the other, he looked more pleased with himself than usual, and more than Agnes had with herself.

"Listening to another customer's conversation—and *repeating* it—is poor form, Ian, and unacceptable," Janet said.

"Tallie's not a customer. She's a shopkeeper. Your actual customers didn't let slip a single syllable about romance, *ssssteamy* or otherwise. And there, you see? Although I did hear what the wannabe wordsmiths said, I refrained from repeating any of it."

"Ever the gentleman," Janet said.

As Ian dipped forward in a bow, Tallie not-quite-whispered in Janet's ear, "Ever the twit."

"What?" Ian straightened.

"Sorry, what?" Tallie looked around, a hand to her ear. "Did you hear that? Someone else sneaking quietly in through the tearoom, no doubt. I'll go see if I can help them find what they're looking for." She put a hand on Janet's shoulder. "I won't be far."

Ian and Tallie bared their teeth at each other as she passed him. Then, hands in his pockets, he ambled over to the sales counter.

"What can I do for you, Ian?" Janet asked. His posturing aside, she didn't like feuding with him. He was good for all three of their businesses—his books sold well and steadily; he enjoyed the attention he received from tourists, and often came to sit in the front window of the tearoom to attract them; and they'd heard from B&B guests, more than a few times, that they chose Bedtime Stories because of "Atkinson sightings." He also made a decent neighbor. Janet had come to see his nosiness about who came and went from her house as added security. She doubted that he'd run to anyone's rescue, but thought he'd at least peek through a window and phone the police.

"I've come to brag," he said.

"That's refreshingly honest, Ian. Brag about what?"

"A consulting job. Something rather interesting. The sort of thing with which it's nice to have one's name associated."

"Good for you," Janet said. Also possibly good for Yon Bonnie Books. "What other names are associated with it?"

"Deets are hush-hush, as yet."

"Ah. Well. Let us know when the deets have a growth spurt and become actual details." She knew that sounded sarcastic, but Ian was like a duck's back when it came to sarcasm.

"Any new stock for me to sign?" he asked.

"Arriving in the next order," an unseen Tallie called. "Thursday or Friday."

"Very good. Give me a bell." He turned as if to go—a clumsy pretense given his next words. "I say, do you remember that woman we stood behind at the library yesterday? Hannah? Hillary? Hermione?"

"Heather," Janet said.

"That's it." Ian snapped his fingers, the name fumbling almost certainly another clumsy pretense. "Heather Kilbride. Do you know that she's yet another writer?"

"Yes. Do you know her work?"

"Why? Don't you?"

Janet said "Mm" with an inflection that might have meant "of course I do." Then, while Ian tried to decide if it did, she slipped around his defenses. "Heather's fortunate that you're here and have the time to consult on her project."

"How did you know—"

"Oh, please, Ian. It wasn't hard to figure out. Congratulations, though. I mean that, and you have my promise. Until you tell me it's no longer hush-hush, I won't say a word. I'm looking for a bit of information, though, and I think you might be exactly the right person to ask."

"Happy to help. If it's to be found in my vast store of information," he said, tapping his forehead with an index finger, "it's yours."

"What do you know about a lawyer named William Clark?"

The world didn't suddenly hold its breath, and Ian didn't actually freeze in the headlights of Janet's question. Janet *did* silently count to three and a half before he answered.

"Not a thing," he said, already on his way to the door. "I don't know the chap at all."

Tallie rejoined Janet, her poker face at its admirable best. Then she wiggled her eyebrows at Janet and said, "*That* was instructive. Not instructive enough, though. I'm left with questions. Would you like to hear them?"

"You know it." Janet sat on the stool, back straight, eyes like an eager student.

"Do you think Ian hoped we *did* know Heather's previous work?"

"Yes. Because *he's* never heard of her."

"He also wouldn't have been able to find her in a quick Google search like I just did." Tallie held up her phone. "No author site. No Wikipedia entry."

"Not every writer has them."

"True. Do you think he wanted you to guess that he's consulting on Heather's project?"

"Of course," Janet said.

"What do you think she's told him?"

"I wish I knew."

"What do you think he's told *her*?"

"Exaggerations."

"And utter bilge. Agreed," Tallie said. "But—" She wiggled her eyebrows again. "We've found a new way to get rid of Ian. Simply mention William Clark. That's a bit of a win for the morning."

"But it's overshadowed," Janet said, "because it raises another question. Or raises the same question. If Clark is some kind of pariah, why did Gerald make him one of the trustees?"

"Gerald's lawyer might know. I wonder who that is and how public the information about trusts is?"

"Two coaches just went past," Janet said. "With luck, we'll hear the pitter-patter of day-trippers' feet before long."

"With book money burning holes in their pockets," Tallie agreed. "Good. One more question before they patter in. Do you think Ian made a special trip here to brag about consulting with Heather?"

"Entirely possible," Janet said. "The twit. But to give him the benefit of the doubt, he might have been doing his shopping, and dropping by here to tell us was a sudden brainstorm he couldn't resist. Why do we care?"

"I might be totally off base, but when he first poked his nose around the bookcase, I got the feeling he'd been eavesdropping on the crime writers. That he came in through the tearoom because he was sneaking in, and he'd been following them."

Janet ran that thought around in her mind. "We know he does that kind of thing, but maybe he's following Agnes or Derek and not the group. They were both at the library yesterday. He was taking notes while he watched Heather, maybe he's interested in one of them, too.

But why? No. Stupid question. It would be impossible for us, as mere mortals, to know what he's up to. Frankly, I don't want to spend any amount of time thinking about what *he* spends time thinking about."

"'Why' isn't a stupid question, though," Tallie said. "You know there are no stupid questions. There's just sneaking, devious twits."

6

The pattern of bookselling soothed the rest of the day—a pleasant flow and ebb and renewed flow of browsers and buyers. Tea flowed in a similar, though often opposite, rhythm in Cakes and Tales. When the ebbs brought quiet to both shops, the women talked over plans for their celebration of Stuart Farquhar's one hundred and twenty-fifth birthday.

Their plans included refreshments, live music, and a discount on local history books and any books, of whatever genre, that featured bookstores or bookselling. They were also going to unveil the new book bags and tea towels they'd had imprinted with a watercolor of the front of their building. Farquhar's sister Morag had painted the original watercolor. It hung over the fireplace, looking very Beatrix Potter or Tasha Tudor. They planned to surprise the first twenty-five people through the door on the day of the celebration by giving them a bag or tea towel.

They were also working on an idea they hoped would bring people into the shop for weeks after the celebration—a display on Farquhar's life and the history of Yon Bonnie Books. They didn't lack for material. Tallie had searched the archives at the library and found a trove of Farquhar family photographs. Summer, who wrote an advice column for the *Inversgail Guardian*, had been scouring the paper's not-terribly-well-organized archives for pictures and articles. As a former newshound, she told them she was on the sniff for a snippet she could turn into a juicy story that would catch the nose of the national papers.

During a pre-lunch ebb, Christine sailed in from the tearoom. "I've a question and a concern. Question first, for you, Tallie. How's your mum holding up after her experience this morning?" She stopped across the counter from Janet and studied her face.

Tallie peered at her mother, too, then nodded. "She's holding her own well enough."

Janet picked up a book catalog and flipped through it.

"Bottling it up, is she?" Christine asked.

"Processing," Tallie said.

"Ready to shake it and pop the cap if you don't start talking *to* me instead of around me," Janet said to the catalog.

"This saved time," Christine said. "Tallie's answers are always the meat."

"Whereas I wander off into the neeps and tatties, and sometimes as far as the pudding," Janet said. "I actually do that, don't I? Och, well, what's a wanderer to do? So what's your concern, Christine? You asked *more* than one question, so I hope you don't have more than one concern."

"Has she been this cranky all morning?" Christine asked Tallie.

"No. I've only just noticed it."

"We'll take her to Nev's tonight," Christine said. "Calm her down. That might answer my concern, too, if we bump into Rab while we're there. We don't know the logistics of the Farquhar display. How big it will be, where to put it, cost of supplies and materials. He put himself in charge of it, and he's become conspicuous by his absence. *More* conspicuous, because it seems to me he's more absent."

"We have two weeks, and he's always come through for us," Janet said.

Christine studied Janet's face again. "Aye. You believe that and I have faith in your beliefs. See you later."

During another ebb, after the lunch rush and before the onslaught of afternoon tea, Summer shared her latest idea with Janet and Tallie.

"See if you can picture this for the refreshment table's centerpiece—a gingerbread stone circle." Summer's hands, choreographed to the vision in her head, measured and arranged her creation. Her blonde hair sleeked back in a ballerina's bun, Summer met any experience with the swing-kick exuberance of a jazz dancer. "Massive. At least eighteen inches in diameter. Bigger, if I find the right platter or pan to build it on. What do you think?"

"Perfect," Tallie said.

"Perfectly perfect," said Janet.

Summer effervesced and headed back to the tearoom.

When she judged Summer to be out of earshot, Janet nudged Tallie and said quietly, "This really *might* be a stupid question, but, why?"

"You missed her news this morning, and I forgot to tell you. She found the snippet she wanted. Farquhar was an amateur archaeologist. He cataloged and photographed local sites, including the Stuart Stones."

Janet stared. "O.M.G."

"That's the meat right there."

"I'd always assumed they were Stuart for the House of Stuart. Are they named for *our* Stuart?"

"Summer thinks so. She's found other names in the records and on old maps, but nothing that stuck. Our Stuart talked about them in a *Guardian* article back in the thirties. The circle captivated him when he was a lad and they've been called the Stuart Stones ever since. Summer's planning a couple of freelance articles. One about Farquhar and the bookstore. Another about him and his stones. She's totally stoked."

The Stuart Stones weren't as famous as the Heart of Neolithic Orkney. Nor were the circle and its landscape as breathtaking as sites in Lewis, the northern part of Lewis and Harris, the largest island in the Western Isles. But the stones had gained a small following thanks to *Outlander* tourists—fans of the bestselling novels by Diana Gabaldon, and the even more successful television series. "Ots" came from around the world searching for the romance and mystery of the Scottish Highlands. Castles, isles, banks, and braes called to them and they answered.

But stone circles—in the presence of standing stones, with their lichen, moss, and rugged, five thousand years of endurance, Ots felt connected to the roots of the universe.

Or so Janet imagined. She'd never seen the Stuart Stones. When the children were young, Curtis, who'd been quite a good father, had taken them on an expedition to find the circle. They *had* found it—on a hillside not too far from Inversgail as the gull flew—and the children had come home exhausted but in raptures. Curtis had come home and poured himself a large whisky. He'd chased that with another, smaller one, and complained to it about what some people called a road, and what some people considered a bit of a hike, and what happens to traction when you park in a mire of mud, and how sometimes it can't be helped but children who need to pee need to get over the fact there's no place except the open hillside or these god- and druid-forsaken rocks. Janet wondered if GPS had changed some of that.

"Do you have visions of *Outlander* tourists dancing in your head?" Tallie asked.

"Well-heeled Ots stopping at Yon Bonnie Books to learn more about the captivating Stuart Stones? Oh, yes."

"Hey, do you know who didn't stop by this morning? Your friend Heather Kilbride."

"I wonder if we should worry about her? Suppose something's happened for real and she's still out there?"

"Maybe she's helping Norman with inquiries," Tallie said.

"Not unless he went back. He left when I did and wasn't interested in inquiries. She was hiking down the burn." Visions of turned ankles now limped through Janet's head.

"She didn't say for sure that she'd stop by, though, did she?"

"No."

"Then we won't worry, because we can't worry about every Tom, Dick, and Heather who doesn't stop in for a cuppa."

❧

When Heather had arrived in Inversgail, and stopped at the library, Sharon the librarian recommended the pub called Nev's for lunch. Nev's would fit anyone's need or desire for a twee-less venue. Away from the High Street, slotted into a narrow space between Smith's Funerals and offices for the *Inversgail Guardian*, Nev's presented itself as dark, smoky, and possibly closed for health code violations. Possibly closed for good and abandoned. Not one of those perceptions was accurate. Danny Macquarrie, the publican of record, cultivated Nev's exterior look intentionally. He wasn't interested in attracting Inversgail's many tourists. He wasn't interested in looking or acting the part of Nev's owner, either, and cultivated his own look as simply the man behind the bar.

"Evening, Janet," Danny said when she opened Nev's door that evening. "Tallie and Summer are having a game." He nodded toward the darts room. "Christine joining you?"

"Helen and David, too. I just got a text that said, 'wrangling the wrinklies, running late.'"

"New man in the kitchen. Quite good with Scotch pies. Fancy one?"

"Aye, and a half of Selkie's. Ta, Danny." Janet took her half pint of the local ale, Selkie's Tears, to the door of the darts room. She was feeling very local herself. Summer looked around and waved. Tallie concentrated on her next throw. No Rab and Ranger. Janet found a table large enough for four or five, and before she had a chance to take her coat off, Christine called from the door.

"A hand, please, Janet?" Christine had a parent on each arm, and getting them through the door wasn't going well.

Janet and Danny both went to the rescue. Janet grabbed the door before it swept the trio back out onto the pavement. Danny took a pink-cheeked Helen on his own arm and walked her to a corner table where another elderly couple greeted her. Christine delivered her father to the chair beside her mother.

"The fish, Dad?" Christine asked.

"A plate between us, love. Extra chips."

Christine kissed them each on the tops of their heads, and went to place the order. When she joined Janet, she set her half pint carefully on the table and dropped into a chair. "I nearly dumped the pint in the chair and sat myself on the table, I'm that knackered."

"You're that good with them," Janet said.

Tallie and Summer came to join them. Danny brought four plates with pies. "Hard to believe you have trouble keeping those old dears in line," he said to Christine.

"Not keeping them in line, keeping up with them. Mum was fashed tonight trying to find a lipstick. Then the two of them went into fits with Dad helping her put it on. And it's *their* fault," she said waving a fork at Tallie and Summer.

"I object," said Tallie.

"Overruled," Christine countered. "Mum and Dad are chuffed over the Farquhar exhibit. When I told them you two posted online requests for people to share their memories of Farquhar, they decided to make an appeal as well. 'We'll do it the auld, non-electronic way,' they said, 'by going down the pub.' Mum wanted the lipstick to look her best."

"I'll tell her she's *gae* bonny when I take the fish over," Danny said. "Tuck in and let me know how you like the pies."

Janet had already tucked in, but before she could say more than "mm-mm," Danny had returned to the bar.

"I should interview your mum and dad and their friends," Summer said. "In all my spare time. Did you know that Farquhar kept a lending library for children at Yon Bonnie?"

"The more I hear about him, the more I like him," Tallie said. "I hope we never learn anything awful."

Janet, her mouth full, nodded.

"But we've all been in businesses where rocks get turned over," Christine said, "and secrets wriggle out. Some die a quick death, some live on, and some are diseased and contagious."

Janet looked at the next bite on her fork and put the fork back on her plate. "Lovely."

"You know it's true," Christine said.

"I do. I also worry about seeing wriggling contagion where it doesn't exist." She glanced around to see who was within earshot. "I'm thinking about Heather Kilbride. She's an odd duck."

"Finished processing her, have you?" Christine asked. "Tell us."

"It should be called 'The Incident at the Beaton Bridge: A Continuing Saga,'" Janet said, and launched into a vivid retelling of the morning encounter. The others ate their pies without interrupting. She told as far as Heather walking off down the burn, and Hobbs seeing no need to speak with her. Then she stopped and finished her ale.

"It was a rabbit hole kind of experience," she said. "It veered toward surreal, but in the end? I didn't dislike her."

"I'll admit," Christine said, "your call this morning strained credulity."

"You didn't believe me?"

"I always believe *you*, but I was strained to believe the coincidence of the incident. She recreated Malcolm's death scene, and we're to believe that you, who found him *then*, also found him this time?"

"She's a good actor, then," Janet said. "I really didn't get the feeling that she knew me."

"Good actors exist," Tallie said. "That stuff about getting into the scene and needing an emotional connection sounds like something an actor would say."

"They might throw around phrases like 'emotional heft,' too," Summer said.

"Well, she apologized out the wazoo, and it seemed genuine," Janet said.

"But don't forget that you're the rosy-eyed one of us," said Christine.

Janet made a rude noise at Christine. "Here's a question, though: Can I substitute 'out the bahookie,' as in 'apologized out the bahookie,' for 'out the wazoo'? Would it mean the same thing, or near enough? Would it be too rude?"

"Go for it," Tallie said.

"But, Christine, would your mum be appalled to hear it?"

"Listen to the lawyer," Christine said. "She's the head-screwed-on one of us."

"Anyway, wherever Heather's apology came from, she was sorry for the obvious distress she caused," Janet said. "And by distress, I mean I blew up at her."

"Fair and square," Tallie said.

"You blew up and then you believed the bahookie," Christine said, "and probably ended up comforting *her.* I can't wait to meet this researcher with her mad, wee skills."

"I'm just saying that I rushed to my judgment of her," Janet said. "I'd like it if we'd all try to be more careful about doing that than I was this morning."

"Janet," Summer said, "listen to us. You had good reason to rush. And think how hard it'll be for the rest of us *not* to rush. We're cynical. You're sunshine."

"It was actually less of a rush and more of a leap," Janet said. "And I leapt as though I was going for her throat."

"Stop beating yourself up," Christine said. "You're blotting out your bloody sunshine."

Janet tried smiling at each of them, and then fell back into picking at the questions that bothered her most. "She couldn't have expected me. I don't ride that way every day. She *couldn't* have known I'd stop just there, or that I would look down the burn."

"Substitute 'hoped' for 'expected,'" Tallie said. "Hope is a strong motivator."

"I like that better," Janet said. "Norman would stick with 'expect,' though. He thinks Heather knows all about who I am and also knows that's one of my regular routes."

"You saved that for last?" Christine asked.

"Best for last. I also left out that she said she has another angle on the Murray case, and that she has an appointment with William Clark."

"Is he the other angle?" Tallie asked.

"When I asked her how he's connected to the case, her answer was either the truth—that she doesn't know because she hasn't spoken to him yet—or a brushoff. Doggone it," Janet said. "Who *is* this guy?"

"That's my question," Summer said. "Who are you talking about?"

"And why do you two know Mr. Mystery when we don't?" Christine asked.

"You might, though," Janet said. "Do you know a William Clark?"

"There are bound to be several of them around," Christine said. "I knew at least two when I was a child. One was a weedy ginger with the voice of an angel. Then he died. Leukemia."

"That doesn't help," Janet said.

"It narrows the possibilities."

"Not in a useful way. I've seen this one. He's closer to Tallie and Summer's age. We heard about him from James."

"The day of the memorial ride," Tallie said. "Clark is a lawyer, and he's been named one of three trustees for the money Gerald Murray left to aid veterans."

"You two were busy in the tearoom when we heard that," Janet said. "James told Norman and Rab, and all three of them had an odd reaction to Clark's name. The looks that went between them were interesting, and not one of them would answer me when I asked who he was. Rab pulled one of his disappearing acts when I asked him."

"Who are the other two trustees?" Summer asked.

"James is one. Ian is the other."

"To answer your question, then, no. I don't believe I know this William Clark. Describe these interesting looks. Were they surprised? Appalled? Amazed? Worried?"

"I have no idea what they were," Janet said. "Norman's reacted oddly to the name twice since then. At the library, he couldn't get away fast enough. This morning, he got all stiff and huffy."

"Don't forget Ian," Tallie said. "She asked *him* about Clark this afternoon. One minute he couldn't have been more irritating, and the next, he was out the door. It was like a miracle."

"Cagey," Janet said. "That's what I was snarling about on the way back to the shop yesterday, and that covers all of them. They know something and they're not telling."

"I've never liked that game," Christine said.

Tallie held up her phone. "From a quick search, it doesn't look like William Clark is practicing law these days."

"Huh." Summer crossed her arms and settled her shoulders. A smile played across her lips, but it appeared to be as much for the crumbs of piecrust on her plate as for the other women at the table.

"I know that look," Christine said. "Boudicca awakes. What are you thinking?"

"That I like a good game," Summer said. "All four of us do. This is the first I've heard about Gerald's trust, because cagey James hasn't said a word about it. And you can call me Queen Boudicca, if you like, but I'm not declaring war against anyone. To summarize all of that, I say, 'huh.'"

"It's the same as 'the game's afoot,'" Janet said.

"And we're quick on our feet," Christine said, "but we'll tread carefully on this. The name William Clark makes strong men and twits who write run for the door. I'll ask my oldies if they know him, but not here. I'd have to shout the name for them to hear it properly, more than twice, no doubt, and Danny won't be best pleased if we empty the pub this early in the evening."

"Is this the reason Rab's been scarce?" Summer asked.

"Rab being scarce isn't really anything new," Tallie said. "Neither is Rab being eccentric."

"We know all about eccentric," Janet said. "Maybe that's what William Clark is, too. Christine, do we dare see how Danny reacts to the name?"

The four women turned to watch Danny laugh and pour a pint. He looked the part of a sailor home from the sea, which he was. He'd returned to Inversgail after retiring from the Royal Navy.

"It can't be worse than tipping him off the harbor wall," Christine said. She'd done that when they were children before he'd learned to swim. She happily took credit for his successful naval career.

As the women watched, Danny glanced toward his pocket. He pulled his phone from the pocket and, as he read the display, his face shifted from open and smiling to still and focused. He sent a quick reply, then crossed to the kitchen door and spoke to someone within. When he turned back, he nodded to a couple who'd come to the bar. "Shug's on his way, aye?" He walked past the couple, coming out from behind the bar and over to Christine.

"I need to go," he said, bending between Christine and Janet to speak quietly. "Search and rescue's been called out. A kayaker's gone missing. Water temperature's a factor this time of year."

"Who?" Janet asked.

"A woman staying locally. She went out solo this afternoon." He checked his phone. "The name's Kilbride."

7

A few moments of shocked silence followed Danny's departure, and then a few more of hushed disbelief. When the disbelief turned back to silence, Janet said she thought she'd head home.

"Wait another half hour and I'll give you a lift," Christine said.

"Thanks, but I need a walk."

"I'll come with you," Tallie said. "Keep you from missing a turn if the mirk is gathering. Even if it's just your own personal mirk."

Janet shook her head. "Stay and have a game with Summer. I'll be fine. I *am* fine. I'll see you at home." She put on a smile and her coat, and told them again that she was fine. She stopped to say goodnight to Christine's mum and dad and opened the door into the dark and cold. Not so dark, though, because of streetlights, and not so cold, because she was bundled against it and dry. She shivered anyway and started walking to keep her teeth from chattering, glad she wasn't down by the harbor where the black waves might try pulling at her.

Something else did try pulling at her—and succeeded. She found herself taking a detour to Paudel's Newsagent, Post Office, and Convenience. Basant Paudel, Nepali businessperson, proprietor, and sole employee, had a number of skills Janet valued.

"Mrs. Janet, good evening," Basant said when she pushed through the door. He marked his place in the book he'd been reading with an envelope, and set the book aside on the counter. "Are you out of washing up liquid?"

"Do a lot of people stop in for that in the evenings?"

"I'm happy to supply a variety of emergency needs and don't ask anyone to explain their definition of the word, interesting though some of them must be."

Janet hadn't wanted to think about emergencies. "I'll pick up bread and milk as long as I'm here. My feet seem to have brought me in without consulting my brain."

"Thank your feet for safe delivery then, because they know your brain is otherwise occupied."

One of Basant's skills that Janet valued most was the thoughtful way he listened to more than just the words of a conversation. Another was the offhand way he had of eliciting information while weighing apples and ringing up postage stamps. Information he didn't mind passing along.

"Basant, do you know a lawyer named William Clark?"

"Ah." Basant nodded, but he didn't suddenly bolt for the door or push her toward it.

"What can you tell me about him?" Janet asked.

"A question first: Is it true he is one of three named in Gerald Murray's will to oversee a trust?"

"Yes, along with James Haviland and Ian Atkinson."

"An interesting trio," Basant said. "I know that William Clark collects miniature books. I find that appropriate because his life shrank when his wife died. He has not engaged in public life, and I have rarely seen him in recent years."

"I saw him at the library yesterday."

"Perhaps, thanks to Gerald's trust, William's life is expanding again."

"That's a generous thought, Basant."

Basant gave a slight bow. "I hear, though I do not know if it's true, that you have also seen the new writer in Inversgail—Heather Kilbride."

"She's missing, Basant. In a kayak. We heard this evening at Nev's."

He paused, eyes closed for a moment, and then said, "Fearing the worst is often the easier road."

"Easier with experience. Tallie, Christine, Summer, and I—the four of us were out there sinking in that lapping, lapping, lapping black water. I know what she's feeling, or what she felt if the worst . . ."

"And now—*right now*." Basant rapped once on the counter and there was a rap in his voice. "Now, you are here, despite the worst that someone wished." He spread his arms and smiled. "Search and rescue have a good track record. We will keep hope foremost in our thoughts, aye?"

"It's a challenge, Basant. But I like a challenge, so aye. Did you meet Heather? Did you talk to her?"

"I might have said a few words to her. *That* was a challenge, because most of the talk came *from* her, she is that passionate about her research project. Mind you, others might not be so passionate when they hear the subject."

"The Murray case, as she calls it?"

"She is planning to trace key movements in the case," Basant said.

"I wonder—"

"That you wonder is good. A sign of hope. Please, forgive my interruption. What do you wonder?"

"What she means by 'movements.' Only where people were and when? Or does 'movements' include how the case progressed? How theories developed and changed? I wonder if 'key movements' is true-crime writer jargon?"

"There were few opportunities for me to insert a question," Basant said, "but I did not even think to ask those questions. It sounded like such a well thought out plan that I swallowed it hook, line, and sinker. You can ask her yourself if—let us say when—she stops by to interview you and your fellow sleuths."

"I hope—I really hope—she doesn't plan to interview us. I hope we aren't even on her radar. We're happy staying out of any limelight. You didn't tell her that we—"

"Mrs. Janet," Basant said, "I do solemnly swear that the secret of your talents and prowess are safe with me. Mind you, although none of *you* advertise your successful sideline, others, beside myself, are aware."

Norman Hobbs and Ian Atkinson, for two. *Norman, who generally tolerates (and profits from) us,* Janet thought, *and Ian, who thinks we're rivals.*

Janet paid for the bread and milk. Basant asked if she'd like to add something from one of the dozens of jars of old-fashioned sweeties arranged on the wall behind him.

"Thank you, Basant, but not tonight."

"Then hold fast to hope for the lost and let your feet deliver you safely home."

~

Janet looked up from her laptop at the kitchen table the next morning, when she heard Tallie on the stairs. "No news. Coffee's still hot. Pour me another?" She held her cup out.

Tallie took it. She poured herself a cup, refilled her mother's, and sat down across from her. "Have you been up long?"

"Half an hour." Janet glanced at the time and closed the laptop. "An hour. I listened to the early news. Checked the *Guardian's* website."

"Twitter?"

"Yep." She pushed the coffee away. "If I'm going for a ride, I should skip this. I'll reheat it when I get back."

"Have you had breakfast?"

"I'll grab some toast after."

Janet rode down to the Stevenson statue to see if any of her cycling acquaintances were waiting for a group ride. They weren't. She saw a number of small boats on the water, joining the search. She turned her bike toward the library and felt every pedal push up the long hill.

It was too early for the library to be open, of course. She took a small bit of pleasure in leaving her bike in the carpark where William Clark had parked his Mini. Then she walked around the side of the building to look down on the bay, the harbor, the town. The views in three directions from the library's first-floor windows—hills, town, sea, isles—were spectacular, almost unbelievable. Standing in the open, not too near the edge, and catching a hint of salt and fish on the breeze felt more real. She took out her binoculars and swept them along the High Street, tried to read the titles of the books in Yon Bonnie's window displays. She couldn't; the binoculars weren't that good.

Inversgail obviously trusted people to be cautious in high places; the edge of the headland wasn't fenced the way it might be back in the States. Janet pictured Heather calmly standing right at the edge, her toes sticking out into the void. What had happened and where was she?

Janet turned away and caught sight of something on the ground farther along the headland. The size of a carrier bag or a folded blanket—like a pile of towels left on a beach. It wasn't just farther along the headland than she wanted to go, it was also nearer the edge than she intended to get. *Really, this is too much*, she thought. *I should wear blinders when I go out so I stop seeing these things.* But what if a child or a dog were to see it and run over to investigate?

Feeling craven, she drew her shoulders up and tucked her hands in her armpits. She'd wait to see if anyone else happened along, and then happily point out the trash for them to collect. If it were a dog walker, she'd hold onto the dog's leash and let the walker take her chances.

No one came.

"Fine," she said, flinging the word ahead of her as she went to see what the so-and-so slob had left for her to deal with. She paralleled the edge, well back from it, until she stood opposite a pile of brown cloth. The same brown as Heather's jacket? Maybe. Or her brother's. Damn. Now she *had* to go get it.

Janet held her breath and inched sideways toward the pile, toward the end of the earth. She wished she could close her eyes. She wanted a safety rope around her waist. The land might look level to anyone else, but she felt the crazy, teetering tilt of it. And any minute, a giant hand would lift the grass under her feet, like the edge of a tablecloth, and flick it to watch her fly up into the air like a toast crumb and then off into oblivion.

When she reached the small heap on the ground, it didn't start sliding away from her so that she'd have to chase it and grab it before they both went over. It looked blessedly stable and ordinary. Also familiar. A jacket. Janet picked it up and shook it out. Too big for Heather; it must be her brother's. Damp, as though it had been on the ground all night. *Why?*

Janet took the jacket with her, away from the edge, from the unknown. As she folded it into one of the paniers on her bike, she felt something like a book in one of the pockets. She didn't take it out, not wanting to pry further, holding onto hope.

⁂

The four women made a habit of meeting each morning in the interior doorway between the bookshop and tearoom. It was a chance to remind each other of sales and specials, and to share customer comments (or jokes at their expense) in a customer-free zone. They exchanged the kind of news and local interest stories customers might bring in with them. Or, as Christine had suggested the first morning they'd met in the doorway, "They're the kind of tasty tidbits customers will enjoy taking away with them."

When they met the morning after Heather Kilbride and her kayak went missing, there still hadn't been news of a rescue or recovery. Janet told them about finding the jacket.

"I suppose this means her brother's in Inversgail, too. Poor guy. What he must be going through. I'll call Norman so he can track him down and get it back to him."

"Why was it still there?" Summer asked. "Did you think he might have fallen off—"

"Stop! No!" Janet's words were the cry of a mother snatching a child to safety. She put up her hands to hold back the others' shocked silence. "That was—I'm sorry. I know it's an overreaction. But I didn't think that. Or I didn't want to. I was mostly thinking of myself falling off."

Janet's hands didn't hold Christine back. Christine went over and put an arm around Janet, who curled her hands around each other and brought them to her lips before speaking again.

"I'll call Norman," she said. "He'll follow up. How likely is it that he fell?"

Tallie and Summer had their phones out. "It would be dumb to say it couldn't happen, but—" Tallie began.

"But I'm not finding any reports of that kind of accident in the past fifty years at least," Summer finished.

"Same," Tallie said. "So, yeah, he could have fallen off, but it's statistically more likely for a guy who's distraught because his sister is missing to lose track of his jacket in all the upset."

"Maybe," Janet said. "But thank you. Have you had any word from Danny?" she asked Christine.

"No, but it's no wonder, with rough seas, and as black as last night was, and they'd no information to help narrow the search or any idea where to begin."

"I saw on Twitter they called it off at some point because of the danger," Summer said. "They went back out this morning."

"They'll do their best." Christine took her arm from around Janet, and laid one of her hands over the other at her waist. She looked at each of them in turn. "And we'll do *our* best, lasses, by keeping hope and carrying on."

The return of the queen, Janet thought, loving her old friend for her certainty. Since returning to Inversgail, she'd noticed Christine's uncanny knack for channeling an inner Queen Elizabeth II. She'd never caught sight of this regal alter ego back among the flat miles of corn and soybean fields in Illinois. Maybe it was a geographical phenomenon, requiring the heathered hills of Christine's homeland.

Heathered. Heather. Is there any hope?

"Mom?"

The other three were looking at her, and Janet wished she hadn't let her thoughts wander past the queen into the heather and back to Heather. But before she had, they'd been talking about the search. She straightened her spine with renewed strength in answer to the queen's directive about hope, and offered what she hoped might be a pertinent detail.

"I saw two kayaks on their way out of the harbor yesterday morning," she said. "On my way here, after the incident at the bridge. Neither of them could have been Heather—when I left her, she was heading down the burn to reflect on spiritual implications and whatnot. It didn't take me that long to ride home, and I did take a shower, but it was a quick one. So it seems unlikely that she changed her mind about reflecting, packed up, and made it back to town faster than I did. Even less likely that she had time to rent the kayak and paddle that far out into the harbor by the time I went past. But maybe one of those earlier boats saw her later and saw which way she was going. I wonder if that's worth passing along to Norman with the brother's jacket?"

The other three were still looking at her.

"I was blathering," Janet said. "Sorry."

"Worried blather," Christine said. "Perfectly acceptable."

"The kayak rental place should have a record of when she went out, anyway," Janet said. "The authorities won't have missed that detail. But did *I* miss something just now?" She straightened her spine again. "If you don't mind repeating what I missed, we'll do as Christine said. Keep hope and carry on."

Summer gave her a thumbs-up.

"We moved on to something more mundane," Tallie said. "I was telling them about the writing group that asked to have meetings here.

It seemed like a reasonable request, and they seemed like reasonable people."

"More likeable and reasonable than Ian, anyway," Janet said.

"That bar not being particularly high," said Christine. She glanced between Janet's knees and her own. "About knee-high to you."

"In my stocking feet," Janet agreed. "Do either of you know Agnes Black?"

Christine and Summer shook their heads.

"She seems to be in charge," Tallie said. "She's a former primary teacher."

"That tells you all you need to know," Christine said. "They shan't be any trouble at all. Agnes will have the rest of the writers lining up in their gymslips and raising their hands before they dare speak."

"Derek might object to the gymslip," Janet said.

"And I bet Sheila won't raise her hand," said Tallie.

"Do you have any real reservations?" Summer asked.

"No," Tallie said. "We should have an agreement right from the start, though, that we can decide when they're allowed to have their meetings, or if it isn't working out."

"I like this," Christine said. "It's a sign we've been accepted. Hosting a writers group sounds appropriately literary, like the kind of thing we should encourage. Community engagement and all that. Does the group have a name?"

"They haven't settled on one," Janet said.

"I'll give them a hand with that," said Christine. "This could be quite good fun. We can come up with a writers tea blend and put it on special when they meet."

Summer pulled out her phone.

"News?" Janet asked, her focus instantly on the phone.

"No, sorry. Making a note." Summer's fingers danced across the screen, then she slipped the phone back in her pocket. "A writers group that meets in a beloved, local bookshop celebrating its one hundred and twenty-fifth birthday—that sounds like good material for an article, and community engagement is a great angle. It's the kind of local color national papers and TV might pick up."

"The kind of feel-good story people like to share on social media, too," Janet said.

"Will your writers go along with it?" Christine asked. "Maybe we should only agree to meetings here if they agree to Summer's article. Though they'd be daft if they didn't agree."

"If they're meeting in a shop, they're hardly shrinking violets," Tallie said. "But Ian's no shrinking violet and—"

"And he's as daft as they come, as well as several other pejoratives," Janet said, then paused. "Summer, there's something else to consider before you write your article. Our writers feel a rivalry of sorts with the other group, Pub Scrawl. If James is still a member, will an article about our writers annoy him?"

Summer blew a raspberry. "That covers how much he'd care *and* how much I'd care if he did care. Pub Scrawl can meet here, too, if they want. They'd just have to change their name."

"I can help with that, as well," Christine said. "How jolly."

Summer's phone buzzed in her pocket. The other three went quiet while she pulled it back out and looked at it. She sucked in a breath and flicked a glance at the others. "It's James. Search and rescue found a kayak, a rental from Sky View Sea Kayaks. Battered and half-submerged below the headland. He says they couldn't have seen it from the boats they had out last night. Not the way it was tucked into the jagged rocks there."

"Any doubt it's hers?" Tallie asked.

"No. The number on the boat matches the rental record."

"A body?" Janet asked.

"Divers are looking. He's forwarded something from search and rescue, if you think there's time before—"

"We'll open late," Christine said. She looked toward the tearoom's front door then the bookshop's. "No one's waiting. Go on."

"It's from an uncredited source, unauthorized to speak:

> To date, only one kayak fatality is known along this part of the coast. That incident also involved a young woman who set out from Inversgail harbor. Ten years ago, Fiona Clark, another skilled kayaker, lost her life in an unexplained accident. Searchers subsequently found her kayak battered and submerged. Last night's incident is eerily similar, but Ms. Kilbride has not yet been found.

"And here's one more from James. 'In an appeal to the public, Police Scotland asks for anyone with information about Ms. Kilbride to contact them.'" Summer looked up. "That's it."

"Clark," Tallie said. "Fiona Clark. We keep hearing that Clark is a common name."

"But we also keep running into it," Summer said.

"I ran into it last night. Or nudged it. On purpose." Janet pulled her sweater tighter around her. "I stopped by Basant's, not quite on the way home, and asked him if he knows William Clark. He said he knows that Clark collects miniature books and the man's wife died. He didn't say when or how she died, and he didn't mention her name. I didn't think to ask."

"Did you ask your mum and dad if they know him?" Tallie asked Christine.

"Mum remembered a braw lad named Wullie Clark. They were sweet on each other. She was seven. He was six. She spent the rest of the evening calling Dad 'Wullie.' He turned up the telly and pretended not to hear."

"It should be easy enough to find out if Fiona was our William Clark's wife," Summer said.

"But it's all so sad," said Janet. "Let's do what we do best: open our doors and pour tea and sell books."

Halfway through the morning, Janet looked up from counting the postcards a woman was buying, aware the light had subtly but suddenly changed. Or had she noticed the low growl of the motor first? A coach had stopped and stood idling in front of the shop, the debarking passengers moving at the slow trickle of aged pensioners.

"Are they allowed to stop like that and hold up traffic?" Janet's customer asked. "I shouldn't think so."

"It happens," Janet said, ringing up the postcards. "But you're right; it isn't allowed. There are designated carparks." She walked with the woman to the door and held it for her. She continued holding it for a stream of happy day-trippers while looking for an identifying number on the coach so she could report it. Then she thought to look at the driver, but could only see him from the waist down. Could it possibly be the same man who'd caused the stramash in the library carpark? Probably not.

"There," the postcard customer came back to the door and held up her phone. "I snapped photos of the coach from this side of the street and from the other so you can see it's blocking the street and your building. What's the shop's email? I'll send them."

Janet recited the address as the woman tapped it into her phone.

"There. Sent. My brother-in-law drives a coach. I wish someone would report *him*." The woman walked away, muttering, but looking pleased.

The last passenger came off the coach yawning. He stopped at the bottom of the steps to yawn at Janet and ask, "Can I get a bloody coffee in the tearoom?"

"Lovely bloody coffee," Janet said.

He thanked her with another yawn and headed for the door to Cakes and Tales. Janet debated stepping onto the coach to get a good look at the driver. But a car behind the bus honked and another joined it, and she let the shop's door close. There was no point in holding up the coach any further, and it wouldn't do for anyone to think she'd encouraged the illicit stop.

She went back to the sales counter and Tallie mimed smoothing the furrows between her eyebrows. "Were you were tempted to go full Mom on the driver?"

"No, no. I just wondered if it's the guy I saw at the library. It would be a bit of a stretch, though."

"The guy with fists like bludgeons? Don't tell me you considered getting on that bus for a better look."

"But did I get on the bus, dear?" Janet smiled. "Of course not, because I'm the picture of sanity." *And because I can tightrope the fine line between didn't and almost did.*

"Sorry for conclusion jumping," Tallie said.

"Don't be sorry for worrying."

"Did you remember to call Norman?"

"Drat—no. But I will."

One of the day-trippers came to the counter looking for books by Lilian Beckwith, just as Janet's phone rang. Tallie waved and went with the customer. Janet answered the phone.

"Janet Marsh speaking."

"Get your—" The rest of the request disappeared into the static of a poor connection.

"Sorry, will you repeat that?" Janet said.

Static, and then, "—headland."

"Rab, is that you?"

Static. Then more clearly, "—face of the headland. Think of it as noughts and crosses."

"Noughts and—oh, sure, tic-tac-toe." It *might* be Rab.

"Middle square, far left—" more static "—your binoculars."

"Is this a game? Is this you, Rab?"

Silence and she thought she'd lost the call, before static burst into her ear again. "—it's urgent—" And the call ended.

It had to be Rab, but she wouldn't swear to it. *Urgent?* She checked for customers looking for help. Happy browsers only. She got her binoculars from the office and first tried looking through a front window toward the headland. But the angle wasn't right and the panes of old glass with their minor distortions didn't help. She went out onto the front pavement.

The towering rock wall of the headland rose from the sea on the northern edge of Inversgail. *How high? A hundred feet? More.* The library sat on top like a toy from this distance. *Middle square,* he'd said, *far left.* Janet scrutinized the area she thought Rab—or whoever—meant.

Sweeping left and right, she worked her way up the rock face. *Just call it what it is. A cliff. A monstrous, freaking enormous edge.* Left, right, left, slowly, slow . . . until she saw . . . what? Something. Someone? On a ledge. *How far up that—wait. No. It bloody well can't be.*

The shop door opened behind Janet and she heard Tallie call, "Mom?"

"She's there, Tallie, clinging to the headland. Halfway up. It's Heather!"

8

Tallie joined her mother on the pavement outside. Janet filled her in on the phone call, then handed her the binoculars. Tallie trained them on the distant headland, leaning forward as if those few inches closer would make a difference.

"She isn't clinging. She's sitting." Tallie said. "Does she *need* rescuing? She looks comfortable."

"Does she need a psychiatrist?" Janet said. "That's a better question."

"Are you even sure it's her?"

"It's *how* she's sitting. That's how she looked yesterday way up on the hillside. But maybe that's the way anyone nutty enough to look comfortable that close to the edge of oblivion sits."

Tallie tried handing the binoculars back to her mother. Janet didn't take them. She didn't need to look at Heather again. Or that ledge.

"If she's sitting there like that, it isn't an emergency," Janet said, "but people need to know she isn't dead. Why hasn't *she* let anyone know? Is she just sitting up there watching them search for her body?"

"Why didn't Rab call someone besides us? Someone it made sense to call. Like the authorities?" Tallie puffed her bangs off her forehead. "We should get back inside. We abandoned the customers."

"Oh, good Lord. What a way to run a business. I'll call Norman from out here, so we don't alarm the pensioners any more than we already have, and then I'll be in."

Janet made her call to the constable—brief, because she had no information beyond the basics, and extraneous details about brothers and jackets could wait longer than Heather. Then she went back inside. But not through Yon Bonnie's door. She took a detour—also brief—through Cakes and Tales to let Christine and Summer in on the basics, too. Summer immediately sent a text to James at the *Guardian*. While Summer did that, Christine grouched because the tearoom was too busy for her to stand outside and watch the rescue.

"I'm not sure it is a rescue," Janet said. "There might not be much to see."

"At least I can run out for a quick look. Let me have your binoculars." Christine held her hand out, already walking toward the door.

"Sorry, Christine. Tallie has them."

"Well, where is Rab, then? This is exactly the kind of situation where we need him to shimmer in like Jeeves and lend a hand."

"Good question," Janet said.

Christine grouched again, and they each went back to work.

Between lunch and afternoon tea, business slowed enough that Christine got her chance to focus the binoculars on the headland. By then, if there'd been a rescue, it was over. She did see Norman Hobbs walking in their direction, and she popped back inside to let the others know. Tallie offered to cover for Christine in the tearoom if Hobbs came in.

Janet was with a customer at the counter when he did. "Good afternoon, Constable," she greeted him.

"Good afternoon, Mrs. Marsh," Hobbs said, returning her greeting with a nod. He removed his cap and went to browse.

"I'll go swap places with Christine," Tallie said.

When Janet finished with her customer, she found Hobbs in the picture book nook. She spotted a smile on his face as he read *What! Cried Granny.* Upon seeing Janet, he tucked the book under his arm with his cap, and his face reverted to a constabulary blank.

"I can take the book, if you like, Norman," Janet said.

"I'll buy it," he said. "My grandmother's birthday is next week."

"She'll love it," Janet said. "How is Nana Bethia?"

"In her element. She's organized the other knitters at the care home. For every item they knit for a friend or relative, they knit a hat or scarf for donation. I'll add the book to a box of yarn I have for her."

Hobbs's grandmother had spent a number of days knitting in the bookshop soon after the four women took over the business. At the time, they hadn't known she was his grandmother—or anything else about her—as she never spoke. They'd found out later that she'd been waiting for a new set of dentures and hadn't wanted to reveal her toothless gums. They also hadn't known about the creative way Hobbs had found to house her before she could move into her new care home. He'd moved her into Janet's house, telling Janet it remained a crime scene and thus uninhabitable. The women referred to that episode as the Nana Bethia Incident, and they occasionally found it useful to remind Hobbs they hadn't reported it, or him, to his superiors.

Hobbs followed Janet to the sales counter, where they found Christine with a teapot and three cups and saucers.

"Tea, Norman?" Christine asked. "It's our new blend. We haven't decided what to call it, yet. Which do you think? Constable's Cuppa or Bethia's Brew?"

"Bethia's Brew," Hobbs said. "Nana Bethia will be delighted, and—"

"And you wouldn't?"

"I would," Norman said, "but wouldn't it be a shame to waste either name? Why don't you come up with a second blend and use both?"

"That's a wonderful idea," Janet said, and looked at Christine. Christine had probably meant to nettle Hobbs, but a slight narrowing of her left eye showed that his easy response and sweet smile nettled *her.*

"So now, Norman," Janet continued, "I didn't dare look at the headland again. Was it Heather? Did she need rescuing? And what in heaven's name was that all about?"

Hobbs set his cap and the picture book on the counter and took a small purple notebook and matching pen from his pocket. His young niece, upon whom he doted, supplied him with a range of decorative notebooks and pens, often with splashes of rainbows and unicorns. "A few questions of my own, first, if you don't mind, Mrs. Marsh."

"Is this an official interview, Norman?" Christine took out her phone. "Does Janet need representation? Shall I call Lawyer Tallie back from buttering scones in the tearoom?"

Rather than answer, Hobbs sighed. He set his notebook and pen beside his cap and the picture book, and picked up the teapot. "Whilst you're by her side, Mrs. Robertson, I doubt Mrs. Marsh could ask for a more determined advocate. Shall I pour the tea?"

Janet took the first cup he poured and passed it to Christine. Glancing between the two, she couldn't tell if either had won that minor skirmish. Both looked satisfied. She decided to slip in one more question before Hobbs set the teapot down and picked his guard back up.

"Did anyone else phone you about the situation at the headland, Norman? Did Rab phone you?" That was two questions, but, Janet thought, essentially the same one.

Hobbs took a sip of tea and replaced the cup in the saucer before answering. And then he only gave back a question. "Was it Rab who phoned you, Mrs. Marsh?"

"I don't know. The connection was terrible. But if he called me, and didn't call you, then that makes me think it *was* Rab. Not that he avoids talking to you." Janet thought about that and raised her eyebrows at Hobbs. "Or maybe he does?"

Hobbs shook his head.

"But he is somewhat eccentric," Janet said.

Hobbs nodded.

"I might be thinking about it too much, now," Janet said, "but I'm beginning to think it wasn't Rab after all. We haven't seen him for days, Norman. Do you know where he is?"

Hobbs shook his head.

"You've gone wordless, Norman," Christine said. "Why?"

"Shortens the conversation."

"If you're in a hurry to get away, you might have mentioned it when you came in."

"She has a point," Janet said. "Why did you stop to browse if you're in such a hurry?"

"You were with a customer when I arrived, and I stopped browsing as soon as you were free."

"Oh." Janet clattered her teacup into its saucer. "Maybe it was Heather's brother who called. Have you spoken to him? If you haven't, you'll have to now, because I have his jacket. I took it."

"Why would you do that, Mrs. Marsh?"

Janet's mind flashed back to her fear on the headland. "I have to say, it didn't seem like a good idea at the time. I planned to call you earlier, and then this whole Heather-on-the-Headland thing happened. I'll go get it. I'm glad I didn't go through his pockets."

"I'm sure he'll appreciate your forbearance," Hobbs said to her receding back, then to Christine, "Were you in on this, Mrs. Robertson?"

"Heavens, no. You can be sure that I *would* have gone through his pockets."

Janet had left the jacket in her panier when she parked her bike in the storeroom. It was still damp, and frankly, a little gamey now. She held it at arm's length when she took it to Hobbs. "I found it at the top of the headland this morning."

Maybe she'd imagined the smell. Hobbs didn't hesitate before draping the jacket over his arm.

"If that's a book in the lower left pocket, maybe I *should* have taken it out so it could start to dry," Janet said. "Unless that cloth is water resistant, but then it wouldn't feel so damp, would it?" She turned to Christine, who shrugged, then back to Hobbs. "You might want to take it out, anyway, Norman."

Hobbs picked up his notebook and pen. "Do you know how I might reach Ms. Kilbride's brother?"

"Sorry, no idea," Janet said. "I've never met him."

Hobbs looked at the sales counter and briefly touched the bridge of his nose, then looked from Janet to Christine. "How do you know the jacket belongs to him?"

"Don't look at me," Christine said. "I've never met him or his troublesome sister."

"Heather was wearing the jacket yesterday," Janet said. "She said it was his. She has one like it that her tattie-bogle was wearing. Are you going to take the book out of the pocket? The *presumed* book?"

"Not just now, no. May I proceed with my questions?"

"That's right; you did have some, didn't you? Please do proceed." Janet picked up the teapot. "Would you like more tea while you do?"

"No, thank you. Am I correct in saying that you are no longer certain that Rab was your caller?"

"Correct, but I'm pretty sure it was a man. I did ask who it was, but he didn't identify himself. He might not have been able to hear me any better than I heard him. He sounded like he was echoing in a grain silo. Have you ever stood in a silo and shouted?"

Hobbs shook his head.

"Shorten the conversation. Got it. The bottom of a well might be a better description, anyway." Janet saw Hobbs touch the bridge of his nose again. "Terrible signal. Breaking up. Said it was urgent. There. In a nutshell. That's all I know."

"Thank you, Mrs. Marsh."

"Now it's your turn, Norman," Christine said. "What did Hazardous Heather have to say for herself? What's her story?"

"Ms. Kilbride is safe and back on dry land."

"And?" Christine demanded.

"And I shall pay for my book and be on my way."

Janet heard a low rumble coming from Christine who might be about to erupt. Janet put a quelling hand on her shoulder and rang up the picture book with her other hand.

"Heather's brother must be relieved she's safe," she said. "You'll be sure he gets his jacket, won't you, Norman? I imagine he left it behind in his distress last night, and he'll be glad to have *it* back, too."

"Presumably," Hobbs said.

"Why only presumably?" Christine asked. "Do you know something about this situation that we don't?"

"Presumably he does," Janet said.

"Only that the *situation*, as you call it, is curious," Hobbs said. "As well, it's an interesting coincidence that you found Ms. Kilbride yesterday morning and again today, Mrs. Marsh."

"Isn't it? Although I'd substitute 'awful' for interesting, because I didn't enjoy either experience. Seeing her this morning, stuck up there on that almost nonexistent ledge—" Janet shrank from the image.

"Think of something more pleasant," Hobbs advised. He picked up one of the bookmarks Tallie had made advertising the Farquhar birthday. "Your celebration." He tucked the bookmark in the picture book.

"You should bring Nana Bethia," Janet said. "Did the Lawries celebrate Yon Bonnie's centenary in 2019?"

"I believe they had plenty else of a more personal nature going on," he said.

"Nicely circumspect," Christine said. "There's no need to air their marital problems."

"If they'd concentrated on the book business," Hobbs said, looking down his nose at Janet and Christine, "their retirement might have turned out as they'd planned. A cautionary tale, perhaps."

"Nicely judgmental," Christine said.

"I pass no judgment." Hobbs replaced his cap. "However, I have one more question for Mrs. Marsh."

"What is it, Norman?" Janet asked.

"I wonder if you can shed light on something Ms. Kilbride said when she was helped down from the ledge. Do you know why she said it was you who suggested she climb the headland?"

"*What?* No. Why would I do that?"

"Another good question," said Hobbs.

"I want to throw up even thinking about climbing that monstrosity."

"She means it gives her the *boak*," Christine said. "Makes her vomit."

"*Thank* you, Mrs. Robertson. And thank you, Mrs. Marsh. You've been very helpful."

"Baloney. You don't think I've been helpful at all. You don't even believe me."

"All I am saying, Mrs. Marsh, is that it is indeed a curious situation. We'll leave it at that, for now."

Hobbs left, and Janet was too surprised to do more than gape after him.

9

When Christine returned to the tearoom and Tallie to the bookshop, Tallie found her mother in the office. Janet sat in front of the computer, arms crossed, fists jammed in her armpits.

"Christine says you need time alone?" Tallie said. She watched her mother's lips grow thin. "Righty-o, then. Call if you need anything."

I only need one thing, Janet thought. *One answer to one question. Just who does Heather Kilbride think she is?* She took her hands from her armpits and shook them out, then logged into the computer. She limbered her fingers and set them to the keyboard in search of their first access point. So Heather had no author website? Righty-o, Janet would start with the nuts and bolts of this curious situation. She logged into the Inversgail Library and Archives' online catalog.

Before typing, she glanced at the closed office door, leaned toward the computer screen, and whispered, "Heather Kilbride, if you write, then you can't hide."

She typed the name in the search window, and hit enter.

No results.

That's the way you're going to play, is it? Janet rubbed her hands and smiled at the screen. *Oh, honey, you don't know with whom you are dealing.*

She opened a new document to keep a record of the hunt. Two columns: "0" in the first, "Inversgail Library and Archives" in the second. Then she took the search for Heather's writing oeuvre to her favorite access point—WorldCat. With the tap of a few keys, she had the collections of seventeen or eighteen thousand libraries from more than a hundred countries and territories available to her. If she found something in a library catalog, she would have authoritative, librarian-certified details in front of her.

But there were no results for true-crime books by a Heather Kilbride.

Janet flipped to her record and hammered another zero below the first and typed "WorldCat" next to it. She drummed her fingers on the mouse. Then she thought back to the day she'd first seen Heather—two days ago? So much ado in so little time.

Sharon the librarian had been happy to pass along the information that Heather was a true-crime writer, but in fact, she'd qualified that statement. She hadn't said she *is* a true-crime writer. She'd said, "she *says* she's a true-crime writer." As a librarian back in Illinois, Janet had run into more local writers than she could shake a bookend at, many of them talented and some of them quite successful. Others remained in various stages from starry-eyed and eager on through to more cynical and dogged.

Sharon's phrasing didn't necessarily mean she doubted Heather. It might be her way of accurately repeating a conversation—if Sharon's accuracy could be trusted. She hadn't played fair with Heather about knowing William Clark, for instance. Sharon was like that, Janet had learned. Not quite fast and loose with the truth, but willing to be flexible with it when it suited her. But that only meant *Sharon* couldn't be trusted. It wasn't a reflection on Heather's character. Unless it came down to the old childhood taunt: "It takes one to know one."

The next hidey-hole to search was their book distributor's online catalog. A formality, though, to be thorough. If books didn't show up in WorldCat, she probably wouldn't find any at the distributor. And she didn't. Another zero went in the record. Feeling petty, she highlighted the zeroes, made them bold, and then sat back and bared her teeth at the screen.

But hadn't she ended up liking Heather? Grudgingly. Heather was a bit of a nut, but since when had that stopped Janet liking someone?

Why did finding Heather's publications matter? What mattered was finding out why Heather had said *Janet* suggested the climb. Or finding out who Hobbs had heard it from, if not from Heather herself. *I should have asked. I should have made him tell me.*

She took out her phone. She could call him now and ask. Or she could ask him how to get in touch with Heather. She could call Sharon at the library and ask for a phone number. Heather would have given one when she got her temporary card. Janet thought about taking a page from Sharon's own book. She could spin a tale about losing Heather's number and needing it for an event at the bookshop. Not a bad ploy. Maybe they *would* consider having Heather for an event.

She put her phone away. Fussing with Norman or playing Sharon's kind of game wouldn't sit right with her conscience. Books were her calm place. Books always set her on the right track. Never mind that she hadn't found Heather's books yet. That made the hunt intriguing, not hopeless.

Janet set her twiddling fingers back to the keyboard, without success. No books by a Heather Kilbride through any of the online booksellers—new or used—UK, European, or US. Janet fell back on one of her personal search axioms of "less is more." She looked first for H. Kilbride, and then just Kilbride. The first introduced her to a series of monograms dealing with Neolithic, Iron Age, and Bronze Age archaeology in Scotland and Ireland by H.E. Kilbride-Jones. Kilbride, on its own, brought up CDs by a band of that name and a handful of solo musicians. Useless. She made notes in her record, including a reminder to investigate H.E. Kilbride-Jones's work another time. Maybe H.E. had spent time poking around their stone circle.

Nooks and crannies—that was where she'd been poking around. Time to go Google or go home. She asked the search engine to find "Heather Kilbride" and "H. Kilbride," every variation of "Heather Kilbride author" she could think of, and the same for "true-crime

Kilbride." She tried every obscure spelling of either name she could imagine and some that were completely ridiculous, and she came up with nothing every time.

Janet saved her work and stared at a cobweb in the corner above the door. It wasn't a neat, precise web anymore. Ragged. Certainly dusty. It might have been there since before they bought the shop. It didn't bother her, though, because she knew she could clear it away with a broom, with the flick of a cloth if she stood on a chair, or by asking Rab to get it whenever he bothered to show up again. Spiders didn't bother her, either. They went about their business. Did their jobs.

What was Heather's job? More of a dream? Nothing wrong with dreams, unless they brought nightmares along with them.

Janet went back out into the shop to do her real job. When Tallie finished ringing up a sale, she eyed her mother.

"You look peaceful," she said. "What'd you do? Watch five thousand kitten videos?"

Janet told her about the fruitless search.

"Yet you come out here looking peaceful, not frustrated."

"Frustration is an end point."

Tallie pulled her glasses down her nose and peered more closely at her mother's face. "You aren't just peaceful. You're percolating. I see it in your eyes."

"Because I'm stumped, which isn't the same as frustrated. Frustrated is when I throw the knitting needles over my head or threaten to toss the laptop out the window. Stumped is a holding pattern with possibilities still in play. I'm waiting for inspiration and ready to jump forward, because I did pull something useful out of that useless search. I know what Heather isn't. I don't know what she is yet, or what she thinks she's doing, but by knowing what she *isn't*, I have a wee toehold of advantage over her. It gives me a gnat's whisker of power. Also, I found a cobweb."

Tallie took a cloth from under the counter. "Where?"

"Hiding in the corner above the door. But leave it."

"Why?"

"I'm not sure yet. But for now, I like it."

⁂

Maida Fairley came into the shop that afternoon. Maida, a few years younger than Janet, was mother-in-law to Janet's son, Allan. The two women had little in common besides their two small grandsons who lived in Edinburgh, but they got along well, in a subdued sort of way. Much about Maida was subdued, possibly due to a staunch upbringing. Still, Maida managed to surprise Janet from time to time. Not in any kind of earth-shattering way. Even Maida's surprises were subdued.

"Cheers, Maida," Janet said. "We haven't seen much of you lately. All right?"

"Mustn't grumble." Maida came to the counter and stood, purse hanging from her forearm. Christine thought Maida looked like a cross between Mary Poppins and one of the Monty Pythons dressed in middle-aged drag.

And that's one of the surprising things about her, Janet thought, watching Maida flip through their new recipe postcards. *It's a good look. Solid as a cast iron skillet and just as reliable.*

"Business good?" Janet asked.

"Aye," Maida said in tones very much like a grumble. She organized the Inversgail area staff for a cleaning business headquartered in Fort William.

"That's good," Janet said.

"If you want to see it that way."

"We might as well, don't you think?"

"Aye, well. It's all right for some. We've lost staff. I've been filling in where I can, mostly in Fort William. You can't send just anyone to clean a solicitor's office. I don't enjoy the travel." She continued her perusal of the postcards, critiquing either the recipes or the format.

Summer had come up with the card designs—a recipe in the center of each with a photo of a familiar Inversgail sight in one of the corners. The recipes, three so far, were for baked goods they sold in Cakes and Tales. Traditional scones were paired with the Stevenson statue (photographed when a local knitter had warmed Stevenson's neck with a Gryffindor scarf). Pear scones went with a springtime shot of the Sgail River footbridge and a swath of bluebells. The watercolor of their building, painted by Morag Farquhar, held a place of honor, appearing with Christine's mum's shortbread, for which she was widely renowned.

Janet watched Maida tap them into neat alignment in their acrylic display. She thought Maida might have swept a surreptitious finger across the top of the display to check for dust.

"What do you think of the new postcards?" Janet asked.

"What aisle for dictionaries?" Maida countered.

"Halfway along the next aisle over," Janet said. "Let me show you."

"No need. I like a browse on my own."

Maida went down the aisle with the reference and DIY books. Watching her, Janet thought Maida's definition of *browse* must not include the word *leisurely*. She wondered if Maida ever relaxed to a point that someone could identify and label *leisurely*. She'd seen the results of mixing Maida with two glasses of sherry—the evening she'd made *that* miscalculation, Maida had gone straight from staunch to better off spending the night. There'd been no relaxed or leisurely transition period, though her permed hair had remained on high alert.

Maida came back to the counter with a thesaurus, a rhyming dictionary, and *On Writing* by Stephen King. She set them on the counter and her attention returned to the recipe postcards.

"If these sell well enough, Summer wants to add three or four more styles," Janet said.

"I should give you my recipe for tattie scones," Maida said.

"Hey, that's not a bad idea," Tallie said as she passed by with another customer.

Maida looked after Tallie and the customer, and when they disappeared down an aisle, she asked Janet, "Does she expect my ideas to be bad?"

"No, not at all. That's just a backhanded way of saying she likes it." Janet wasn't sure Maida bought that. "Sorry, it might be an American thing. Say, Maida, you know an awful lot of people. Do you know a lawyer named William Clark?"

"No." Maida looked disappointed.

Janet thought she probably looked disappointed, too. Thanks to Maida's self-effacing nature, and her job giving her entrée to homes and offices and various other venues, she was a repository of soundbites and snapshots from Inversgail and the surrounding area. A quiet repository, as she didn't go in for idle gossip. But as she'd told Janet, she knew her moral and civic duty. She also knew a good clue when she swept one up, and more than once she'd provided useful information.

"Have you seen Rab lately?" Janet asked. "I'm beginning to worry."

"He knows where he is."

"Well, yes, I suppose he does, but no one *else* seems to know. Even though he's never had a set schedule here, he does show up often enough that we don't forget he actually works here."

Maida pulled back, obviously ruffled by Janet's sarcasm.

"Sorry, Maida," Janet said. "I shouldn't have directed that at you. Or at Rab. I guess I hadn't realized until now that I really am beginning to worry."

"Och, it's what I just said the noo. *He* knows where he is. So does the dog. Dinnae fash yersel."

Easy for Maida to say she shouldn't be upset. But then Janet noticed that Maida wouldn't quite meet her eye.

"I thought you said you don't know where he is," she said. "You sound as though you might."

"I certainly do not, and if I did, I couldnae nor wouldnae say. It's strictly need to know." Maida paid for her books. Then, somewhat fashed herself, but without another word, she left.

That was so . . . Maida, Janet thought. She hoped Tallie would poke her head from around a bookshelf so they could exchange looks. They'd never added up the eccentrics in their new Inversgail lives, but Maida was definitely one of them. If she were being honest, though, the four of them might be considered eccentric, too, for making their leap across the Atlantic. *And good for us.*

As the background music slid effortlessly from a lament to a lively fiddle tune, Janet celebrated their eccentricity by arranging her arms as she'd seen the lasses do who danced the Highland fling—or maybe something closer to a flamenco. She added an eccentrically celebratory leap that was more of a lurch just as the bell over the door jingled.

The couple who came in smiled and nodded, as though her galumphing maneuver might be a typical and expected greeting. *Good for them,* Janet thought, and went to offer her assistance.

After closing, Christine jumped back into the conversational fray between Janet and Hobbs. Hobbs, having left hours earlier, got the short end of it.

"We don't know if Norman believes you encouraged Heather's climb or not," she said.

"Really?" Summer asked. "Norman believes that?"

"I just said that we don't know," Christine said.

"No wonder you were in a stew," Tallie said, ignoring Christine.

"He acted like it, and he didn't deny it." Janet, who'd been putting on her jacket, pulled it off and smacked it on the sales counter. "That was for him, not for any of you. But you were there, Christine. What more proof do you need?"

"We don't have any proof at all," Christine said darkly, "and I'll tell you why. It's because of his Scrabble face. Hear me out." She held up a hand, as though any of them had tried to interrupt. They hadn't, but their eyebrows rose by varying degrees. "You, for instance, Tallie. You have your poker face. It convinced me years ago that I should never bet against you. And Summer, you use your Boudicca-Will-Have-None-of-That voice to excellent advantage. Then we come to Norman. Just see if I ever fall for his havers about 'shall we play Scrabble in English, Scots, and Gaelic' again. *Never* again. He hides a multitude of wiles behind his constabulary stodginess. Sins, no doubt, as well."

"Wait, wasn't that Scrabble game your idea?" Summer asked.

"Ordinary Scrabble, aye. Not Norman's havering, harebrained version. The point is, he says yon havering Heather Kilbride claims Janet told her to climb the headland."

"Suggested," Janet said. "I think that's how he put it. She's supposedly telling people, or at least the authorities, that I suggested she make the climb."

"*Suggested* is a trickier word," Summer said. "It isn't as specific as *told*."

"It has nuances," Tallie agreed. "It gives her room to say she mistook your meaning, if someone calls her out. And we can easily call her out, because if she said anything like that, it shows she doesn't know you."

"Because here's my Do Not Tell, Encourage, Suggest, or Even Hint That Someone Should Climb Something Even a Tenth as High as the Headland face." Janet did an impressive imitation of the painting *The Scream* by Edvard Munch.

"So, what's going on?" Summer asked. "Why would Heather say it?"

"And why wouldn't Norman believe you when you said you didn't?" Tallie asked.

"Something's up," Christine said. "With him or . . . or there's something we don't know about. Janet's story of the phone call didn't satisfy him, either."

"But again, he didn't come right out and say he thought I'd made it up," Janet said.

"No, he didn't. He was dismissive," Christine replied. "He used the Lawries as a cautionary tale, suggesting they might have avoided marital problems and be enjoying their retirement from Yon Bonnie if they'd concentrated on business. If he tries a line like that again, I've a suggestion for *him.*"

"Think about this," Janet said. "The first time I found her, she was recreating Malcolm's death. This morning, when she was missing and presumed dead, the source from search and rescue said it was only the second kayak fatality in this area. But Heather wasn't really dead, so was her kayak really wrecked? Was this an accident and merely a coincidence? Or was she recreating another death?"

"That's a bit far-fetched if she's prying into the Murray case," Christine said.

"So far, anything to do with this woman defies fetching," Tallie said.

"Agreed," Christine said. "Emotional heft, indeed."

"I fetched something you'll want to hear," Summer said. "We wondered about Fiona Clark, the victim in that first accident. I went ahead and checked the paper's online archive, and, yes, she was William Clark's wife. I texted James to ask why the secrecy, the silence." She looked at her phone. "He said, and I quote, 'Nothing secret. Some deaths are better left alone, but.' End of quote."

"Our trailing Scottish *but*?" Christine asked. "He included that? To what end? It's a characteristic pattern of speech, aye, but it can be a throwaway word or it can be open to nuance and interpretation. Like the wretched *suggestion.*"

"It speaks volumes," Janet said. "The whole answer *shrieks* volumes, and we don't begin to understand any of them."

10

Christine went home to organize the evening meal her parents called "tea." Janet turned down an invitation to join them, and waved off a quick bite and a movie with Tallie and Summer, as well, turning her bike toward the quiet of home, cats, and toasted cheese.

"Pick up some Marmite when you stop at Basant's," Tallie called after her.

Janet waved again without wondering how Tallie knew she meant to stop. Someday she'd surprise her daughter. *And it won't be a subdued, Maida-like surprise, either,* she thought. *But I'll wait until it's worth it.*

Tonight, it was worth stopping at Basant's. She'd pick up the jar of Marmite and ask Basant if he'd picked up any more information or impressions of Heather. And because of the way this day had started, continued, and ended, she would let him sell her something she didn't need. And then, if he was willing, she'd ask what he could tell her about Fiona Clark's death.

She parked her bike against the wall of the small shop. As she straightened from locking it to the handy drainpipe near the door, a young couple with a pram was on their way out. Janet stood back to give them room. Then, seeing their struggle to coordinate carrier bags, pram, and the panic that a suddenly screeching baby brings on, she leapt forward to hold the door. After they were safely through, an elderly woman with a shopping trolley bustled toward the door on her way out. Janet held it again, standing out of the way. It was the folklore- and omen-spouter—the woman with the nonsense about seagulls and death. Janet was almost tempted to say *so far, so good,* but the woman trundled past as though she wasn't there.

"Good evening, Mrs. Janet." Basant, book in hand, smiled at her. "A chilly evening and a narrow escape from a new bairn discovering her lung power, aye?"

"Both, yes." Janet let the door close and glanced around. No other customers. Safe to be honest. "I hate to say it, Basant, but after the day I've had, if those poor parents came back in now, with the baby in full-screech, I'd be outside before you could say 'Scots wha hae.'"

"No need to apologize, Mrs. Janet. Negotiating these narrow aisles while dodging that pram, which barely squeezed between my well-stocked shelves, while also trying to ignore a wailing wee banshee, would have been too much for a patron saint, let alone any person's sanity. As well, you should be aware that if they were to return, I would join you out the door and away on your bicycle. But I am sorry you have had a hard day. How can I help?"

"Marmite and answers to some questions?"

"Marmite I can do. Answers, I will try."

Janet located the Marmite. She had never developed a liking for the salty yeast spread, but Tallie loved a thin schmear of it on toast. She took the small jar to the counter where Basant waited.

"Marmite accomplished," he said. "Let us tackle your questions."

"Thank you. First, did you hear that Heather Kilbride was found safe?"

Basant nodded. "Hopes answered."

"Yes, thank goodness. Has she been in again?"

"No."

"Have you heard anything more about her?"

"I can only offer a few favorable impressions I have gathered from our fellow shopkeepers. They worried, as did you and I, until she was returned safely. From our friends at the cheese shop, for instance, I heard this—she endeared herself by falling in love with the shop's aromas. She also bought Mull Cheddar, Strathdon Blue, and Highland Brie, and promised to return for Caboc and Red Anster. But that does not help you."

"It kind of does," Janet said. "We like the same kinds of cheese. She's unusual, though. A puzzle. But I found myself liking her when she and I talked, so it's good to know other people seem to like her, too."

"And that is also a puzzle, is it not? When we seek reassurance about something as simple as liking another person?"

"I guess that's what's going on in my head." Janet thought about that for a moment. "But am I more puzzled, troubled, or irked?"

"Unsettled?"

"That works. Here's another question, though, and it's part of why I'm unsettled. Have you met, seen, or heard anything about Heather's brother?"

"None of the above and nothing at all." Basant cocked his head. "What have you heard?"

"Only that she has one. She was wearing his jacket yesterday at the burn. She said it was his, anyway, and it was way too big for her. I found it this morning on top of the headland."

"Left behind in worry?"

"Or in a hurry," Janet said. "Towels and T-shirts get left behind often enough at a beach. I gave it to Norman Hobbs."

The door opened, held by Derek Spiers, and bringing in a laughing Agnes Black and a rush of cold air. Basant greeted them. Agnes fluttered a wave, but turned back to Derek for another round of laughter, and then the two moved down the nearest aisle.

"Anything else at the moment?" Basant asked quietly.

"Digestives?" Agnes called from the back of the shop.

Basant, looking over Janet's head, called in return, "Along to your left two feet, at elbow height."

"Chocolate," Agnes called. "Milk, not dark."

"Six inches more to your left, please," Basant replied.

"I can show her, if you like." Janet raised her eyebrows at Basant.

"No need. It is the same question every fortnight. She has great strength of will to make a packet last that long."

"Good Lord. I could never." Janet smiled and stood aside when Agnes approached to pay. Derek trailed behind. "Nice to see you two, again. I meant to call you, Agnes. We'll be happy to have your group meet at Yon Bonnie Books."

"I thought you might," Agnes said. "Didn't I say that, Derek?"

He was looking out the door and didn't answer. He might not have heard; he'd turned and leaned his head close to the glass and seemed to be looking up the street to the right.

"Is something going on out there, Derek?" Agnes asked.

"Sorry, what's that, Agnes?" Derek straightened and looked back at her. "Finished here, are we? Any other stops before I drop you home?"

"Ta, no. You've been more than kind enough." Agnes put the digestives in a carrier bag and said quietly to Janet, "More than he wanted to, I'm afraid. No good deed, though, eh?" Then, at normal tone, "We'll see you Friday, then. Cheery-bye."

"Where were we?" Janet asked Basant when the door closed behind them.

"A happy ending," Basant said. "Sister and jacket were both returned. Forgive me, though, if I say that you still look puzzled, troubled, irked, or unsettled."

"Because I have one more question. But it's one you don't have to answer it if you don't want to."

"Understood."

"We—Tallie, Christine, Summer, and I—have learned that William Clark's wife was the young woman mentioned in reports this morning. The one who died in what looked like a similar kayak accident."

"That is sadly true."

"Why do people tiptoe around William Clark?"

"Who does this tiptoeing?"

"Not you. You told me, last night, that his wife died and that he collects miniature books. But Constable Hobbs, James Haviland at the paper, Rab. That reminds me, too, have you seen Rab lately?"

Basant shook his head.

Janet blew out an aggravated breath. "Ian Atkinson practically ran from the shop when we asked him if he knows Clark. You gave me a glimpse of the man, and I thank you for that, Basant. But what's going on with the others? What is this force field around the man? James sent a text to Summer that said some deaths are best left alone. I can understand why that might be true—to avoid inflicting pain or out of respect for privacy. But it's been, what? Ten years?"

Janet picked up the jar of Marmite, weighing it in one hand, then passing it to the other and back again. Not as useful as a stress ball but serving the same purpose. She remembered thinking about threats and protection on yesterday's bike ride. About how Heather's research might threaten people. She glanced at Basant and saw his worried eyes intent on her hands now tossing the jar back and forth.

"Sorry, Basant." She set the jar on the counter.

"And I am sorry. I cannot answer your questions. Although I am on good terms with the people you mention, I do not travel in the circle involved in this force field."

"Don't be sorry, and don't worry about it. Maybe the answer is as simple as force of habit."

"No doubt. Mind you, to tiptoe for ten years must require the same strength of will that keeps Agnes Black in check so she does not devour an entire packet of digestives in less than a fortnight. Milk chocolate, not dark."

Janet looked at the smile playing on Basant's lips and then at his serious eyes. Gentle humor tempering an interesting truth. Time to head home.

"What are you reading today?" she asked. He almost always had a book in his hand.

Basant held up a mass-market paperback. "An account of a dreadful case of abduction and murder that happened in Yorkshire. True crime is a genre I have not read before, but in honor of our visiting writer, I thought I should broaden my reading horizons. I have often told my sisters that it is good to get a new perspective."

"It is. You're right. Heather believes it, too. She likes viewing situations from different perspectives when she's doing research. What do you think of the book?"

"I find that my stomach does not appreciate this perspective. This came as a surprise, as I like Ian Atkinson's murder mysteries quite a lot."

"Reality can leave a lot to be desired."

"Desired and often discovered between the covers of a novel." Basant reached around and stood the book in front of the cash register. "There, I have set it free. Anyone who wishes to may take it. And I will turn to something that will bring the desired refreshment."

"For your soul?"

"For my palate. Although, something else I have found is that my soul and my palate are closely related." He bent and brought a book from somewhere below the counter—*Scottish Baking* by Sue Lawrence. "My sisters gave it to me for my birthday. I am sorry I did not buy it from your shop."

"Ah, but *they* did."

"Ah, and it might be that I gave them a hint. So now, if you can spare another few moments, I have something I think will help you through your puzzles, troubles, irks, and attempts to settle the woes of the world or at least those in our own small corner of it. But not," he said with a wave at the shelves behind him and at the dozens of jars of old-fashioned sweets the shelves held, "from our jars of nostalgia. I will be right back."

Janet picked up the jar of Marmite and thumped it into her cupped left hand. She wondered if a shinty ball would feel as good. She could ask Basant where to buy one. Or she could buy a second jar of Marmite.

She put the jar down when she heard Basant returning. He held a plastic container in both hands, like an offering. It might hold two baseballs. Or two cake squares.

"I've been experimenting with a recipe," Basant said. "If I put this in a bag, it should travel safely in the panier on your bike until you arrive home. Mind, I am not the baker either of my sisters is. This might not be ready for my case." He nodded toward the small bakery case sitting on the end of his counter that held a selection of meat pies and a variable selection of cakes and puddings.

"I bet you're being modest. Who taught Arati and Puja to cook?"

He acknowledged the compliment with a bow. "At any rate, it is not yet ready for large-scale production or the problems of how long it will keep and can best be transported."

"What is it?"

"The night sky brightened by a path of moonbeams and sparkling stars."

"Good heavens."

"As you say. In reality, it is chocolate cake with a swirl of lightly sweetened mascarpone and sprinkled with flakes of Himalayan salt. The cake is moist and quite rich."

"It sounds like a slice of heaven, in more ways than one."

"That is my goal. If you will take this, I believe we can help each other. You are in need of a path to light your way through puzzles, et cetera, and chocolate is the answer to many questions. For my part, I would like to know if I am on my own correct path with this recipe. You and Tally can be my beta testers. There is enough here for two."

"Thank you—for more than the cake," Janet said. "Thank you for not waving off my worries or telling me to stick to my own business."

"That might be the easier way to go. But if one approaches life with a good heart?"

"But do I have a good heart?" Janet asked. "Or am I a nosy besom?"

"I hear your questions and counter with my own. Are the two mutually exclusive? Can you say for certain that either is bad or wrong?"

~

The immense number of stars arcing from horizon to horizon on a clear night in Inversgail could astound any visitor who'd only ever known light-polluted skies. By the time Janet left Basant's, clouds had arrived like a flock of gulls following a fishing boat. No Milky Way like sweetened mascarpone with sparkling Himalayan salt. The moon shone only briefly between the clouds now flying inland, and then it stayed hidden. *No matter,* Janet thought. *I have my own slice of the heavens.*

A bicycle passed in the street. Janet glanced toward it. Something about the jacket and the hair made her think of Heather. She unlocked her bike from the drainpipe, peering after the other bike. The rider stopped under the next streetlight, not that far along. Heather—it was definitely Heather—fiddled with her brakes or gears. Janet didn't think Heather had seen her or recognized her, or she might have waved or stopped. Too dark. Although not really all *that* dark in front of Basant's.

Heather still fiddled. Janet waited. If Heather turned and saw her, Janet decided she would wave and ride forward. If Heather didn't ride on, Janet would have to pass her to continue homeward. She could stop and see if Heather needed help.

Janet got on her bike just as Heather dusted her hands and started out again, pedaling slowly. Janet started, too, happy to hang back, pedaling just as slowly. The more she thought about it, the more she didn't want to catch up to Heather. Alone. At night.

But the streets were hardly deserted. A few cars passed. People on foot, though not so many in the quiet streets on the way home. But she could turn at the next corner and take a different route. Or turn around and ride to Christine's. Or Nev's.

Where was Heather headed?

Heather's bike had a flashing light on the rear fender where Janet's had only a reflector. *Smart,* Janet thought. *I'll get one.* Up ahead, Heather made a left turn where Janet would make a right. When Janet reached the corner, she didn't hesitate. She turned left.

The flashing rear fender light made it easy to keep Heather in sight. Janet still didn't want to catch up to her, but as long as it was this easy. . . . She took a hand from the handlebars to reassure herself that her phone was in her pocket.

Heather made another turn, this time uphill. Her pedaling slowed. Janet imagined the younger woman puffing, barely holding on. Three months earlier, Janet would have fallen off her bike, gasping. *What will I do if she stops?*

Heather turned the next corner onto a street that leveled out.

Janet braked at the corner and wondered what she thought she was doing. Hoping to find out where Heather stayed? Who she might be going to see? Why? Nosiness in the dark of night?

Heather's fender light grew smaller as she pedaled on, and Janet didn't think she knew she was being followed. Janet pedaled faster so she didn't lose sight. But what good would it do her to know where Heather was staying or who she was visiting? If Heather stopped and went into a house, Janet couldn't *know* it was her bedsit or B&B. And what if she got lost in an unfamiliar part of town?

Janet pedaled on, matching the pace of the fender light. She wasn't terribly worried about getting lost. She only had to find her way back to the harbor. Just turn her bike downhill and let it roll.

At the next turn, she knew she wasn't lost. She'd driven down this street *and* ridden her bike here, and down the one where Heather turned next. The memories weren't warm and fuzzy. Malcolm Murray's house lay ahead on the right. Malcolm Murray, central figure in Heather's research, avid cycler. Deceased. Was this nighttime ride another effort to gather facts and feelings? To develop a connection to Malcolm?

Heather's fender light stopped blinking and shone steadily in front of the Murray house. Janet coasted to a stop in the shadows of the privet hedge two houses before, far enough back, and shadowy enough, that Heather wouldn't easily see her. Far enough that if Janet hadn't known it was Heather, she might not have guessed.

Heather propped her bike on its kickstand, put a hand in a jacket pocket. Pulled out a phone—Janet recognized the bowed head, the cupped hand held at reading distance, the light of a display like a candle in the dark. Then Heather walked a short way up the footpath toward the house, holding the phone up in front of her. Taking pictures? Making a video? What feelings did she hope to gather here in the dark?

The first time Janet had seen the house—imposing, square, cold—she'd felt as though it stared past her, behind her, at something she couldn't and wouldn't want to see. An illogical feeling, she knew. But even when someone had lived in the house, and let yellow lamplight spill from every window upstairs and down, the effect had been more of keeping something at bay than one of cheer or invitation. Now the house sat like a hulk in the dark. Janet hugged herself and rubbed her upper arms. Whatever feelings Heather was gathering, Janet didn't want to share them.

A car turned onto the street farther down, normal people going about their normal lives. It was a good time to go home and leave this unhappy house and puzzling woman behind. Janet turned her bike. With a last look over her shoulder, she started to pedal away. And stopped.

The car had parked across from the Murray house. Straddling her bike, Janet watched the driver get out. Heather waved and went to meet him. Him? Maybe. Taller, anyway, but Janet couldn't tell who it was at this distance. Heather put a hand on his arm, showed him her phone. Then she turned and pointed toward Janet. *At* her. Then Heather held her phone up, pointed it toward Janet. Taking a picture? Filming? Janet didn't wait to find out. She put every bit of strength she had into her pedals.

11

Janet's thoughts churned faster than her bike pedals as she raced home. *What just happened? Did Heather know I was there all along? Me, specifically, or just someone?* She turned the first corner she came to, then the next and the next, hoping to put enough of a tangled route between her and the car to lose it, if it came after her. Janet's heart and breath sounded louder in her ears than any car engine.

Who was that with her? Did she know I was following her? The way she stopped and fiddled while I unlocked my bike—fiddled with what? What if she followed me to Basant's in the first place? But she couldn't have known I'd follow her to the Murrays'. Maybe she was going to follow me, and she changed plans when I stayed behind her. But why? Am I one of Heather's experiments? Because that's what all of these "Heather" situations are beginning to feel like.

Janet chanced a look behind. No one. Maybe there never had been. But her feet didn't slow down. Neither did her mind.

I could've confronted her. Found out what was going on. Or simply talked to her. Said hello instead of hanging back when I first saw her. Treated her like a friend. Janet was beginning to feel foolish. Almost. *Next time,* she thought. *Next time, I'll talk to her, ask her. But not if we're alone in the dark.*

She only slowed when she reached Argyll Terrace. She didn't want to arrive home with a bigger clatter than usual, which could alert Ian of her arrival and give him something to wonder about or pry into. He liked to keep tabs on their comings and goings, and she'd become used to seeing him at the window in his upstairs writing room. Though she didn't like his nosy ways, she was grudgingly thankful for his eyes and ears on the neighborhood.

She locked her bike, took the package from the panier, and went through the garden gate to the back door. Once in the house, she locked the door, leaned her back against it, and closed her eyes. *Safe. With chocolate cake.*

Then she heard footsteps.

Paw-steps, rather, and a double-base purr accompanied by a high, piping mew. "Evening, lads," she said, opening her eyes. "All right? Got your fur lounge suits on, I see. How about a bite?"

Butter wound himself once around her ankles then led the way to the kitchen.

"Coming, Smirr?" Janet asked the old tom. He stretched a front paw in a half-hearted attempt to trip the kitten. "I've got fish for those who keep me company while I toast cheese," she told him.

That suited him and he followed. She fixed the cats' meal, and while her sandwich toasted, she called Norman Hobbs. Speaking to him, while she might sound like a meddler, made more sense than telling the cats about her evening's experience. They would hear her agitation and might think she was scolding them. It didn't bother her that Hobbs might feel the same way.

Hobbs took her call and listened without interruption. Janet didn't delude herself, though. From the muffled sounds on his end, he wasn't quietly intent on her information; he was finishing his own supper and trying not to be obvious about it. She knew she might be taking advantage of his manners, but went into more detail about following Heather than she'd planned. Her sandwich finished toasting at the same time a stifled belch came from the other end.

"May I know why you would follow someone in the dark without knowing where you were going, Mrs. Marsh?" Hobbs asked.

"Not just anyone. And I was on my way home—until I made a detour. This wasn't the wee hours of the night, Norman, and I didn't follow her to some dicey dockyard or out onto a deserted, moonless moor." She was getting nicely worked up and she pushed her sandwich away. "I'm not calling to make a complaint against myself for doing something dumb." She heard another stifled belch, and possibly a stifled sigh, and was glad she hadn't spewed all that at the cats. Janet didn't stifle her own sigh. "I'm not making a complaint against Heather or the mystery man, either, Norman. I just thought you might want to know about more of her odd behavior in case it escalates."

"Thank you, Mrs. Marsh."

"It also made me wonder if anyone's living in the house. Malcolm needed a good housekeeper, but the place is full of valuable things. I really don't mean to tattle on her—to be a *clype*—but considering the other things Heather's done, can you honestly say she wouldn't try to get into that house? Is someone keeping an eye on it? Checking doors and windows in case someone *does* try?"

"I believe that is in hand, but I will make inquiries. Now, if that is all, Mrs. Marsh?"

"No. One more thing. Did you get her brother's jacket back to him? Could that be who I saw with her tonight?"

There was a hesitation on his end. "My understanding is that he is not in the area. I returned the jacket to Ms. Kilbride."

"Did she say where he is? How do you know he's okay? Norman, I'm genuinely worried about him. Call me a meddler, call me nosy, but if you haven't seen him or talked to him yourself, how do you know he didn't fall off the headland? What if he jumped?"

Silence on Hobbs's end.

"Sorry, Norman. I didn't mean to sound hysterical."

"Dinnae fash. You're worried. What put the notion in your mind that he might have fallen or jumped?"

"It was always there. It's the go-to function of my brain in high places. The jacket was so near the edge. Abandoned."

"If he jumped, why bother to take the jacket off and leave it? Mrs. Marsh, Janet, I understand your worries, but when I gave the jacket to Ms. Kilbride, she assured me she knows where her brother is and that he is safe."

"You asked her if he was safe? Do you always ask that when you return someone's jacket?"

"She offered the information."

"Isn't *that* kind of odd?"

"Much of the information I receive from the public might be considered odd."

Hobbs was quiet again. Janet screwed her lips shut, refusing to rise to the bait.

"To put your mind further at ease," Hobbs said, breaking the impasse, "Ms. Kilbride told me that *she* left the jacket on the headland. She forgot it and was well-chuffed to have it returned. She's grateful to the thoughtful person who found it and turned it in."

"You didn't tell her it was me."

"No."

"Why did she forget it?" Janet asked.

"People, being people, leave things behind, Mrs. Marsh. You might be surprised at the extent and variety. I've a cousin who works in lost property at Waverly Station in Edinburgh."

"It wasn't just the jacket," Janet said. "It was the book, too. In the pocket."

"Which you assured me you did not look at."

"I assured you and it's true." Janet put a finger on her toasted cheese. Cold. She pulled it back toward her anyway. "Well. I'm glad she's safe. And her brother. And the jacket."

"And presumably the book," Hobbs said.

"I worry about books left to molder in odd places almost as much as I worry about people teetering in high places."

"I appreciate that, as I'm sure the books do."

A teakettle whistled in the background. Janet heard the scrape of a chair and the whistle abruptly cutting off.

"I did ask Ms. Kilbride why she thinks you encouraged her to climb the headland," Hobbs said.

"*Did* you. I'd love to hear the answer to that."

"You left her a note."

"I did not."

"She did not keep the note, so we cannot know if that's true."

"Yes, you *can.* I did *not.* I would *never.*"

"Mrs. Marsh. *Janet.*"

Was he shouting at her? No, she'd been shouting at him. "What?" She wasn't ready to be more polite.

"I believe you. Can you describe the car Ms. Kilbride's companion drives?"

Janet swore quietly at herself and pushed the cold sandwich away again. "It was dark and I wasn't thinking. So, no."

"Here's something else, then. I've called in a favor and hope to have the brother's address and phone before long."

After hanging up, Janet brought her laptop in from the family room and put it on the kitchen table. She reheated her sandwich and took a bite—sharp and strong. *And so am I.* She set her plate on the table, sat down, and said *oof* when Smirr helped himself to her lap. She opened the laptop and the "Where's Heather" document she'd started at the bookshop and saved to cloud storage. The kitten started playing with her shoelaces, and she started a journal.

"It's more of a ledger than a Dear Diary account," she told Smirr after the last bite of sandwich. Smirr blinked his eyes and cleaned his paw.

Janet wiped her fingers, and went back to recording every detail she could remember of her interactions with Heather. She couldn't expect Hobbs to share all his information or hunches—she and her partners had learned to respect those hunches—but she'd be ready to share *hers* if he needed them.

Tallie brought a shiver of night air in with her when she came home from the movie. It flittered into the family room where Janet sat reading with the cats. The shiver woke Smirr and settled with the weight of a feather across Janet's shoulders. The kitten sneezed. Janet pulled an afghan around herself.

"Bit of a chill out there tonight," she said when Tallie joined them. "How was the movie?"

"More than I bargained for. Pretty violent. And there's more than a chill out there. It doesn't help that it's getting dark so early."

"Are we ready for the cold and dark of a Highland winter?"

"The lads are." Tallie rubbed each of the cats between their ears. "They've got fur pajamas. We can be ready, too. We'll knit nightcaps and sleep snug as bugs."

"Let's get Nana Bethia to knit them for us. She's faster and more competent."

"True, but I'm more than competent at *pouring* nightcaps. Fancy a sherry?"

Janet showed her a small measure with finger and thumb.

Tallie went to the kitchen for glasses. The kitten followed, ever hopeful. "Thanks for the Marmite," Tallie called. "What's in the bag?"

"I can't believe I forgot that! It's from Basant. An experiment he wants us to try. The way he described it—bring it, will you? I haven't even looked at it."

Tallie came back with two glasses then went back and returned with two plates. "Basant described this to you, and you forgot about it?" She handed one of the plates to Janet. "Look at that. Smell that. Now, tell me what happened. Because for this piece of Oh My God to fly right out of your head, something had to have happened."

"Taste first, then tell."

"Deal."

The night sky, Basant had said, *brightened by a path of moonbeams and sparkling stars.* The description suited the square of cake on Janet's plate. He'd swirled an arc of mascarpone across each piece and sprinkled the whole with flakes of salt.

"There's more of the white stuff inside," Tallie said through a mouthful. She put her hand over her mouth. "Sorry, couldn't help it. Don't wait, or I'll grab yours when mine's gone."

It was so moist it was almost a pudding cake, and neither it nor the mascarpone was too sweet.

"Notes of cardamom?" Tallie asked.

"And almond? Both subtle, though."

They finished in contented silence, then Tallie took the plates to the kitchen. "After that, I'm not sure I care what happened," she said when she came back. She scooped up Smirr and settled him on her lap. "Blissed out." She kicked off her shoes. "But tell me anyway."

Typing her detailed notes had organized Janet's thoughts and she was able to give a concise summary. "I think what it adds up to," she said when she'd finished, "is a path. That's what the cake from Basant was about, with its path of stars. I'm puzzled by this woman, so I laid out the path of my interactions with her. The trouble is that I can only look back and see where I've been. My path of notes doesn't tell me where I'm going."

"I detect notes of eccentricity. Hers, not yours." Tallie finished her sherry. "I've known about yours for years."

"It's nice to be noticed. Thank you, dear. Any other thoughts?"

"Yeah, about the McGonagall at the door."

She was talking about the framed embroidery hanging over the front door. Janet had hung it there for Curtis. He'd loved the coincidence of their house being built in 1880, the same year William McGonagall, the Scots poet infamous for his overly dramatic doggerel, had written his ripped-from-the-headlines "The Tay Bridge Disaster." Janet had embroidered the last lines of the poem on linen: "For the stronger we our houses do build, The less chance we have of being killed." They'd hung it as a talisman. The house and the embroidery had both proved to be more robust than the marriage.

"What's wrong with my McGonagall?" Janet asked.

"Not a thing. It's perfect. But this thing with Heather makes me think you could write up your adventures with her in the style of McGonagall and call them 'The Beaton Bridge Not-Quite-Disaster,' 'The Sea Kayak Near-Catastrophe,' and 'The Incident of the Woman Who Biked Alone in the Night.'"

"They'd be ridiculous, and I doubt there'd be a market for them."

"I'm pretty sure McGonagall faced the same problem. He and his wife depended on the charity and kindness of friends. But you don't need to sell your doggerel. It'd be for us, for our entertainment. Or—oh, hey! What do you think of this? We can have a McGonagall write-alike contest."

"Dare I say you're brill?"

"Sure, but I owe it all to Basant's cake. It made my little gray cells sparkle."

"I'll add that to my cake critique for him. Any other thoughts before I head upstairs?"

"Not about the cake," Tallie said. "And I hesitate to bring it up only to bring us down. But from where we stand, looking back at the way your path has come, it doesn't take much imagination to guess where it's going. Or maybe it isn't imagination. Maybe it's experience."

"Or both."

"Mm. Hand me your glass. I'll do the dishes. Anyway, I don't think your path is heading in a direction anyone expects, or that anyone will want to go."

12

When Janet heard the bell jingle over the shop door the next morning, the man who walked in was the last person she expected. "Welcome to Yon Bonnie Books," she said.

"Cheers." William Clark glanced around as though getting his bearings. He nodded at Janet and crossed the room to a glass-fronted case set into the wall opposite the fireplace. The case, framed as though it was a painting, wasn't much larger than two medicine cabinets side by side, but a good twelve inches deep. Stuart Farquhar had set the case into the wall and kept a selection of rare and antique books on its three shelves. Each of the shop's subsequent owners had followed suit.

With Clark's attention occupied, Janet scooted from behind the counter to look for Tallie. Tallie had gone down an aisle with a customer wanting gardening books and, from the look and sound of it, a good long chat, as well. Janet didn't interrupt. She thought about texting Christine, who would be as intrigued as she was by Clark's visit. In fact, she might be downright tickled. She might abandon her teapots for a look and—

Janet left her phone in her pocket. Christine could be intrigued or tickled after the fact. As much as any other customer, Clark deserved to shop in peace.

Good customer service, friendly yet professional, was a different matter. Janet approached Clark, who was still perusing the titles in the glass case.

"If you'd like me to take a book out for you, let me know," she said. "You're welcome to have a seat and look at anything for as long as you want."

Clark gave an offhand wave over his shoulder. Janet tried to gauge the height of that shoulder in comparison to Heather. Had he been the man who met her the night before? *But how tall is Heather?* Janet wondered. *Taller than me, but. . . .* She couldn't remember well enough.

She went back behind the counter and picked up a review journal. Book browsing habits were more interesting, though, and William Clark's in particular. She put the journal down and watched. He seemed to be reading the titles on each of the spines in the locked case and studying the covers of the few books there was room to display face out.

The boxed set that held Clark's eye longest was Janet's current favorite item in the case. The box—a shadow box, really, with a glass front of its own—housed five miniature books published by David Bryce and Sons in Glasgow in 1905. Bryce had specialized in producing books so tiny they boggled Janet's mind. These five, including a book of Robert Burns's poetry, each measured just one inch by three-quarters of an inch. They were bound in red roan and nestled face out, each in a compartment of its own. A sixth compartment held a portrait of Burns and a magnifier to make reading the wee things easier. The box, lacquered in a tartan pattern, was in nearly perfect condition. Janet lived in hope for the day they sold the set for its very dear price. She also knew she'd mourn its leaving when they did, or wish she'd taken it home herself.

Clark left the case and went to look at the watercolor that Farquhar's sister had painted of their building. He stopped short of the fireplace, resting his hands on the back of a chair. It happened to be the chair Rab's dog Ranger usually napped in. Clever dog that he was, he'd bring his own tea towel with him and arrange it in the chair before arranging himself on top of it.

As if reading Janet's thoughts, Clark asked over his shoulder, "Does Rab MacGregor still work here?"

"He does." Janet wondered how Clark knew that, but she didn't see any reason to volunteer more information about her sporadic—and still absent—employee.

Clark didn't ask for more information. Maybe he was satisfied by the answer or had just been making small talk. Janet wondered how he would react if she asked him if he knew Heather. He hadn't introduced himself, so it would come as a question out of left field. *And am I prepared for how that conversation goes if I start it?*

He came to the sales counter wearing the quiet smile she'd seen as he walked past the threatening coach driver in the library carpark. The smile softened his high cheekbones and prominent nose. Janet couldn't tell if the smile reflected his mood or was part of his natural resting face. It gave him a slight air of absence, as though his mind was already moving on to another thought.

The day had turned cold, and he wore gloves and a tartan scarf with an overcoat. He took the gloves off and tucked them into a pocket. "Grand to see Morag's picture still hanging," he said. "And the Bryce miniatures still in the cupboard. Bittersweet, that, aye? Colonel Farquhar told me that every time customers asked to see the set, he hoped they would buy it and prayed they would not."

"I hadn't realized they'd been here that long," Janet said, "but that's exactly how I feel about them, too. I'm Janet Marsh, by the way, one of the four new owners of Yon Bonnie Books. I don't think I've seen you in here before."

"Maybe at the library." Clark turned the quiet smile toward her and then directed it to the Farquhar birthday celebration bookmarks. "I haven't been in the shop since Colonel Farquhar died. I have something he gave me." He opened his coat and took a small, white cardboard box from a trouser pocket. It had the look and size of a jeweler's box for a ring or pin. "He had this with him during the war."

Clark lifted and set the white lid aside on the counter. Then, with forefinger and thumb, he carefully lifted another box out of the white bottom and put this second box down in front of Janet. Ornate metal—possibly silver. Not quite square, it wasn't much bigger than an inch by an inch and a bit more. With forefinger and thumb again, Clark adjusted the box slightly so that, although *it* wasn't square, it sat square to the edge of the counter.

"I think I'm afraid to touch it," Janet said.

"It gives that feeling." Clark's smile warmed as he gazed at the small treasure. "That's a magnifier set in the cover. Still no?" He glanced at her.

"You go first."

Clark rubbed his hands as though about to do a trick. And it was like a magic trick when he undid a clasp at the side of the box and turned the lid back on its hinges. Inside was another miniature book—much fancier than the Bryce books in the locked cupboard. This tiny gem had a cover of fine brown leather with an ornamental gilt border, and in the center a lozenge of green leather and gilt.

"He said it brought him luck." Clark tipped the book out onto his palm and then turned it face up. "He passed that luck on to me when I joined up. You'll be fine holding it. Aye?"

Janet nodded, and Clark moved the book from his palm to hers. She stroked the leather cover with one finger.

"Open it."

Gingerly, she opened the cover and turned past the marbled endpapers to the title page. It was another Bryce edition of the Burns book in their set, *Poems, Chiefly in the Scottish Dialect*, this one published in 1895.

"What is it about something so small and perfect that makes it thrilling to hold?" Janet said, more to the book than to Clark.

"The beating of its heart."

Janet looked up. Clark still had his eyes on the book. "Wouldn't you love it," she said, "if you could time travel? Visit David Bryce and Sons, in Glasgow, and watch them make these?"

A genuine, conspiratorial smile lit Clark's face. "Aye, and go back a bit further to visit Robbie Burns. Watch his 'honest, *sonsie* face' to see what he thinks of a wee miracle like this."

"Maybe not so plump, but honest, I'm sure," Janet said with a laugh. "This edition, in this condition, must be quite rare."

"I've never seen another as fine."

"But we're not really in the market to buy—"

"And I'm not looking to sell," Clark said. "You might say I brought it for a visit. I spent a great deal of time here when I was a lad. Getting away from life."

"Life with books—the life in stories—can be more real, don't you think?" Janet said as she looked at the postage stamp–sized pages, carefully turning them. Clark didn't answer. Janet glanced up from the book and saw that his attention had drifted to the zhen xian bao Rab made for them. Clark picked up the information card displayed with the folded books.

"Beautiful, aren't they?" Janet said. "Open one, if you like."

Clark replaced the information card and picked up one of Janet's favorite zhen xian bao. Rab had used a combination of handmade papers and decorative origami papers for it. The range of greens, purples, and blues were the shades of Inversgail's hills, seas, and skies. They were the colors that made visitors stop in their tracks and believe, hand on heart, that somehow they must be a Scot who'd returned home.

Clark didn't immediately run his fingers over the texture of those papers, as Janet had when she first saw that zhen xian bao. He flipped the book to look at the back, then flipped it face up again. Without exploring it further, or trying to open any of the folds, he returned it to the display. *A glance-and-a-shrug reaction, if ever I've seen one,* Janet thought.

"MacGregor made them?" he asked. The question was a shrug, too. "I used to be indiscriminate in my book collecting. When I started, I let emotion lead me. Nothing wrong with emotion, but Colonel Farquhar taught me to focus. It was good advice." Clark flicked a finger toward the zhen xian bao display. "Nothing wrong with crafts, mind, artistic or otherwise."

Janet handed the miniature Burns back to him. He put the book into its metal box, and that into the jeweler's box, then slipped it back into his pocket. He turned in a half circle, gazing around the shop again. Janet thought his smile looked wistful now. She wondered if he was looking for the shop as it had been when he was a lad—or if maybe he actually saw it.

"Will you come to our Farquhar birthday celebration?" she asked.

"I might do." His back still turned, he answered the bookshelf in front of him rather than her. He pulled his gloves from his pocket, slapped them into the palm of his hand, and started for the door. "Cheers," he said, as he had when he came in, and went out the door.

Janet didn't call cheers in return, as she might with another customer. Clark's focus had moved on, and he wouldn't have heard her.

Tallie appeared, leaning against one of the bookshelves, watching her mother, and pointed to the door. "Who was that?"

Janet crooked a finger and waited until Tallie joined her behind the counter before she answered. "Is your customer still browsing?"

"After gardening books, she wanted help choosing a knitting book for her grandmother. I warned her I'm an admirer, not a knitter, but I described Nana Bethia and showed her the books *she'd* bought. Then, when she finally chose one, the cookbooks caught her eye, and with scones in the mix, everything was up for grabs again. Long story short, she went next door to settle her mind with tea and treacle tart, and she promised to come back refreshed for round two."

"That'll soothe her to the point she'll go home with two or three books," Janet said.

"Tranquilized by treacle tart. Excellent. What about your customer? Who was it?"

"He was a curiosity, not a customer. That was William Clark."

"No kidding."

Janet admired her daughter's ability to assume a poker face when needed, but she'd always loved watching Tallie process intriguing information, the tip of her head, right, then left, as though catching sight of something furtive or slippery.

"Did you hear any of our conversation?" Janet asked.

"I'll fess up. I heard from 'honest, sonsie face' to his parting 'cheers.'"

"Then why didn't you join us? Until he dissed the zhen xian bao, he was charming. You missed seeing the most gorgeous little book. It belonged to Stuart Farquhar. He carried it during the war and said it brought him good luck."

"How did Clark get it? I mean, a gorgeous thing like that, his good luck piece? Why would Farquhar sell it?"

"Farquhar gave it to him. When *he* joined up."

"Huh."

"You don't believe him?"

"I used to get paid to be skeptical," Tallie said. "Why did he come in?"

"He brought the book in for a visit."

"I heard him say that."

"It made sense at the time." Janet dropped onto the stool. "You think there's something fishy."

"You said he was charming?"

"He was. When I asked him why it's thrilling to hold something so small and perfect, he said 'the beating of its heart.' And I honestly almost felt it beating in my hand."

"Charmers aren't always on the up and up."

"I know that." Janet thought of Curtis the Rat. "But is this really a case where I was a chump for a charmer?"

Instead of answering, Tallie asked her own question. "So you held the book, and now your fingerprints are on it?"

13

Janet arrived first at Nev's that evening. She stood at the bar, making small talk with Danny between customers asking for pints and ordering meals, waiting for their usual table to open. Danny gave her a nod when it did, and she took her half of Selkie's Tears to sit and wait for the others. She'd called a meeting of SCONES—the Shadow Constabulary of Nosy, Eavesdropping Snoops. A visiting author had thus dubbed the four women from Yon Bonnie Books. They'd never been sure if she meant it as an insult or a backhanded compliment, and finally decided that embracing it was the way to go. Janet considered it a badge of honor.

Her only worry now—a half-worry, she told herself—was that she hadn't told the others this was a SCONES meeting. She'd saved her "Where's Heather" file to the cloud account the four had used for previous SCONES activities, and she'd meant to tell Christine and Summer about the file at their morning meeting. But they'd filled that time with actual business—going over plans for the birthday celebration—and then Tallie had brought up her McGonagall contest idea. Summer had hooted in delight. Christine had immediately regretted that, as one of the organizers, she wouldn't be able to enter. Then it had been time to open their doors and, between books and teapots, they'd all stayed busy for most of the day.

At least, in addition to her half-worry, Janet had an agenda. She would ask for their insights and take notes. She would especially record any notes of skepticism—a barely discernable brow furrow from Summer, a guffaw from Christine. But even Tallie's unease over Heather, the mystery man, and William Clark's tiny book were only that—unease with no clearer idea of what or if anything was going on. Still, her remark about Janet's fingerprints on the tiny book had added a new strand of disquiet.

The women often used an evening at Nev's as a way to wind down and touch base on their lives apart from their business. *Tonight, I'll just wind things down in a pre-planned direction,* Janet decided, *and hope I don't get anyone, including myself, too wound up.*

That wasn't one of her real worries, though. They'd all been competent and successful professionals in their pre-Yon Bonnie lives. Their combined experience in helping people untangle personal or legal problems—Christine as a school social worker, Tallie as a lawyer—or in helping them find and use information—Summer as a journalist, Janet as a librarian—made them a force. *I reckon, anyway,* Janet thought. *A force for finding solutions. Ooh. A SCONES motto?* In her excitement, she set her glass down with a thump.

"Steady, there, Mom," Tallie said. She set her own half pint down, hung her jacket on the back of a chair, and sat. "Summer says she'll be in later. Have you ordered supper? Something smells like soup."

"How late?" Janet skipped over the supper question, trying not to sound disappointed about Summer.

"Her column's due. She's working on it there, though." Tallie pointed her thumb over her shoulder in the general direction of the *Inversgail Guardian*'s offices next door. "She's probably working in Summer Time—faster than a speeding typist. Shouldn't be long. So what about supper?"

"There comes James," Janet said. "*He's* not next door working late."

"Good. Maybe she'll finish even faster."

"Evening, James." Janet smiled, expecting the editor to join them for a chat, as he often did.

"Tallie. Janet." James returned the smile and raised a hand, but passed them by.

Janet swiveled to see where he went. "Must be a meeting of Pub Scrawl. He's joined Maida. Maybe Rab will show up. And there are Rhona and Isla. You don't mind holding the table, do you? I'll go say hi."

"Want me to order something so it's here when you get back?"

Janet was already up and out of her chair. "Let's wait for Christine." She took her glass and passed between tables to reach the back of the long, narrow room.

Rhona McNeish, active in the local environmental movement, and Isla Strang, a district nurse, were two of the friends she sometimes joined on morning bike rides. They'd been touched by the Murray case. A third friend, Lynsey Maclennan, had lost her husband, Lachlann, to the killer.

"Join you for a bit?" Janet asked. Rhona and Isla raised their glasses, and Janet sat. "Is Lynsey not coming in?"

"Out of town," Rhona said.

"I'm sorry to miss her," Janet said. "But kind of glad she's away. Have you two heard about or met the true-crime writer who's in town?"

"Not met," Isla said. Sharp, terse—the answer and Isla.

Rhona, with her brush of red hair and general air of calm, made Janet think of a sturdy Highland pony. A pony that always wore one of the green T-shirts her environmental group sold. This evening, perhaps in a nod to dropping temperatures, she had a green sweater draped around her shoulders. "We've heard about her," Rhona said. "I've not heard from her. Have you, Isla?"

"No." The twist of Isla's lips added several impolite words without wasting breath.

"It's all in the papers and court records for anyone to read," Rhona said. "If she's any good at what she does, hearing from her might be inevitable, I reckon. But I hope we don't."

"Me, I'll be insulted if we don't," Isla said. "But, aye. I'll be glad, as well. I'm prickly as a bare-arsed—"

"Wheesht, Isla," Rhona said with a shake of her head, like a pony resigned to the inevitability of a fly.

"Havers," Isla buzzed back. "Nothing wrong with a wee bare-arsed hedgehog." She grinned wickedly. "I dinnae ken where or how far this woman's research is taking her, but I ken well enough what she'll accomplish by mucking about doing it. And if she comes looking for me, I'll havetae say something to her about that mucking. Then, no doubt, someone else will tell me I should regret having done that."

Rhona laughed. "And regret *that* themselves."

Isla sat back, looking pleased for defending honor and friend.

"How did you hear about her?" Janet asked. "Sorry, dumb question. After that business on the headland, who wouldn't have heard? Has Lynsey, though? I've been worried about her. If she knows about the project, I can't imagine what she must be feeling."

A look passed between Rhona and Isla. Isla's share of the look turned into thin lips.

Janet sat forward and asked quietly, "What's the look for? I'm not trying to pry or muck about."

Isla's lips went a bit thinner.

Rhona answered. "She's at her mum's. Soon as she heard about the writer and her research, she left. Best that way."

"Not a word." Isla and her eye held Janet's.

Proof, Janet thought, *that my worries about Heather's research hurting people I know and like aren't overblown.* She didn't feel the least foolish putting her hand on her heart. "I'm glad she's with her mum. When did she go?"

"Monday evening?" Rhona looked at Isla. "Och, well, it's no wonder I'm fuzzy. Monday morning, I was in casualty." She pointed at her right arm. "A dog ran in front of me, and I went over my handlebars. The elbow's dislocated." She pulled the sweater back and Janet saw the plastic splint and sling.

Janet winced. "Ouch. Sorry I didn't notice."

"How would you?" Isla asked. "Our Rhona's not one for waving her arms about like she's sending semaphore signals. And you cannae tell it's the sadly nonalcoholic ginger beer in her pint. You were mistaken earlier, as well. We heard about the true-crime wave arriving well before she went mucking about in the kayak. That was Monday, as well."

"Someone phoned me," Rhona said. "I'd been back home a few hours."

"Phoned you, not Lynsey?" Janet asked.

"She uses caller ID," Rhona said. "Ever since Lachlann . . . aye, well, ever since. She only answers for a few of us."

"Sick of reporters," Isla said.

"I'm sure she is. Do you know who called?" Janet asked.

"No," Rhona said. "I was not at my best, and he didn't say much. He sounded genuinely concerned. He sounded familiar, as well. His voice. But not as though I knew him. I don't think he knew me, either. Likely I was a bit off my head."

"Casualty has the *good* drugs," said Isla.

"Wheesht," said Rhona.

"If it was me, I would've asked for a double dose. Do you remember what he said?" Janet asked.

Rhona stared at the ceiling, and then a corner of the table as she worked through her memory of the call. "He asked could I pass a message on to Lynsey. That this woman is here and stirring up the Murray business again. Said he didn't want her to hear it in the shops, or be surprised if the woman herself showed up at her door." Rhona sat back and looked at Janet. "Just that and no more. He told me her name, but I muddled that. I've since learnt it. He disconnected before I could thank him or ask who he was. I muddled that, too. It was a good deed."

"It was," Janet agreed. "Was the call clear? Any static or breaking up?"

"No. Why so many questions?" Rhona asked.

"I'm just—"

"Nosy," Isla said.

The way Isla said it, and from the look on her face, Janet thought she meant it as a compliment. Coming from Isla, it was a fine one. It also saved Janet from answering Rhona's question. Rhona was occupied telling Isla to wheesht. Janet gave a nod of thanks and was pleased when Isla nodded back.

"Well, whoever he was, I'm glad he called," Janet said. She glanced to where Maida and James sat for their Pub Scrawl writers' meeting—just the two of them—at the table in the corner. James had a pint next to his elbow. Maida had the stack of books she'd bought the day before. By the lack of conversation and the tilt of their heads, they were busy scrawling away. If Rab planned to join them, he hadn't shown up yet.

Janet looked over toward her own table and saw Christine just sitting down. "How long before you can ride again, Rhona?" she asked, turning back.

"Four to six weeks," Rhona said. "Maybe sooner."

"At the minimum," Isla said. "This is your prickly nurse speaking."

"Will I see you, Isla?" Janet asked.

Isla's thin lips again. "How long will she be in town?"

"I don't know."

"I heard about what happened at the bridge. Better you than me, no offense. But I'll not take any chances of meeting up with her. I've a stationary bike. I'll stick to that. Thanks for asking, though. I didn't think you'd miss me."

"Always, Isla. Rhona, could it have been Rab MacGregor who phoned you?"

"Rab? It's the kind of thing he'd do." Rhona gazed at the ceiling again, then shook her head. "I was muddled, but no."

"Have you seen him lately?"

"Sunday? Monday, before I tumbled?" Rhona tipped her head toward her arm. "Don't ask where. An awful lot's gone oot the windae with ma bum."

"She means it could be naught but blether," Isla said. "She's aye poetic. The harbor wall's a good guess for Rab. He's like a lamppost. All around, but you don't go out of your way to notice and say hello."

"One more question," Janet said. "Nosy as can be. Do you know a lawyer named William Clark?"

Rhona and Isla shook their heads, and Janet didn't see even a flicker of recognition in their eyes. She asked Rhona to give her best to Lynsey and made her way back to her own table. Danny, with a steaming bowl of soup, arrived as she did.

"Ta, Danny," Christine said as he set the plate in front of her. "Not eating, Janet?"

"We were waiting for you."

"Were you? That was kind. I thought I'd give a try to phoning in the order ahead. Works a treat. This way, we arrived, I maneuvered Mum and Dad to their table, fetched their drinks, and almost as soon as I sit down myself, they have their meals and here's my bowl of Cullen skink, piping hot, and oatcakes on the side. *Doesn't* that smell good. We'd have been here sooner, but we seem to run on 'wrinklie time' more often than not these days. I'm famished."

"So am I," Janet said wistfully.

"It's all right, Mom. I've got your back." Tallie nodded toward the bar. "Here comes Danny with ours."

"Thank you, dear," Janet said. "And thank you, Danny. Smoked haddock, onions, and potatoes. *Doesn't* that smell good." She dipped a spoonful. "Mm. Hot. Tastes good, too. Before you two sink too far into soup bliss, there's something I want you to do."

When Christine and Tallie looked at her, each with a spoon halfway to her mouth, Janet told them about the "Where's Heather" file. "If you don't mind, I'd like you to read it while you eat. Discussion to follow."

Tallie had already put her spoon down and found the file on her phone. "'SCONES Meeting Agenda'? When did you decide to do this?"

Janet had added that headline to the file, and below that an item—*Look for insights, and a goal—to be prepared for the path forward.*

"Fascinating," Christine murmured.

Tallie continued looking at her mother.

"What?" Janet said.

"Did you think we might not come if you said this was a meeting of the SCONES? How often have any of us turned down an evening in our alternate living room?"

"This way I didn't need to explain ahead of time. Or eat up business time in the shop."

"True." Tallie read some of the file, ate some fish, and looked back at Janet. "This has you spooked. That isn't really like you."

"You're the one whose mind leapt to fingerprints this morning. You're more likely to do that than I am, but you don't go around just generally thinking about people leaving fingerprints, do you?"

With her glass to her lips, Tallie shook her head. She took a sip and put the glass down.

"Christine?" Tallie said. "Here's something you should both hear, even if it's short on details. Summer heard James talking on the phone as he walked past her. She didn't hear much, but she caught enough—that we haven't seen Rab because he's following Heather. But when Summer stopped James and asked what he meant, he said she'd misunderstood. He didn't elaborate, and then he left."

"What does James know about Heather or Rab that gives him that idea?" Christine asked. "More to the point, why didn't Summer tell me first? We work next to each other all day."

"I'm sure she would have," Tallie said. "This happened this evening when she went to finish her column. She told me about it when she let me know she'd be late."

"Maybe James saw the two of them somewhere," Janet said. "First Heather, then Rab. Do you suppose Ranger is a good tracker?"

"Rab following Heather is purely hearsay," Christine said. "Inadmissible in a court of law."

"We aren't in court, and that's not always true," Tallie said. "Hearsay isn't automatically a load of bull, anyway."

"A lot of hearsay is interesting," Janet said. "Bull, too. And sometimes they lead to snips and snatches that *are* true."

"Such as the fact that Rab is possibly nosier than y—" Tallie stopped at a noise from her mother. "That he's possibly nosier than *we* are."

"A beautiful save, dear. I'll try getting in touch with him again."

"Why don't you try getting in touch with the Empress of Selkies instead?" Christine said.

"It might be easier to get in touch with Ranger, too." Janet mused on that, and Christine went back to reading the file.

Janet spoke quietly to Tallie. "You can say I'm spooked, or curious, or that I'm curiously spooked, but it's like there's something just out of sight waiting to swoop in. Whatever 'it' is."

"It's those three seagulls of doom." Tallie glanced at Christine. Christine hadn't heard, or at least didn't flinch. "They're circling in the primitive part of your brain. What's that part called?"

"The bird brain." Janet shrugged a shoulder. "That's not it, but it's probably what I am."

"Mom." Tallie wiped her fingers and pulled her glasses down her nose. "Stop cutting yourself down."

Janet started to shrug her other shoulder, but stopped. Instead, she gave her daughter a thumbs-up. Then she ate her soup and oatcakes, watching the other two as they read, waiting until they'd finished.

14

Heather left the Hart and Hare. A posh place. Posh views and a posh menu, unless you were vegetarian. She wasn't. She'd had the local salmon the first time. He'd paid, so why not? The rabbit curry was excellent tonight. Meat tender and sweet, just the right amount of heat to the sauce, perfect mushrooms.

But a repeat of last time was not on—his arm round her shoulders as they walked back to the car. She might be chilly, he'd said. Tonight, she'd made certain to mention Owen, making it clear they were attached and he'd be coming down at the weekend. He'd winked and touched her hand. She wondered when he'd notice she'd not returned from the loo. A shame about running out before the lovely sounding pudding, but she patted herself on the back for bringing her own car this time. Calum's car. Dodgy old thing.

A shame about this lead, too. It had sounded promising when they'd first talked. He claimed outsider status. Said he had the perspective of someone who moved around the edges rather than wading through. He'd laughed at her joke, when she asked if that didn't just mean he was standoffish. But it was a view of events in Inversgail that she'd hoped would be as clear and broad as the one from the Hart and Hare's wide windows.

By the time they'd had their starters tonight—he'd suggested the cock-a-leekie and she'd opted for Scotch pancakes with smoked trout—signs were as clear as a broad hand on her leg that he had nothing for her. All talk and no useful details beyond scraps of gossip that wouldn't take her any further down either of her trails—the Murray or the Calum one. No worries, though. He was harmless, a bit of a twit in the short run, and his publishing contacts might yet be helpful in the long.

Slow and steady wins the race—and never burn bridges, Calum's voice said in her head.

"Not original, Calum, but aye, you're right." She'd phone and apologize. Say she'd been called away. True, or near enough. And the text that hastened her leap away from the Hart and Hare promised a better lead. Or so she hoped. On this narrow road, she didn't dare take a chance to read the text again.

❧

Christine was first to put her phone down and move her plate aside. "Tell me about William Clark," she said. "Not about his wee book, which you describe in almost indecent detail in the file. Tell me what *he* looked like, and tell me the other bits you left out of the file. Then tell me what this meeting is really about."

"What it's about is in the file's headline," Janet said.

"Insight? Path forward? No," Christine said. "Too abstract. Give me specifics." She settled herself comfortably and waved her hand for Janet to proceed.

Welcome to Nev's, Queen Elizabeth, Janet thought. *Glad to have you here.* "Midforties, five-foot-ten," she said. "Those are guesses, obviously. Slim to the point of thin. Prominent cheekbones; hair short and dark brown. No sign of balding. If he spent as much time in Yon Bonnie as a lad as he claims, he must have lived an easy walk or bike ride away."

"Did you ask Isla and Rhona if they know him?" Tallie asked.

"They don't. But I asked if they know a lawyer named William Clark. Maybe that's the wrong question. It was too specific. That's often the way a database or internet search goes wrong. If I'd left out 'lawyer,' I might have gotten a different answer."

"Then we'd be back to the problem of both names being common," Christine said, "and Mum dumping Dad for the foggy memory of a lad in short trousers who probably needed a nose wipe."

"Is she still talking about him?" Janet asked.

"No. Dad brought out photos from their wedding, and she said she's fallen in love all over again. Then she asked him to take out the rubbish, and all's well. Carry on with your report, Janet."

In her mind, Janet curtseyed before the queen. "Basant was right that he's a collector. Mr. Clark says Stuart Farquhar taught him to focus his collecting habits. Something else that struck me about him, something I'm not sure I can put into words, is that not much about him seemed *light*."

"Examples," Christine said. "Specifics. Because sometimes they *are* what we need."

"I don't exactly mean weighed down. He said 'cheers' when he came and went. But it was just a word. There was no feeling behind it. He reminisced, but the memories were fairly buttoned down. No gushing."

"Not everyone gushes," Tallie said.

"I know, and maybe I'm projecting or overanalyzing, but it felt like he stayed on one side of a line and kept the memories on the other."

Christine cleared her throat.

"Let me think." Janet stared at her plate, wished she still had an oatcake or two, and thought back over the visit. *There was something about him*, she thought. *About the way he looked around that I can't quite put my finger on—but there it is!*

Janet took an oatcake from Christine's plate, broke it in two, and pointed half of it at her. "Here are your examples. He went to look at Morag's watercolor. He said it was nice to see it still hanging over the mantel. But he stopped behind Ranger's chair. He could have gone right up to the painting, but he stayed behind the chair. It isn't even the closest chair to the fireplace. And here's another example. The locked bookcase. He spent most of his time looking at the books in it—but through the glass. I offered to open the case and let him sit and read any one he wanted. He said no. Actually, he didn't even do that. He waved me off with his hand."

Christine and Tallie remained silent.

"I've been thinking about this too much, haven't I?" Janet ate both halves of the oatcake.

"Possibly." Christine pushed her plate closer to Janet.

Tallie shook her head. "No, it's like his memories are in a museum. He came to visit them, but he doesn't want to, or can't, touch them."

"That's it." Janet took the last oatcake from Christine's plate. "He even said he'd brought his miniature book to Yon Bonnie for 'a visit.' That sounds whimsical, but I didn't get a sense of whimsy or joy from him, otherwise. Not that he was dour, or unduly dour. *Except*—" She widened her eyes. "Except his eyes. When he showed me the tiny Burns, his eyes were very different."

"When he saw your obvious delight?" Tallie asked.

"He was delighted, too. Very much so. At the time, I thought we'd made a connection, but in the end, he was just as vaguely pleasant and minimally informative as his smile. Like this." She tried to imitate the smile for them, but gave up. "Anyway, what do you think of our visit from Mr. Clark, Esquire?"

"Is that what he calls himself?" Christine asked.

"I was being overly dramatic," Janet said. "He didn't introduce himself. But that's why I didn't ask him if he knew Heather or if he'd met her. I didn't want to let on that I knew who he was."

"Why not?" Christine asked.

"Part of that keeping on one side of a line thing?" Janet said. "I'm not sure."

"I am," Christine said. "It was instinct." She lowered her voice. "You generally have good ones. All four of us do, which is why I want something to call him other than William Clark. Because we have concerns. Hence, this discussion." She looked quickly around at the tables nearest them. "Further hence, we should take precautions against eavesdroppers. Here, in the shop, wherever. We hardly know the man, so calling him William is too familiar. Not to mention the problem that already stirred up for Mum and Dad. Other suggestions?"

"Simple," Tallie said. "Call him Clark."

"Too reminiscent of Superman," Christine said. "That might sound silly to you, but I think I must have been traumatized by the thought of his X-ray vision when I was a small girl. We'll call him WC. That should keep open-air discussions on the q.t. No one will want to listen in on a conversation about a WC. But would you like to know my main takeaway from this visit of his today?"

"That's part of the reason for this meeting," Janet said. "So, yes, please."

Christine sat back and looked at them. "That's it?"

"That's what?" Tallie asked.

"That's my takeaway." Christine raised her empty hands in a shrug. "That's it? For all your pleasant book chat with WC, you learned precious little for us to go on, Janet. Other than wondering if you'll be taken in for theft, if his wee book disappears, what else is there to wonder about?"

"And just like that, your insights have cleared my cobwebs away."

"In a *fankle*, were they?" Christine asked.

"A tangle is sort of the definition of cobweb, isn't it?" Tallie asked.

"And Christine is the cure," Janet said. "So let's get another half pint each and we'll talk about what we can do."

Tallie took their empties to the bar while Christine went to check on her parents. Janet tried calling Rab, and then tried to leave a message, but his voice mailbox was full. She didn't bother with a text. She'd sent two already and received no replies.

"Right," Christine said after helping Tallie bring the fresh ale to the table. "What do you want us to do, and to what end?"

"Let's add to the information we have," Janet said. "As to what end, I'll get to that in a minute."

"The information we're looking for, is this focused collecting?" Tallie asked.

"That, but with eyes and ears open and receptive," Janet said. "If we're too focused, we might miss something small. Something on the periphery—*beyond* the periphery—that could make all the difference. Take note of odd behavior."

"*That* is hardly focused at all," Christine said. "How does that book go, 'From there to here, from here to there, odd behavior is everywhere'?" She took out her phone. "I'll make a note of it, anyway. 'The odd note of odd behavior,'" she said as she tapped the phone. "Got it. And there goes odd behavior now."

Janet turned to see James Haviland rushing toward the door and through it. The customer at the bar, waiting for the pint Danny held, called Danny's name twice before he brought his gaze from the door and handed it to him.

"Text from Summer," Tallie said, looking at her phone. "A man's been attacked. Beaten. Head injuries."

"Pub brawl?" Christine asked.

"She hasn't said—here's more. At the church on Victoria and Albert. The minister."

"That's the Church of Scotland," Christine said.

"That's Derek Spiers," Janet said. "One of our writers. Good Lord."

Tallie's phone buzzed again. "No further details. She says she'll wait around to see what else she hears, and then be over."

"Not to be flip," Christine said, "but is this odd behavior we should make note of? I can't remember hearing of such a thing as a minister being attacked. And *at* the church?"

"I think we have to take note," Tallie said.

Janet nodded and tried to relax her shoulders. "Information," she said with a slight wobble in her voice. "I want to know who the mystery man or men are. There might be just one, or there might be two or three."

"Tell us what you know," Christine said.

"Practically nothing," Janet said. "I've heard one, heard *of* one, and seen one. I'll start with the one who met Heather at the Murray house last night. Taller than Heather. By how much, I don't know. He didn't look heavy, but he was wearing a loose jacket."

"What kind of car?" Tallie asked.

Janet shook her head. "First the headlights blinded me, and then I only looked at the two of them."

"And he wasn't generous enough to give us a limp or some other recognizable gait?" Christine asked.

"He didn't move far from the car. Heather walked over to him. That's all I can tell you about him, and I've already told you what I can about the call from Heather's guardian angel yesterday. The third one is Lynsey's guardian angel from Monday night. He called Rhona to pass a message along to Lynsey. That's the day Heather arrived in town."

"The day she *said* she arrived," Tallie said.

Janet looked at her daughter and took a swallow of ale.

"I'll make a note of that," Christine said.

"Rhona has more information to go on, although she was on pain-killers after going over her handlebars," Janet said.

Tallie mouthed a silent *ow*.

"She thought his voice sounded familiar," Janet said, "but only familiar from hearing it before, not like she knew him. She didn't think he knew her, either. He told her about Heather and her research. He didn't want Heather surprising Lynsey, and didn't want Lynsey hearing about Heather in the shops. He hung up before Rhona thought to ask who was calling. It was a clear connection. She's sure it wasn't Rab. She called Lynsey, and Lynsey is—" Janet remembered Isla's *not a word*. "I'll put it this way. She's safe and won't be bothered."

"That's all we need to know," Christine said. "I'm glad the mystery caller had the decency to look out for her."

"It made me feel a bit better," Janet said. "One of the things I've worried about is how Heather's research will affect people. Nothing like having someone come to town and start picking at a scab. Obviously this guy worried, too. Isla—you know prickly Isla—she heard about Heather's playacting at the Beaton Bridge. She'll ride her stationary bike at home until Heather leaves."

"So caller number one knew to call you, and had your phone number," Tallie said, "and caller number two—or the first guy with a clearer signal—is someone who knows that Lynsey can be reached through Rhona. Interesting."

"The phantoms of the phone," Christine mused. "But yours might have been Rab, Janet?"

"It's possible, but Rab wasn't the man who met Heather."

"Could one or all of them be WC?" Tallie asked. "Is that too left field?"

"No," Janet said, "but we don't have enough information."

"I wonder if Heather isn't making sure people notice what she's doing," Christine said. "Some of the children I worked with did that sort of thing. Not the class clowns; they seize the moment and act out for the laughs. There were a few, though, who created situations. They planned and presented them, and then stood by during the uproar as though waiting for an A-plus. One lad in particular excelled. Out of his hearing, staff called him 'the showman.'"

"There is that feeling about what she's been doing," Janet said.

"So the question becomes: who is she presenting her brand of uproar for?" Christine said. "People in general, or is she making sure one person in particular notices?"

"Could she be getting help?" Tallie asked. "Maybe from her brother? Could he be the mystery man who called Mom?"

"How did he get my number?"

"From the same place Heather heard about your bike-riding habits," Tallie said.

"*If* she did," said Janet. "If that's what she's been up to, though, who was she performing for in the headland scene?"

"Again, what about WC?" Tallie said. "I wonder if we can find out if he saw her on the ledge. Or could he have helped stage that bit of uproar?"

"We've already established that we know next to nothing about him," Christine said. "Why do we suddenly believe he's in cahoots?"

"We don't," Janet said. "We need more information. We know Heather said she had an appointment with him. I heard her at the library on Monday. We don't know if she *actually* had one."

Christine nodded and finished her ale. "It's difficult to *know* anything. All our questions might just be part of the whole seagull of doom vibe. There, you see? Some good is coming from our discussion. I've worked my way through the angst suggested by multiple seagulls."

"That's excellent, Christine." Tallie pointed at her mother's face. "But wait, there's more."

"There's Norman," Janet said. "I've been thinking back over my conversations with him, starting with the one at the bridge. It's pretty clear to me that he's just as curious about Heather as we are. And he knows what we're like."

"Nosy?" Tallie said.

"Yes. See? *I've* worked through the angst that comes with people equating nosiness with the liveliness of a curious mind. So here's my deduction. Norman didn't so much ask us to nose around—"

"Wait—he didn't ask us at all," Tallie said.

"Because he didn't have to. He hinted, because he knows we're good at picking up on things like that. He wasn't trying to dissuade us; I think he was actually urging us on."

"Do you think you might be obsessing on Heather and her shenanigans?" Tallie asked.

"I'm going to call it focus. But I won't focus on your implied criticism."

"It was mild criticism, anyway," Christine said, "and Heather's shenanigans *are* fascinating. Do you know what else is fascinating? Maida. She's still here, a meeting of one back there in the corner. It gives me a start every time I see her in here. She's like an old fishwife out of water."

"She looks comfortable, though," Tallie said, "so maybe she's more like a selkie. Instead of hiding her sealskin when she comes on land, she hides her old fishwife skin when she comes in Nev's."

"Did you ask Maida and James why Rab wasn't with them when you were over there talking to Rhona?" Christine asked.

"I didn't want to interrupt them," Janet said. "I asked Maida about him yesterday. She said she doesn't know where he is, but *he* knows where he is."

"A selkie might talk more sense than Maida," Christine said.

"I think *she* knows where he is, or has a good idea," Janet said. "She might not know exactly where, but not being able to pinpoint it gives her wiggle room so she doesn't have to lie."

"I don't get the secrecy," Tallie said, "but what if Rab's doing the same thing as Lynsey and Isla? Lying low as long as Heather's here?"

"But why?" Janet asked. "I can't see Rab being afraid of anything, can you?"

"We haven't seen Rab at all lately, so it's hard to say. Good, here's Summer."

Summer dropped her purse and jacket at the table, but didn't sit. "Sorry I'm late. It's been a bugger of a night. Can I get anyone a refill?"

Before anyone answered, Danny arrived to collect empties—bringing a half pint for Summer. "Selkie's Tears all right? On the house. You look knackered."

"That's a charming thing to say, Danny," Christine said.

"I am, though." Summer dropped into a chair. She massaged her forehead then lifted the glass to Danny in thanks. "I finished the column, then hung around in case there was more news about the attack. Did you hear about that, Danny?"

He checked the bar and sat. Christine told him the few details they already knew.

"Good news, though," Summer said. "Medics treated Derek at the scene and released him. He's home, and some of the church members are rallying around."

"Did they get anyone for it?" Danny asked.

"Long gone before he was able to call for help. He couldn't give a description or say how many."

"He was at the church?" Janet asked.

"Leaving his office there. He said the blow staggered him, literally, and he couldn't say if it happened in the building or outside. Norman found him outside. If it was attempted burglary or theft, they might not have expected Derek to be there, and used the first weapon to hand. Nothing seems to be missing."

"Do you know Derek, Danny?" Janet asked.

"I'm not much of a church man. I hate to hear this, but." He stood to go. "Anything else for the rest of you tonight?"

They shook their heads. When he'd gone, Summer took a packet of folded papers from her purse. "This is another reason it took me so long. It took some digging, but I found an article about Fiona Clark's kayak trip. She was planning to recreate a trip up the west coast made by two guys in 1934. One of them, Alastair Dunnett, wrote a book about it. The article hasn't been digitized, so I made a copy for each of us." She handed the copies around.

"Recreating the trip, but she was going solo?" Christine said as she scanned the article.

"If two men could do it, why not one woman?" Tallie asked.

"One woman could do it better, no question," Christine said. "My remark referred only to the accuracy of the recreation, but accuracy might not have been her goal. Even without knowing how it ended, the trip sounds a daft idea. Was she a romantic?"

"Or loved an adventure," Janet said. "I like the idea. But how awful, to plan what might be the trip of a lifetime and end up in tragedy before you'd hardly started. So now, is it still too far out there to think Heather was recreating Fiona's death with that stunt at the headland?"

"Is that what you've been talking about?" Summer asked.

"It's a small part of what we've been talking about," Christine said. "And I *want* to say it's so far out there as to be complete and utter rot."

"It's really too much of a coincidence, though, don't you think?" Tallie asked.

Janet spoke for all of them. "Absolutely."

❧

Heather sat on the harbor wall. With the hush that descended after closing time, Inversgail might as well roll up the High Street and put it away for the night. Nice, that. Protective. The way folk closed ranks around those who'd been hurt in the Murray case. If only there'd been folk like that for Calum. How many days had she been here? Four? And what had she accomplished? Not enough. She banged a fist against her temple.

Not all progress is forward.

"Thank you, Calum," she said. "Not all comments are helpful, either."

She spotted an abandoned beach chair on the muck below the wall. Darker down there. She thought about jumping down, but the harbor muck wouldn't make a nice landing. She walked along the top of the wall, headed for the stairs she'd seen farther along, balancing as though on a tightrope. Or walking a plank.

The harbor smells intensified with each stair step down. Salt, seaweed, fish, mud—they swirled together into the pervasive eau de muck. Not so bad as *mingin*, though. Not a nasty smell. She rescued the chair, pulling the legs free. Moved it back against the base of the wall and sat. Now she was alone on her own private beach.

With the tide out, not much to look at down here. She pulled her phone out, read the text, and tried the number again. No answer. She tucked the phone away safely, the phone more precious than the honking huge map she'd crumpled and tossed into the back seat. Time to take stock. Firstly, what had she done so far? Already been over that. Not enough. Secondly, what was she doing now? Sitting like a lump in the muck.

Thirdly, what was still to do? Places to go. People to see. And if they wouldn't take her calls or be clearer in their texts? Then she'd be happy to make house calls, announced or not. And that was the way she'd get through this—*we'll get through.*

"This is for you, Cal. You aren't alone, and I'll prove you weren't alone then."

She got the feeling of being watched. Or was that just a cliché tiptoeing across her scalp? "Who's watching me, Calum?" Of course, he didn't answer. She leaned forward, looked up and over her shoulder. On top of the wall sat a wee dog, a sandy-haired terrier, looking out to sea.

"Good lad. Is this your chair, then?" she said.

The dog interrupted his superintendence of the horizon to glance at her, then returned to work.

"No, maybe not."

A bird called. From the dog's reaction, she thought if he owned a watch, he would have looked at the time and marveled. Instead, he shook himself, trotted a short way along the top of the wall, and then hopped down on the other side.

15

Crime writers Agnes, Sheila, and Derek arrived together at Yon Bonnie Books shortly before ten the next morning. Sheila held the door and Agnes held Derek's arm.

"Derek, oh my goodness," Janet said. "We heard about last night, and I wasn't sure we'd see you this morning. How are you?"

"Feeling a bit peely-wally," Agnes answered for him as she steered him to a stop in front of the sales counter. "But you'll do, won't you, Derek? Here we are for our first meeting of the—" Agnes looked at Sheila and Derek, who looked with some apprehension back at her. "Murder of Crows."

Derek, eyes closed, groaned. "As I've said about your other name offerings, it's majority rules. If you two want this one, I'll fall in line, but—"

"But you'd like something more macho." Sheila saluted, then said to Janet, "Can you imagine Ken Follett or Tom Clancy or anyone else writing military crime belonging to a group called the Cozy Quills? We'll keep thinking. No worry, no hurry. Right, Agnes?"

"Och, well, it is the writing that counts."

"Thank you, Nessy." Derek patted her hand. "Thank you for everything you've done." He turned to Janet. "She's organized meals and rides if I need them. She called round this morning to make sure I hadn't popped off overnight. Sheila, too; she came round and here we all are."

"Wonderful," Janet said.

"He's havering," Agnes said.

"Not a bit of it," Derek said.

Janet wanted to roll her eyes at Sheila over the mutual admiration binge. She behaved herself, though. Just because Sheila wasn't contributing to it didn't mean she wasn't a fan.

"Anyway," Janet said, "TLC is what anyone needs at a time like this. Tallie, will you bring a cup of tea? Make it tea for three."

Tallie, already on her way to the tearoom, called over her shoulder, "Coming right up."

Janet turned back to Derek. "Besides peely-wally, how are you feeling?"

"Not my best, but good to be on my feet. The medics who looked me over said my skull is made of granite. That makes me a blockhead, but that's hardly news. I should mend without much fuss."

Looking at Agnes, Janet thought fuss might be inescapable.

Or maybe not. In a deft move, Derek disengaged from Agnes and side-stepped along the counter. *The practiced move of a well-loved minister,* Janet thought.

Derek picked up one of the birthday celebration bookmarks as Tallie returned with teapot, cups and saucers, and a plate of shortbread on a tray.

"Lovely," Agnes said, and she, Derek, and Sheila followed Tallie and the tray to the chairs near the fireplace.

Soon enough, Janet and Tallie heard the murmur of voices mixed with the clink of cups and saucers. Yo-Yo Ma's cello played in the background.

"So far, so good," Janet said. "This might work."

"I thought about finding a recording of that piece of music by Leroy Anderson, 'The Typewriter'," Tallie said. "We could play it at the beginning of their meetings. Turn it into a theme song."

"Tallie, don't move." Janet, facing her daughter and the windows, skipped sideways so that Tallie stood between the windows and her. "It's Heather. Looking in."

"Looking dangerous?"

"No. But what's she doing here?"

"Mom, get a grip. We're a bookshop. She's a writer. Writers like us. We sell their books, and we currently have three chairs full of them swilling tea right over there. Now, breathe in and breathe out. If she comes in, maybe you'll get the chance to ask her some of the questions you have. But remember that we like customers, okay?"

Janet squeezed both of Tallie's upper arms. "Thank you."

The bell at the door jingled, and Heather Kilbride walked in.

Tallie turned around and welcomed her to the shop. "Let us know if we can help you find anything."

"Ta. I like your waistcoat. Are those bookshelves and moggies all over it? Perfect for a bookshop. I'll just look round on my own."

Janet took her phone out as Tallie turned back to her. "The odd note," Janet said quietly. "And a heads up to the tearoom."

"She likes my cat and bookshelf vest."

"And I ended up liking *her*," Janet whispered. "But I think she might have a screw loose."

"Just remember to breathe."

Janet took in a deep breath and let it out to show she could do it. Tallie patted her mother's arm, and then went to help a couple who'd come through from the tearoom.

Janet found a duster under the counter and ran it over surfaces she'd cleaned first thing that morning. *But in times of stress,* she said to herself, *cleanliness is next to calmness.*

Still, when her phone buzzed with a text, she jumped. The text was from Christine: *If we don't see her in C&T, will try to stroll through YB.*

A moment later, Christine sent another: *Neither of us knows her. How to recognize?*

Brown cargo jacket, Janet sent back.

Tallie came back to the counter with the couple and rang up a book on the art of Charles Rennie Mackintosh. Janet put a bookmark in the book, smiled, and handed it to the female half of the couple. The woman pulled the bookmark out and dropped it on the counter.

"Not necessary," she said on the way to the door. "Save a twig."

"If a twig snaps in the forest and no one hears it, does it need saving?" Heather asked, watching the door close behind the couple. She came to the counter, flipping through a guidebook.

"Hello, nice to see you again," Janet said, while thinking, *There, a pleasant greeting without a hint of miff.*

Heather put the book on the counter, picked up the abandoned bookmark, and tucked it into one of her pockets. "I wonder if you can give me directions to the Stuart Stones. I looked through your guidebooks. This one's great in other respects, but no joy." She nudged the book she'd set down. "Your local megalithic site must be too obscure to make the big time."

"Google?" Janet suggested.

"Neither Google nor GPS have discovered them yet, either. Nor has my map." Heather took a map from another of her pockets and started to unfold it. "This thing is like a tent once you get it going."

"It looks like it's had some refolding issues," Tallie said.

"Wrinkles happen to the best of us." Heather took the map to the floor, spread it out, then refolded it into a slightly tidier square that included Inversgail.

"What's the scale?" Janet asked.

"This bit should be twenty or thirty miles. I've a general idea where to find them."

"But you don't want to waste time just wandering around," Janet said.

"Not that I object to wandering in general."

"Summer might know," Tallie said. "I'll go ask."

"Summer's in the tearoom," Janet explained. "She's a wonderful baker, and she's fallen in love with the Stuart Stones. They're named for Stuart Farquhar, who started this shop. She's going to make a model of the stone circle out of gingerbread for our celebration of his one hundred and twenty-fifth birthday."

"I might have to come see that," Heather said. "I'll have a lovely wander now and put this back."

Heather took the guidebook and went off down an aisle. Janet grabbed a piece of scrap paper and a pen. Her thumbs weren't fast enough to keep up with odd behavior. First, Heather hadn't acted surprised to see her behind the shop's counter. She also hadn't greeted her. She didn't act as though they'd met, much less that they'd stood over a "body" together. She also didn't act like someone who might have been recording or taking a picture of the woman behind the counter after being followed by her in the dark on a bicycle.

Janet knew she was getting worked up. She put the pen down and the scrap of paper in her pocket. *Flaunt your pockets all you like,* she told Heather in her mind. *I've got pockets, too.*

Heather wandered back to the counter with *The Claymore in the Cloister,* one of Ian Atkinson's Single Malt Mysteries. Janet took a breath in and let it out, rested her hands loosely on the counter, and smiled. She used the nonconfrontational voice she'd practiced as a librarian. "Were you waiting for me at the bridge the other morning?"

"Waiting, yes. For you?" Heather gave her head a noncommittal wag. "I discovered that waiting is an oddly stimulating activity. There are so many ways and reasons for waiting. Have you ever thought about what waiting requires? As well, there's the question of what those who wait hope to gain."

Janet tamped down an urge to drip sarcasm, but a droplet got away from her. "Am I part of your research? Did I pass your psychological exam?"

"I'm not sure I follow," Heather said. "Why do you think I was examining you?"

"You said you were looking for other perspectives in the Murray case, other angles and points of view. So were you studying the crime scene from my point of view? Examining my reactions?"

"Your reactions were certainly interesting, and I noted them, of course. It was a dreich day, but fruitful for research. Back to your first question, was I waiting there for *you*? No."

Tallie came back with a piece of paper torn from a notebook. "Summer's written out the directions. I've never known her to get lost."

"Brilliant." Heather tucked the map and the directions away in a pocket.

Janet, afraid her opportunity to ask questions was about to walk out the door, pounced. "Do you know who called me Wednesday morning to say you were up there on the ledge and I should call 9-9-9?"

"The police told me someone phoned it in, but didn't say who that was. Well done, you!"

"Thank the anonymous caller. He said it was urgent. It *looked* urgent. Do you have any idea who that was?" Janet asked.

"A Good Samaritan, but no, I haven't a clue."

"It wasn't someone you're working with?" Tallie asked. "Someone helping with your research?"

"No. It strikes me, though, that the urgency mightn't have been for me. It might have been for the searchers out there, wasting their time looking all over watery creation for me. Honestly, I feel terrible about all that. I was never in any danger. I was well-equipped for my overnight stay. The searchers couldnae see me, the way the ledge is situated. I didnae see or hear them. I'd no idea the kayak had disappeared."

"You meant to stay overnight?" Tallie asked.

"I was quite comfortable."

"How did you know you'd be safe?" Tallie sounded like a district attorney cross-examining a witness. Janet was happy to stand aside for the expert.

"Insider information."

"What information? Inside where?"

"Who, not where," Heather said. "My brother. A great rock climber. Aces at keeping notes. He taught me everything I know."

"Is he staying here?" Tallie asked.

"No."

"Did he teach you to secure a kayak for an overnight on the water?"

"I failed that, didn't I? I'm sorry for all the bother. I thought I'd secured it. In the morning, when I looked, it was gone. As well, my cell died, so I'd no way to phone for help. I'd a flare, but it was in the poor kayak."

A customer jingled the door on his way in. He waved off assistance and went to browse. Janet treated the jingle as a signal to bring the conversation around to something more apropos of the shop. "You've made a good choice, there, with Ian's book. Are you a fan?"

"It looks like good fun, but I don't read much fiction."

"We'd love to get in something of yours for the shop," Janet said. "I've had trouble finding it on our distributor's site."

"I'll get back to you with some promo material, shall I?"

"Wonderful. Would you like to browse more, or shall I ring you up?"

"Sorry, I hope I've not been holding anyone else up." Heather looked behind her, then handed the book to Janet. "And I'm still so sorry about the scare I gave you at the burn. I'd like to make up for it. I feel I owe you more of an explanation. Set things straight about my research aims. But I don't want to take up anymore of your time the noo. I'll get back to you, aye?"

"Sure. I look forward to seeing you again." When the door closed behind Heather, Janet turned to Tallie. "I meant that. I do look forward to seeing her again."

Tallie lifted her chin toward the fireplace area behind Janet. "Don't look now, but I think our crime writers have been more interested in our conversation with Heather than their meeting."

"And I worried about *them* creating a spectacle."

"I'll go collect their tea things," Tallie said, "so you can get started on the odd behavior I know you're itching to note."

"Notes galore," Janet said as the door jingled again.

That was the beginning of a decent and continuing stream of customers that kept Janet from all but the briefest of notes jotted between sales. When the stream turned to a trickle, she and Tallie thanked each other for a job well done. At that point, the crime writers adjourned their meeting and came to say goodbye.

"What do we owe you for the tea and shortbread?" Derek asked.

"Not a thing. Our treat," Janet said. "To wish you a speedy and full recovery."

"Kind of you, but I don't believe in dwelling on the negative," Derek said. "We'll call it a celebration of our first meeting in Yon Bonnie Books. And what do you think, Sheila and Nessy? Let's the three of us say we'll be here for this birthday celebration." He held up one of the bookmarks. "This promises refreshments. Will that include more of your delicious shortbread?"

"Shortbread, an assortment of scones," Janet said, "and a special gingerbread creation Summer is planning."

"The Stuart Stones," Agnes said. "We heard you telling that woman with her ridiculous map." Agnes mimed refolding something threatening to get the better of her. "*She's* the one search and rescue went looking for, is she? And caused you some trouble, as well."

The implied tut-tut in her words created a moment of silence. After observing it, Derek changed the subject. "Our stones aren't much to look at. Why not a gingerbread bookshop?"

"Derek has a place in Callanish," Agnes said. "Their stones are much more impressive."

"I've seen pictures," Janet said. "I'd love to see them in person."

"Worth it," Derek said, "though I didn't mean to insult our own."

"But a gingerbread bookshop's a wonderful idea," Janet said. "Maybe Summer can make one of those for Christmas."

"It might be too cute for you, Derek," Sheila said. "Too cute to take apart and eat, at any rate. I'll gladly have a slice of the Miraculous Stones."

"Are miracles associated with the stones?" Tallie asked. "Summer will love that."

"Not the meaning for miraculous that you're thinking," Agnes said.

"Miraculously drunk," said Sheila, "from the way some of the stones lean and some have fallen over. They look like they're staggering—staggering being another word for drunk. As well, I've heard a lad or two call them the Stoatin' Stones. Have you heard that one—stoatin' aboot? Drunk again. Here I am, with this wealth of information, and I don't drink at all."

"But you write," Agnes said. "And it's that wealth of information and the local color you bring to your work that sets it apart. Sets it *above*."

"Rubbish, but thank you."

"Speaking of local color," Janet said, "did you know that our Summer, in addition to being a baker, is a longtime journalist? She has an idea for a local color story about your writing group meeting in the bookshop. What do you think? Is that something you'd be interested in?"

"I should say so," Agnes said, then turned quickly to the others. "But I shouldn't say so for all of us. Derek? Sheila?"

"We're rather new at the writing game. Would it not be premature?" Derek asked.

"It works for me," Sheila said. "It puts our names out there and puts pressure on us to keep at it."

"I'm outvoted," Derek said. "Apparently we are happy to cooperate with your journalist."

"Great," Tallie said. "We'll tell Summer and she'll be in touch."

"And we'll see you back for your next meeting. Will that be next week?" Janet asked. "Next month?"

"Next week for a meeting. Tomorrow for drop-in writing," Agnes said. "The vibes here are good for our creative energy."

"Are they?" Janet asked.

"Och, aye," said Agnes, miming another threatening map. "Things seem to happen here."

16

Heather woke early on Sunday, the sun not yet up. She sat on one of the hard chairs at the small table rather than the squeaky bed to pull on her socks and lace her hiking boots. She put on her jacket, checked for the map and directions in the pocket. She was dying for tea, but left without. The less clatter, the better. She left the car and took her bike. The less obvious, the better, too.

Water and mist lapped against the harbor wall as she coasted along the High Street. She passed the bonnie bookshop and dreamed of seeing her books in the window. She turned away from the water at the next street, puffing now as the street climbed its way out of Inversgail and became a road winding away through the hills. At the top of one hill, she stopped to check the map and catch her breath, and turned to look at the roofs and chimneys of the waking town.

Calum would have liked settling in Inversgail. She liked it and wouldn't mind staying on. Relocating, even. The people were good. Most of them—not all. Cal had found that out. And she was doing her best to fix that.

"I've backtracked from that trip I wish you'd not taken, and from there, your flapping great map brought me here. And now I've poked and prodded and listened between the lines and found the evidence to build my case. Rock solid. Fitting, that, for an ace rock climber like you."

She searched in one of her pockets for a tissue, then rode on, looking for the next turn. Looking forward to this meeting, she pedaled faster.

Fools rush in, Calum warned.

She didn't answer, took a hand from the handlebar to blot her nose again. He never answered *her* anymore. Just chucked helpful comments into her thoughts now and again. And since when was the title of an Elvis Presley song helpful? This morning, she needed quiet, inside and out. Stealth. That's why she planned to arrive first and wait. Calum had taught her that, too, to wait—for a salmon in the river, a badger's sniffing nose at the entrance to its sett. Compared to any of that, waiting at the stone circle would be a doddle.

No need to rush a plan. Calum, repeating his favorite worry.

"I'm not, Calum. *I'm* not rushing and I'm not rushing into any*thing.* You always say that. Said that. *Stop* saying that. Experience is a hard teacher, but give me credit for learning. I learnt from you how to wait, and to *listen* while waiting, and to *see* what's waiting in front of me. And what's been in front of me, all this time, is the plain fact that no matter what anyone's told me, there was nothing straightforward about your death. I also learnt from you not to trust. And trust *me*, it's not a coincidence I learnt that when you died."

She pedaled on, climbing the next hill. The directions she'd got from the shop were taking her *somewhere*, and she hoped it was where she meant to go.

She turned onto the single lane road, and then made the last turn onto something not much more than a track. She bounced along, glad she'd left Calum's ancient car out of this, until—*there.* Across a field of sheep, on the rise beyond, were the ancient standing stones. And a small herd of Highland cattle. Nothing wrong with a hairy *cu.* And they'd be fitting witnesses; Calum had been a ginger, too.

She dismounted from the bike and wheeled it the rest of the way. "Are you in a curious mooood?" she said to the cattle who watched her coming. "That's fine, gather round, lads. But dinnae blink. This'll be over before you ken."

Walking into the circle, reaching a hand toward the tallest stone that still stood upright, she felt the cold before she touched it. But she felt more than the cold, felt it somewhere deeper than her heart, and growing. "The sooner this is over—"

Building properly takes patience.

"Wheesht. That's why you joined the Royal Engineers and I write. You had the brain for building things. But building this trap took imagination."

⁂

Janet agreed with the cats—time to roll out of bed. She often slept later on Sunday mornings, making the cats work harder for their breakfast with paw pats to her nose. This morning, though, Summer wanted to take better pictures of the Stuart Stones than she'd found in the old newspaper article and online records, and Janet wanted to see them for herself. She dressed for a ramble across fields, in jeans and two layers in case it warmed up or cooled down. She'd add hiking boots and a waterproof jacket after breakfast. A glance out the bedroom window looked promising for a clear sky. She'd take the waterproof anyway. And put wellies and the umbrella in the car.

A seagull, perched on Ian's roof next door, flew off. Then movement at ground level caught Janet's eye—Ian, wearing worn jeans and an anorak instead of his usual writer's costume. This was awfully early for someone who wasn't typically a get up, get dressed, and get going kind of guy. No matter how quiet she tried to be, on most mornings, when she opened the garage to get her bike, Ian appeared at his writing room window, often with a cup in one hand, a saucer in the other, and wearing—or so she assumed, because it irritated her—a silk dressing gown and cravat.

Ian got in his car without looking toward her window and drove away. Janet enjoyed twiddling her fingers at him anyway. *The table's turned, twit. Where are you off to?* Janet and the cats padded downstairs.

When Tallie came down half an hour later, she found her mother reading something on her laptop, an empty coffee cup dangling from her finger.

Tallie rescued the cup. "More?"

"A lot more. Christine got up way earlier than I did. I don't know if her questions get us anywhere, but here's what she added:

"Can we trust Heather?

"Is what she's doing real?

"Is it malicious?

"Is it dangerous?

"Is she a name and face muddler?

"Or is she an adept at excuses and convenient sidesteps?

"The 'or' is in italics."

Tallie, pouring her own cup of coffee, said, "I meant more coffee."

"In that case, no, thanks. I probably shouldn't have had *any* if I'm going out for this ramble with Summer. Are you sure you don't want to come with us? Look at the sunshine out there."

"Nope. The lads and I are going to put our paws up and read the morning away. The stones have been there five thousand years, give or take, so I can wait, and I'm pretty sure they will, too. Sorry, though. It does look like a nice day."

"Heather apologizes a lot," Janet said.

"And?" Tallie sat down across from her mother.

"Is it a habit? Good manners? Does she have a lot of regrets?"

"Regrets are a jump."

"Hang on, I'm adding those last few questions. There." Janet looked up. "I'm not saying I believe she has a lot of regrets, I'm just asking. You know what's bugging me? A couple of things I could've asked her, when she came in the shop, but didn't. I could've asked who the mystery man was."

"How was that going to work, though? Like, 'S-o-o-o, Heather, I couldn't help but notice the other night, from where I was hiding behind the bushes in my trench coat with my magnifying glass, that you met a mysterious man outside the old Murray house. Would you like to share his name with the rest of us, and tell us what you were doing there?' *Awkward.*" Tallie put an operatic spin on the last word. "Which, I'm sure, is why you didn't ask her." She got up. "Are you sure you don't want more coffee?"

"You might have had enough for both of us. I also didn't ask her about the jacket or her brother, but that was because I wanted to see if she brought it up. She didn't. Not a peep."

"What does that prove?"

"I don't have to prove anything. That's for her to do."

"But Norman didn't tell her you found it, did he?"

"Phooey. You're using your superior powers of logic and memory."

"That's just the caffeine being clever," Tallie said.

"I liked her smile, and the way she sounded tickled when she said she'd bring in promotional material," Janet said. "Even if she did say she'd have to do it later, which made me wonder if she really has any."

"Do you want to know my impression of her? She's plausible."

"You're right. Weird, but plausible."

"Yet questions remain," Tallie said. "She did all that planning for her kayak 'adventure,' and she prepared well enough to survive the night on an open ledge, not uncomfortably. But her phone died? And she left the flare in the kayak? *And* she totally blew it when she secured the kayak for the night?"

"And someone conveniently called me to get her down. How convenient is too convenient? I'm not sure that question makes sense. But here's Summer, so I'll just conveniently leave it with you."

"Give my best to the Stoatin' Stones. If they're buying, have one for me, too."

⁂

Janet said she'd drive so that Summer could navigate and give her a summary of her research on the stones.

"Head out of town on Buchan. We'll stay on it for three or four miles," Summer said. "It isn't the easiest place to find. I found it once, though, so we should be fine. I would've taken pictures then, but that was before I found out photography wasn't one of Farquhar's many talents."

"Are people going to know if the stones in your gingerbread circle aren't completely accurate?"

"Most won't care, but *I'll* know. Farquhar's measurements were meticulous, so an accurate model will be a tribute to him. Even if we cut it up and eat it afterwards."

"It'll make a good story for an article, too," Janet said.

"I love good stories for articles." Summer rubbed her hands over that idea.

"Do you think about going back to writing full-time?" Janet asked.

"I like writing on *my* time. The agony aunt column for the paper is enough pressure these days. I'm working on a profile of Farquhar—what a cool guy. Totally into Neolithic and Bronze Age archaeology, and did a decent job of not ruining the sites he worked on. Of course, we're talking about megaliths—twelve feet of granite sticking out of the ground. Some of them are only six feet, but it's not like he broke them in half with a careless tap of a rock hammer."

"*Only* six feet."

"I know, right? And, yeah, some of the stones have fallen over, but no one's going to be at their best after five thousand years. That's hardly Stuart's fault," Summer scoffed. "A professional—or what passed for a professional in the 1920s—accused him of digging around the bases of the stones to see how deep they went, and said that's why they fell. But Stuart proved he hadn't. He had sketches of the ring that Morag made when they were children, and they looked exactly the same. He did his serious work after the war, after he started the bookshop. He had one of the few cars in Inversgail, and he'd go out on long summer evenings, when it stayed light until ten or eleven. He tied a ladder to the side of the car and used it to get the height measurements. He measured the diameter of the circle, too. It's forty feet across. And where he could, he measured the circumference of each stone. I might have a crush on him."

"Are there pictures of him at the circle?" Janet asked.

"I haven't seen any. Maybe he was camera shy."

"Or maybe he needed an enthusiastic partner. Was Morag married by then? Why didn't she go with him?"

"She died of influenza. Soon after she painted the picture of the shop."

"I had no idea," Janet said. "Now I might cry."

"I did when I read about it."

Janet briefly put her hand on Summer's, then gripped the steering wheel again. Buchan Street had turned into a narrow hill road. "Are we still on the right track?" she asked.

"Coming up soon, we should see an even narrower road on the left. You'll turn there, and after that, before too long, we'll see a farm track on the right."

"I'm surprised there aren't signs for the stones," Janet said. "How do the *Outlander* tourists manage? They're mad about visiting any circle they can get to."

"'Get to' is the key. Uh-oh." Summer swiveled around in her seat, twisting to look over her left shoulder. "I think that was it."

They found a wider place in the road, farther along, and corrected course. The narrower road, when they located it, wound them between lower hills and became increasingly iffy. Janet slowed, and Summer sat forward, ready to let her know when to make the next turn.

"There, on the right," Summer said. "And now you'll want to go even slower."

"It would take money for infrastructure and a good bit of road engineering to make this more accessible." Janet took the car around a rock crowding the right side of the track, and jounced them through a stretch of water she'd assumed was a puddle but might be the cousin of the mire Curtis had complained of all those years ago.

"There's been talk about working on the site," Summer said. "Letters to the editor and to the Council. People who want to put the fallen stones back on their feet, and pave or at least grade this track."

"Expensive talk."

"And not a lot of support for it. Historic Environment Scotland would almost certainly have something to say about messing with the stone circle. HES is one of those public bodies that has some kind of relationship with the government. It doesn't like it when people make 'improvements,' and you sure wouldn't want it breathing down your neck."

"Outlanders might prefer their stone circles as is, anyway," Janet said. "Scraping a hole in your undercarriage to get here probably makes the experience more mythical and mystical. More so than a carpark full of exhaust-belching busses. How much longer? The suspension and my kidneys are wondering."

"Around the next bend should do it."

Janet gritted her teeth around another rock and around the bend, and rolled to a stop. "*That,*" she said, staring across a field toward another low hill. The sun seemed to light the stones especially for them. "I'm a convert. I'm a druid. Let's go dance around them."

"Naked?" Summer asked.

"Whatever the stones tell us to do. I'm all in."

As they walked across the field, catching sight of sheep in the distance, Summer said, "Can't you picture Stuart Farquhar over there, pacing off the distances between the stones, measuring heights and angles? Wearing—what are those things called? *We* call them knickers, but I'll never make that mistake here again."

"Plus fours?" Janet said. "Or are those only worn for golf? What about breeches with puttees?"

"That's it. A habit leftover from the Great War. I hope he wore a pith helmet, too."

Summer stopped several times to take pictures of the drunken circle as they approached. The sun that had shone on the stones now spilled over into the field and splashed onto the women. Despite the late fall nip in the air, Janet felt warmth soaking into her shoulders. A herd of long-haired, long-horned, red Highland cattle watched them from a distance.

"What do you think," Summer asked, eyeing the cattle in return. "Are there dozens more waiting around a corner?"

"It's a small herd," Janet said. "And no corners. Think of them as the great-great-grandchildren of the cattle who watched your friend Stuart and envied him his pith helmet. Is that a puddle in the middle of the ring?"

"It's not quite in the middle, according to Stuart, and seems to be a naturally occurring pool, probably a spring." Summer took pictures of the pool before asking, "Do you think fairies swim in it? Do you think Stuart and Morag believed that when they were children?"

"Easily," Janet said.

"Or what about one of those shape-shifting black horses that come out of lochs and pools?"

"No, no water kelpies. They're beautiful and seductive and murderous. If there was ever a water kelpie in this pool, the druids got rid of it by building their circle around it."

"Would that work?" Summer asked.

"We're going to say it did. But you don't believe in kelpies, and neither do I, so let's stop talking about them. It takes the warmth right out of the sunshine. You go ahead and take your pictures. If I disappear, you'll know I found a stone with a time travel portal, and I'm back visiting Morag and Stuart as children."

"Before you wander, stand next to the tallest stone to give it perspective."

Janet stood next to it, then in front of it, leaning her back against it. The cold of the granite drained all the warmth she'd absorbed from the sunshine. *Not an unpleasant cold, though,* she thought. *An ancient cold.*

"Thanks. That's good," Summer said.

"If I get in the way of your other shots, let me know. And don't go near anything that climbs out of that pool."

Now that she knew where to find the stone circle, Janet wanted to see it in every season and every kind of weather. It struck her as a wilder, less couth relative of Stonehenge. These stones stuck out of the earth like monumental teeth. She twined her way in and out of the stones that still stood, and commiserated with the ones beginning to stagger, then went to mourn their fallen comrades. One of them—a twelve-footer, Janet estimated—had not only fallen over, but had also fallen from its proper station in life, now serving as a picnic table big enough to seat a dozen.

"A picnic table for slobs," Janet said, going over to pick up cans and crisps packets littered around it. She straightened up when she heard a low mooing. Two of the hairy cows watched her from thirty or forty feet away. Youngsters, by their gangly legs. "Here's an apple core," she called, and lobbed it toward them.

The low mooing came again. But no, not a moo, and not from the cattle. A moan from the other side of the fallen stone. Except for the hair standing up on the back of her neck, Janet froze. A useless reaction, she told herself, and made her feet carry her around the end of the stone.

Heather lay up against the stone, curled on her side. Blood from a wound to the back of her head soaked her hair, her shoulder, the ground.

Janet froze again. *Trick me once,* she thought. *Trick me twice . . .*

Heather held something in her open hand—a miniature book? Janet recognized it, she was sure of it—William Clark's miniature Burns. But that blood. The metallic tang of it hung in the air between them. She saw no rise and fall of breathing. Heard no more sounds. "If this is an act and all part of your process, so help me I'll—"

No response.

Janet leaned down and felt for a pulse at Heather's wrist, then her neck. Thready at best. Not an act.

"Oh, dear God," Janet said, and hoped that was enough of a prayer for the emergency training the library had required every year to kick in full throttle. She hoped her delay hadn't cost a life.

"Summer!" Urgency snapped her voice across the stone circle. Summer, her back to Janet, whipped around. "I need you here. Now!" Janet shouted. "Medical emergency!" When she saw Summer on her way, she tried rousing Heather—calling her name, taking her hand, patting her cheek.

"What's—" Summer said, coming around the end of the stone. "Oh, geez."

"Call 9-9-9. Tell them it's a head wound with a lot of blood lost. Weak pulse. I don't think she's breathing. I'm going to start CPR."

"You're going to move her?"

"I have to."

"Wait. Pictures of the scene. Real fast." Summer took the pictures while she talked. "Got them. Calling now."

Janet moved Heather, apologizing to her as she pulled her onto her back. No response, and none when she tilted Heather's head and lifted her chin to straighten her airway.

"Okay, lass, you're staying with me. Understand?" she said.

No response, so Janet started chest compressions, singing the song she'd learned to keep the rate steady, but changing the words: "Aye, aye, aye, aye, you're staying with me, you're staying with me." She repeated thirty compressions and checked for breath. With no mouth-to-mouth shield, and all that blood, Janet didn't blow in a rescue breath. She apologized for that failure, and started another thirty compressions—and heard a mewling noise from Heather.

"Are you here, Heather?" Janet felt for her pulse, tried to rouse her. Still no sign of breathing. She started compressions again, feeling it in her arms, her interlaced fingers, and the heels of her hands. She changed the song and sang louder. "It's a beautiful day in the neighborhood, a beautiful day for a neighbor."

Another noise. Eyelids fluttering.

"You're staying with me, Heather. Do you hear me? It's a beautiful day, and you're staying with me."

A shallow breath, more of a gurgle, and a barely whispered, "It's dreich."

"No, it's not, you numpty. It's beautiful."

No whisper. No movement. No more gurgles or breath.

"No!" Janet started compressions again and didn't stop until Summer pushed her aside and took over.

"What about the dispatcher?" Janet picked up Summer's phone. "You ended the call?"

"She did. She got. Norman," Summer said, timing her words to her compressions. "He knows. How to. Get here. On his. Way now. Who you. Calling?"

Janet held up a finger. "Christine. It's me. And it's Heather. I think she's dead."

"Oh, aye?" Christine said. "And how has she done it this time?"

17

After phoning Christine and giving her the barest details, Janet took over from Summer. They continued spelling each other even as Norman Hobbs arrived, driving his all-wheel-drive vehicle across the fields with a bounce or two that might have smacked his head against the roof. Summer continued, even after he loped over, compressing and counting loudly, until Hobbs had called her name twice and Janet finally pulled her away.

"It isn't defeat," Hobbs said. He'd put on gloves and checked, as Janet had, for a pulse or signs of breathing. "If you've been working steadily since your call, you've done all that you could do and done it well."

Summer, sitting with her arms clamping her knees to her chest, didn't answer.

"Was there hope when you found her?" Hobbs asked as he turned Heather's head, looking at the wound.

"She was alive," Janet said. "She said something, so I thought there was hope. *We* had hope."

"What did she say?" Hobbs asked.

"'It's dreich.'" Janet watched him scanning the area around them.

"Dreich. Aye, from her point of view, I reckon it was. Medics should arrive shortly. Will you come with me? It's warmer in the car."

Janet appreciated Hobbs's circumspect way of saying they *would* sit in the car, whether they cared to be warmer or not. After he handed them in, he went back to the circle, and she thought he might be taking pictures of his own with his phone. She saw him bending close to the fallen stone, and wondered if he should be walking around quite so much.

"I'm not sure I can wait until the medics get here, and then for the Major Investigation Team," Janet said. "I'll have to hunker down behind one of the stones or one of the cows. Look, they're lying down. Back in Illinois, we used to say that meant rain is on the way."

"That's as useful here as the one about a cat washing its ears." Summer stared out the window, away from the circle. "Heather could have been standing on the rock and slipped off. Fallen backward."

Janet agreed, but Heather hadn't slipped. Janet knew that. Summer hadn't seen the wound—how it looked like one central, specific blow, and not at all like the back of Heather's head had hit a slab of granite—and Janet didn't want to tell her about it. Hobbs or the team of investigation specialists would do that soon enough.

"How can you be so normal?" Summer asked.

"I'm not. We might both be shocky. I can't believe she's dead. I liked her and her loopy ways, and I'm dealing with it by being inconsequential on the surface. Did you ever see the cartoon by Booth with a couple of ducks floating on a pond? The caption is something about being calm on the surface, but paddling like hell underneath. That's me. Will you be all right here? I really need to pee. I'll paddle over to warn Norman what I'm up to."

Janet skirted the stone circle so she didn't disturb the scene any more than they already had. And of course that was useless. The killer might have skirted the stones, too. And where was Norman? In the ring, looking into the pool. She told him what she needed to do.

"I shall be . . ." Hobbs pointed his hand toward the fallen stone, and without finishing his sentence, followed his hand there.

When Janet finished, she decided that protocol called for her to let him know. Rather than call out to him, at such a sad and solemn time, she crossed the circle to where he stood like a sentry. And then she couldn't help the questions that spilled from her in place of tears.

"Shouldn't an ambulance be here by now?" she asked.

"They've got lost. I've been in touch and told them there's no urgency. They shouldn't be too much longer."

"Did you see the metal box in her hand? It's a case. There's a book inside. An antique miniature book that William Clark brought to the shop a few days ago."

Hobbs turned to look at her.

"I didn't touch it, Norman. It's distinctive, and I recognize it. At least I think I do, and if it *is* the same one. . . ." Doubt tangled her thoughts. She batted it away. "I'm sure it's the miniature that belongs to William Clark, so why does she have it?"

Hobbs took out his small notebook and wrote in it.

"There's no question about this being murder, is there?" she asked. "It wasn't an accident. It wasn't suicide."

"Mrs. Marsh."

"Norman." She held his gaze. "You don't have to answer me, but I'm going to ask all my questions, and then I'll go sit in the car. Do this for me, please. I'm coping with something horrendous . . . just listen. Okay?"

"Aye."

"Why didn't the killer make sure she was dead? Why take the chance that someone would come along and save her? What kind of—" She stopped a moment to collect herself. "Was leaving her alive cruelty on top of horror? Was someone *sure* that no one was going to come along in time? Was it someone who thought no one would come along at all? Is this the same person who attacked Derek Spiers at his church?

"There. I'm done. I'll stop. No, wait. I'm not. I have two more, and I *would* like answers to these. First, how long will we have to sit here waiting before we can leave? Then, can't your murder specialists come find us at home or the shop if they have questions for us?"

Hobbs didn't immediately answer.

"Am I putting you in a bad position by asking that?"

"Not at all. I was thinking how best to answer. I've had word from the inspector in charge of the MIT. He asked that all witnesses remain until he arrives."

"Your face is telling me it isn't Inspector Reddick." Janet liked Reddick. She also trusted him.

"I wish my face had better news," Hobbs said. "I spoke with Inspector Russell. He expects to arrive within the hour."

"Well." There was nothing else to say. Janet also had previous experience with Inspector Russell. She'd never thought of weasels as likeable or trustworthy. With this particular weasel, the feelings seemed to be mutual. She started back to the car.

Hobbs called after her. "You can add this to your other questions. Is the person who did this someone not used to killing people?"

When Janet got back into the rear seat of Hobbs's car, Summer made a soft quacking noise.

"Are you paddling all right, now?" Janet asked.

"I'm afloat, anyway. And reinforcements are on the way. Tallie and Christine should be here soon."

"It might be a race, then." Janet turned in the seat so she could look back across the fields toward where she'd parked, and told Summer about Inspector Russell. "Norman made it sound like a request that we stay, but you can bet it's an order. If Russell gets here before Tallie and Christine, he'll probably run them off."

"If they get here first, can he make them stay?"

"I guess we'll find out. Christine's pulling in next to my car—no, she's not. She's pulling a Norman and driving straight for us. Lord love a duck. I hope she doesn't wreck the car."

Christine drove her parent's ancient Vauxhall skillfully across the fields. Hobbs met the arrivals as they got out of the car. Janet and Summer climbed out of Hobbs's car and joined them.

"Did one of you warn him?" Christine asked, swinging around toward the others, and then back to face Norman. "I can tell by that thing you're doing with your eyes that you're not surprised to see us."

"No one here warned me, Mrs. Robertson, but may I ask if you offered directions to a policeman consulting a map by the side of the road quarter of an hour ago?"

"Christine!" Tallie's voice fell just short of the decibel Janet would consider a wail. "You told me he asked the way to Ardtoe, and when you got back in the car you said you were laughing because he was going in the completely opposite direction."

"And by then he was," Christine said.

"You lied to a policeman," Tallie said, "and when you came back and asked me the quickest way for them to get to Ardtoe, you made me complicit. I'm a lawyer. An officer of the court. And now I've lied to the authorities investigating a murder."

"Dinnae fash." Christine thumped Tallie between the shoulder blades. "They can't take your license to practice away; you don't have one here. And considering that we *are* facing a murder investigation, I had to think on the fly. When I recognized D.C. Shaw with his map, and the odious Russell sitting in the car, I knew we'd need time to get our stories straight before they arrive. I'm sure they'll think your misdirection was simply a misunderstanding, Tallie."

"If I asked you to leave now, before Russell arrives, would you go?" Hobbs appeared to be making eye contact with one of the young hairy cows—his eyes resigned, the cow's sympathetic. Four of the cattle now stood close enough to their group that Janet could admire their eyelashes.

"Here come what look like an ambulance and two more police cars," Summer said.

The four women, four cows, and one constable watched as the vehicles came over the fields toward them, one behind the other, driving with more care than Hobbs or Christine had. Janet imagined them mincing their way around hillocks and stones and whatever the sheep and cattle left behind.

"It's too late now," Janet said, as the vehicles came to a stop. "But there's no story to get straight, anyway."

"We should wait to see what sort of muckle mess Russell makes of the investigation before we decide that," Hobbs said. "And if none of you repeat that, I will be forever grateful. Now, will you please wait in my car?" Then, in a rare show of overt authority, he pointed a finger at each of them and said, "In my car. Wait there."

As they headed for the car, Christine asked, "Did he leave the keys in the ignition?"

"No." Janet had no idea if that was true. With hand signals to Summer behind Christine's back, they successfully got Christine into the rear seat, sitting between them.

"I almost, almost yelled 'shotgun,'" Tallie said after getting into the front passenger seat and closing the door.

"The enormity of that mistake puts your rather poor map skills into better perspective," Christine said. "I don't like that they're assembling behind us. We'll all get neck strain trying to see what they're up to. Ah, but there they go toward the stone circle. That can't be the entire team, can it?"

"They're just the first to get here," Tallie said.

"They'll call in all kinds of forensic and crime-scene people," said Summer. "It'll depend on who's available, what expertise they need, and what they decide they're looking for out here. And who knows where they'll all be coming from. Could be Fort William, could be as far as Glasgow or Inverness."

"Which I'm sure works wonderfully well for them, but hardly seems efficient," Christine said. "And in our experience, yon wee stoatin' stoat, with the nasally voice to match, is hardly efficient, either." Russell had just stumbled over something.

"Is he a drunk?" Janet asked. "He's certainly not as intelligent as Reddick. I've been thinking of him as a weasel."

"Weasel works," Christine said. "I've no idea about his drinking habits, but he's mean as drunks often are. So now, before he comes to stretch us on the rack, tell us what we need to know."

The women settled into their seats, and Janet and Summer took turns filling in what they'd left out of their earlier, brief calls. Tallie took out her phone and recorded them as they talked. When they'd finished and fallen silent, Tallie said, "Your arms and shoulders will be sore from the CPR tomorrow."

"It doesn't matter," Janet said.

"I know." Tallie reached behind her, between the seats, and put her hand on her mother's knee. "D.C. Shaw, the one with map, to whom *I* gave bogus directions to find this place—is he the one who found a home for Gerald and Malcolm Murray's dogs?"

"He is," Janet said. "His uncle took Cyrus and Tapsalteerie. I hope I get a chance to ask him how they're doing."

"You might get it now," Summer said. "Here come Norman, D.C. Shaw, and the stoatin' weaselly stoat."

"Let's meet them on our own terms," Christine said.

In tacit agreement, the four women got out of the car and stood shoulder to shoulder, Janet and Summer in the middle, between Tallie and Christine. Inspector Russell marched to a halt barely two steps from them. *A small weasel's effort to intimidate*, Janet thought, *but not good enough.* Looking him coolly in the eyes, she moved two inches forward.

"I'm happy to see that you're eager to cooperate," Russell said. He held up a black wallet, and with a practiced move, let it fall open, showing his warrant card.

Drat the man for not understanding reverse intimidation when it tries to bite him. Janet wanted, very much, to see what he would do if she moved two more inches forward, but she felt a hand behind her back give a sharp tug on her jacket. Tallie's, at a guess.

"You've had a chance to warm up in the constable's car?" Russell asked.

"We have," Janet said.

"And chat, too, no doubt. That would not have happened if I'd been here sooner. Constable Hobbs tells me it's not a problem. We shall see about that. He also tried to convince me that two of you, Mrs. Christine Robertson and Ms. Natalie Marsh, are not involved in this incident. He said you arrived shortly before I did, and that being so, you should not be counted as witnesses."

"Constable Hobbs is correct," Tallie said.

"But I asked the constable if he knew, for a fact, that you had not been here earlier. Been here, maybe, and left before he arrived. And what did you answer, Constable?"

"That I do not know, for a fact, sir, that Mrs. Robertson and Ms. Marsh had not been here earlier and left."

"I can state, for a fact, that we had not," Tallie said.

"That's what makes a good witness," said Russell. "Clear, direct statements. Means bollocks, though, if you can't prove them. So, as you are here now, and as you have no doubt been exchanging information with your comrades, *I* am considering all four of you to be witnesses. Tainted witnesses, no doubt, but I'll need to get your statements just the same."

"Is that a legal term, Inspector?" Summer asked. "'Tainted witnesses?'"

Russell ignored her. "If you continue to cooperate, I shan't have to keep you long. We'll go over here, shall we?" He marched off toward the stone circle.

The women looked at each other, then at Hobbs and Shaw. Shaw ushered them forward as though inviting them to the ball.

"A question, though," Christine said, as they fell in behind Shaw. "Were we cooperating?"

"You wouldn't have to ask that if you had left when I asked you to," Hobbs said, bringing up the rear.

"You didn't ask us to leave," said Christine. "You asked if we *would* leave *if* you asked us to. The answer makes no difference now, anyway. But so that you know, Norman, I'm not sorry we're here. So let's not bicker."

"That's good advice, Christine," Tallie said. "We should all try to relax and not worry. Answer questions clearly and briefly. We don't need to guess. If you don't know the answer, say so."

"Your advice is good, too, Tallie," Janet said. "You'll see, Norman. We'll make you proud. We'll be impeccable witnesses."

"We will," Christine said. "We shall put the absolute *imp* into impeccable." With that, she strode ahead to walk beside D.C. Shaw.

Tallie fell back to assure Hobbs that the rest of them would try to keep a rein on Christine.

"Is that possible?" Hobbs asked. "To look at her"—they did, and saw a slightly taller than average, somewhat angular woman with a cloud of graying hair, wearing a comfortable skirt and trainers—"you would never know that she carries, in some wee corner of her heart, a burning desire for chaos."

"Oh, no, you know she means well," Tallie said. "She has the best interests of all of us in mind and she's never done anything to disrupt the police or get in the way." Tallie looked at Christine again. "Much. She's certainly never created chaos."

"But with Russell in charge, if she did," Hobbs said, sounding wistful, "wouldn't it be grand?"

18

The beasts, Shaw." Inspector Russell eyed the hairy, horned cattle that had followed the constables and witnesses in a wide arc around the stone circle to where he stood on the far side. "Any chance you can move them along?"

"Not advisable, sir. I've been on the phone to my uncle. He has a herd. Says it's best to ignore them. Warns they're docile until provoked, sir."

Janet watched the process of Russell digesting that information. It gave the man's sneer a twist of sour and added calculation to his eyes.

"Any chance the victim provoked them?" Russell hooked a thumb toward Heather's body, mercifully obscured by a wide police officer with a camera. "Could one of them have done this?"

"An orangutan, possibly, if you think your villain's a ginger," the officer with the camera cut in. "Your basic hairy cu cannae pick up a rock and bring it down with sufficient force to cause the damage the victim suffered."

Shaw, standing between Janet and Christine said quietly, "Those two don't get on."

"*Will* the beasts attack if provoked?" Christine asked.

"Not likely," Shaw said. "Just winding him up. I don't get on with him much, either."

"Which of you lot says you found her?" Russell asked.

"I did, Inspector," Janet said. "I—"

"How did she get here?" Russell cut in.

"Here? I have no idea."

"So you found her laid out like this." Russell said. "Interesting. I was told you'd moved her. Are you changing your story?"

"No—*oh.* I thought you meant *here.*" Janet spread her arms to take in the whole site. "Yes, I did move her."

"Sir," Shaw stepped in. "The witness found the victim in a *kreesal.*"

"What? Where?" Russell whirled in a circling scan of the area, then stopped and directed his snarl at Janet and Summer. "Why was I not told this? Where was she and why did you move her here?"

"Sir." Hobbs stepped forward before Janet could react. "I believe the D.C. means the witnesses found the victim curled on her side. Kreesal—the way a dog or a cat curls up when it sleeps."

"Yes, exactly. I found her in a kreesal," Janet said, as though she'd known the word and had been using it for longer than thirty seconds. "Summer can show you. She took pictures of the scene. Then I repositioned the victim so I could do CPR."

"You're an expert, are you?" Russell asked. "In emergency medical treatment as well as selling books?"

"Would you like to see my CPR certification card?" Janet asked. "I'm trained and I've taken a refresher course to renew my certificate every other year for the past twenty."

"Perhaps this is one of your off years, then."

Russell's attention shifted momentarily to a cow grazing to Janet's right. Janet wished she could bring his attention back with a slap, but instead brought it back with a question. "Would you like to know what her last words were, Inspector? She seemed to be coming around." To keep her voice from cracking, Janet concentrated on Russell's unblinking eyes. "Her eyes opened very slightly. I told her it was a beautiful day. She took an awful-sounding breath and said, 'It's dreich.'"

"Sounds more like a weather report," Russell said.

"Then would you like to know something about the victim as a person?"

"Not if it's a heartfelt outpouring of dreich, no."

"You've mistaken Mrs. Marsh for someone else," Christine said. "She does not waste *valuable* police time. Carry on, Janet."

"Thank you, Christine. First a question, Inspector, so I *don't* waste your time. Did Constable Hobbs fill you in on why Ms. Kilbride was in Inversgail and her activities since she arrived?"

"We've had a chat, aye."

"Okay, so I did an exhaustive online search, and if she's a writer—traditionally published, self-published, or published in the form of a blog or vlog—then I've failed as an information specialist."

"She means librarian," Christine added.

"Online searching is my superpower," Janet said, immediately wishing she hadn't. "What I mean is I haven't found anything she's written. Anywhere. That means she's not the writer she claims to be. Not a published writer, anyway. It's possible she's written hundreds and thousands of pages we have no access to."

"What does it matter that Ms. Kilbride wasn't published?" Russell's smile patted him on the back, as though he'd crossed a finish line before Janet. "Right. D.C. Shaw, move these people back, but don't let them go far and don't let them provoke the beasts. Get the photos from that one's phone. Or take the whole bloody phone. You, Hobbs. What are you staring at? If you haven't anything useful to contribute, why are you hanging about?"

"Sir," Hobbs said, "I've no idea if this will help in solving the case at hand, but I've found that most of our local crime depends on the convergence of possibility and nerve."

Russell stared at Hobbs, then walked away.

"You should have said that in Gaelic, Norman," Janet said. "It would have had as much impact as what I said."

"I wish I were that talented, Mrs. Marsh."

"It probably sounded like Gaelic to him, anyway," said Tallie.

"It was a nice turn of phrase, Norman, and an interesting premise," Christine said. "But when you can't dazzle him with your own Gaelic, you can always trot out your Monty Python homage and tell him his hovercraft is full of eels." She bumped him with her elbow. "I'll give you a nudge and a wink when the time's right, shall I?"

"How is it you both know about a cat in a kreesal, but Russell doesn't?" Summer asked. "Do you know it, Christine?"

"I've never heard it or read it."

"I saw it on Facebook," Shaw said.

"Aye," Hobbs said. "That's where my sister saw it. Someone with a blog says it's a Scots word worth using more widely."

"It's not often I get such a fine opportunity as this," Shaw said.

"My sister thought it might be a joke," Hobbs said. "She tracked it down in a Scots language dictionary. It comes from the Norwegian."

"I should do a story on you and your sister," Summer said. "You're in the same line of work. Here you are investigating, and she's a word detective." She offered her phone to Shaw.

"I shan't need to take it," he said. "If you'll just show me the photos, then you can send them to me here." He handed Summer a card, then handed one to each of the others.

Janet tucked hers in a pocket. "How are Cyrus, Tapsalteerie, and your uncle getting along?"

"Like the greatest of friends," Shaw said. "They're lovely dogs."

"I'm glad. I'm also glad that my memory of you is right. You're kind to dogs and badgered witnesses."

"There's nothing difficult about being kind to either, Mrs. Marsh, but thank you."

"My memory of Russell is playing nasty tricks on me," Hobbs said. "The last time I saw him, he was looking forward to retirement."

"I was looking forward to his retirement, too," Shaw said. "The paperwork got buggered up."

"A shame," Hobbs said.

"A shame he buggered it himself," said Shaw.

"A shame he's coming back so soon," Christine said.

Russell marched back over to them. He stopped in front of Summer, but spoke to Shaw first. "Did you get the photos from her phone?"

"Sir."

"Ms. Jacobs, is it?" Russell said. "What brought you out here this morning?"

"I came to take pictures," Summer said. "I'm going to make a model of the stones out of gingerbread."

Lips pressed together, Russell moved on to Janet. "Constable Hobbs says you can identify the object in the victim's hand and tell us who it belongs to. That's convenient for us. You might save us *valuable* time. Unless you're mistaken, of course. She might have picked it up at a jumble sale."

"That's always possible," Janet said, "but in this case unlikely. It's a rare miniature book inside a metal case. It belongs to William Clark, a collector, given to him by Colonel Stuart Farquhar. Mr. Clark said he's never seen another like it, and I certainly haven't. If you look inside, on the title page, you'll see Farquhar's name. When you dust it for fingerprints, you might find mine on the case and the book, unless the killer wiped them before putting it in Heather's hand. And when you *do* dust it, do it carefully. It's an exquisite book and should be treated like a . . . like a piece of treasure."

Janet looked from Russell to Shaw. Had Shaw just winced?

"You're very knowledgeable, Mrs. Marsh," Russell said.

"Not really."

"No? Let's see. You ken the book well enough to recognize it immediately on sight. You can describe it inside and out. You ken the killer put the book in the victim's hand. You found the victim. You ken we'll find your fingerprints on the wee treasure. You ken more than you let on, I reckon. And that makes me think back over the question you thought I asked earlier: *How did she get here?* You didn't give her a lift, did you?"

"No."

"If I have forensics go over your car, they won't find anything she left behind? In the American crime shows you might be fond of, they call that 'trace evidence.'"

"No."

"One more question, then, Mrs. Marsh. Something for you to think about, maybe use your superpowers on. How is it that you know the book is still inside its box? That is, unless you opened it. Ta, Mrs. Marsh. I'll be in touch."

"Are we free to go?" Tallie asked.

Russell ignored the question. He ordered Shaw to follow him, then walked away. Shaw lagged behind long enough to salute the women and wave them off.

"Shaw!" Russell barked.

Janet turned her back to him. She wasn't sure he'd notice, but if he did, she was positive he wouldn't recognize it as the snub she so heartily meant it to be. Fuming, she flipped the conversation back to the information *he'd* snubbed, addressing an imaginary Russell at the end of her jabbing index finger.

"The question of whether or not Heather is published, given that she presented herself as a writer, gives insight into her character, and *that* should interest you, you irritating blister," she said. "Her writing, *if* we could find it, would give even *better* insight, you annoying, small-thinking waste of skin, snot, and sinew."

"That's rousing and Shakespearean of you, Janet." The rant had roused Queen Elizabeth, who nodded her thanks to Janet and then stared after Russell. "I, for one, take Inspector Russell's foul mood personally. What is this? A habit? Ask him a question he doesn't like or he can't answer, or merely chooses to ignore, and he turns round and walks away."

Janet saw the queen tuck that detail away and wondered how she hoped to use it. Janet turned to Hobbs. "In the grand scheme of things, of course it doesn't matter that Heather is published or not. But it *is* an insight. It's a nuance. And *they* matter."

"In the grand scheme of things, Russell doesn't matter, Mrs. Marsh," Hobbs said. "Would you like further insight on the ways in which he doesn't matter?"

"No, Norman. I wouldn't want you to get in trouble."

"So if we can leave, shouldn't we do that?" Tallie asked.

"You'll likely make him suspicious or nervous if you continue standing here," Hobbs said. "So you needn't rush."

"Good man," the queen said.

"What about Heather's brother?" Janet asked. "Have you located him yet, Norman?"

"No."

"Do you know where Rab is?" she tried. "There's some question about him following Heather. I have no way of knowing if that's true, but if he was, he might have seen something."

"If he'd seen anything to do with this tragedy, he would have called 9-9-9, as you did," Hobbs said.

"You're right. Of course."

"To put your mind at ease, he has not been following Ms. Kilbride. Their paths might have crossed, but that is all."

"Then you do know where he is."

"No, Mrs. Marsh, I do not."

"A point of procedure, Norman," Christine said. "Does our agreement still stand? If we, SCONES, share our questions with you, will you answer the ones you can without jeopardizing your investigation?"

"Technically, that agreement was with Inspector Reddick," Hobbs, looking wary, said.

"But we are stuck with the irritating blister." Christine eyed him in a way that momentarily increased his wariness.

But Hobbs drew up into a more official posture. "The agreement stands."

"Then let's set the ground rules," said Tallie.

Hobbs thought for a moment then nodded. "I will trust you not to involve yourselves in police business in any way that jeopardizes the investigation, or that puts you knowingly in danger. Aye?"

"Aye," the women said.

"I will answer what questions I can without jeopardizing the investigation, although, as you probably realize, I will not be directly involved, or involved at all, depending on the whim of yon blister of skin, snot, and sinew. Aye?"

"Aye," said three of the women.

"Yea, verily," said Christine.

"If you hear or learn anything that might help the investigation, I will appreciate knowing that information. Aye?"

"Aye," said Janet, Tallie, and Summer.

"You won't be disappointed, Norman," Christine said. "We've been honing our ESP."

"Aye, well." Renewed wariness made a subtle but telling adjustment to Hobbs's eyebrows.

"I'll send you our file this afternoon," said Janet, "and for now, we'll get out of your hair."

Christine offered to give the others a lift to Janet's car. The four of them walked silently past the circle, now filled with more MIT officers. After they were in the car and bumping back over the fields, Janet said, "Norman can be a pain in the bahookie, but he's our pain in the bahookie."

"Speaking of our pain in the bahookie," Tallie said, "you might have upset him when you mentioned ESP, Christine. He might not remember it stands for 'educated speculation and probing.' *I* hardly remember."

"Did we *ever* tell him?" Summer asked.

"If we had real ESP, we might remember," Janet said.

Christine slowed for a faction of cattle that had split away from the herd. They'd regrouped in the only level area between the Vauxhall and the track where Janet had parked.

"The beasts have converged," Tallie said. "Do you have the nerve to drive through them?"

"Possibly," Christine said. "Slow and steady should do it. Norman's point about convergence and nerve is brilliant, though, don't you think? I wonder if he borrowed it from somewhere. Put it in your cloud document, Janet, so we keep it in mind."

"As long as we also keep our eyes peeled for complicating factors like intention versus reality," Tallie said. "Or the odd hairy cu."

"Very good, Tallie," Christine said. "We'll keep complicating factors firmly in mind. If I may say, it will be*hoove* us to do so."

"You only get to do *that* once," said Summer.

"How you can be comfortable and make jokes around highland cattle, but turn into a gibbering fool in front of sheep, I'll never know," Janet said. She took her phone out and started tapping.

"Notes?" Summer asked.

"Text. To Norman. I asked the wrong question back there, so I just sent the right one. It shouldn't have been 'Do you know where Rab is?' It should've been, 'Do you know what Rab is doing?'" She paused. "He's not answering."

"He might not," Tallie said. "He's at work. At a crime scene."

"If he were bored at home and staring at the toes of his regulation boots, he wouldn't answer," Christine said.

"Because he *does* know what Rab is doing." Janet put her phone away. "And by not answering, he's just given us an aha moment."

19

Janet dropped Tallie and Summer at the shop. Sunday to Sunday bookings were the most popular at Bedtime Stories. Summer managed the B&B in exchange for a small flat separate from the guest rooms. But with so many rooms turning over on Sundays, Tallie usually pitched in. And after the shocks of the morning, she'd told Janet she wanted to make sure Summer didn't feel alone or overwhelmed.

"Not that I'm ignoring *your* feelings, Mom. But you have a pattern for working through traumas and worries. It's got a rhythm, and you don't need me throwing you off."

"It's called being sadder but wiser. It comes with age, if you're lucky enough to live that long."

"*Do* you need me?"

Janet held her daughter's face and kissed her forehead. "I'll be fine. If I'm not, you'll be the first one I'll call. The first person—I might snatch up the cats first. You stay and help Summer, and I'll see you later."

When Janet pulled into the drive at home, she saw Ian appear at his upstairs window. He stood, looking down, until she opened her car door. That was *his* pattern. Though he'd broken it that morning by driving off so early. Maybe just to the shops for something he needed for breakfast.

But she'd rarely seen him dressed in anything but author formal or casual. Curious.

Smirr and Butter met her at the door, sniffing with cautious interest at her boots.

"That's mostly whatever grows on a brae with subtle overtones of Highland cow," she told them.

Butter attacked her bootlaces as she undid them. She left him to the battle and went with Smirr to the kitchen.

"Here's *my* pattern, old man," she said. "It starts with tea, and lots of it. Then, for a while, we're going to push every thought of vile killing and vile killers right out of our heads."

Her cup from the morning still sat on the counter beside the sink. She gave it a sniff, and her nose tempted her toward coffee over tea. "No. We'll stick with the pattern." She rinsed the cup and looked at the cat. He blinked. "But is that approval, or is it your unending love for me?" He blinked again. "Ah, Morse code for 'Snacks are good.' I could not agree with you more."

She gave each of the cats a half dozen of the treats meant to clean their teeth. Then she fixed a tray with teapot, milk, cup, and a plate of oatcakes and sliced cheese. On the way past the fruit basket, she put the tray down and added a stem of grapes, then went through to the lounge. Tallie had left a CD of Rachmaninoff's "Rhapsody on a Theme of Paganini" on the player. Good enough. She sat in her favorite chair, looking out the large window into the back garden. Took a sip of tea. Nibbled cheese and oatcake. Then went to get her laptop.

"Because there is *no* way in this *world* that I can push the picture of Heather out of my head." Janet's voice and her fist shook with anger. "And I will do whatever I can to find out who did this."

She read over the "Where's Heather" document and started a new one. The tea grew cold as she typed up her notes and questions. When she noticed, she warmed it in the microwave. When she couldn't think of any more questions, she created a new document for Hobbs, copying and pasting from the first two. Then she hit SEND.

The cats napped in kreesals on the couch. Feeling calmer, Janet decided to join them, but first she sent a text to the SCONES.

Rain threatened that evening. But because the threat of rain was occasionally not as wet as actual rain, the Marsh women left the car at home and walked to Nev's. They often walked in actual rain, too, crowded under an umbrella, their feet protected by rubber boots.

"Did you set up your cozy teatime when you got home?" Tallie asked.

"I did, dear. Thank you."

"And sat down to relax?"

"You'd think my life is hobbled by habit."

"But before you sat, you raged around, shaking your fist at villains and killers?"

"This time, I actually sat and had a sip of tea before only a very short rage. But a little variation in routine is nice now and then. I sent a file to Norman, but haven't heard back from him. That doesn't worry me."

"What does worry you?"

"That I'm *not* worried."

"Well good, because you wouldn't be *you* if you weren't worried about something."

Tallie and Summer had cleaned the B&B's rooms that afternoon, changed linens, checked in new guests, and then shared a pizza. Janet had eaten a salad while reading online articles about the history of miniature books.

"Is there anything in particular you think you should be worried about but aren't?" Tallie asked.

"No, and that worries me, too. But talking it over with the three of you should help."

"Bring all your worries into focus like a swarm of bees."

"Like a flock of seagulls flying in groups of three."

Tallie held Nev's door for Janet, just as the threat of rain became a downpour. Helen and David, Christine's parents, waved them over, and they went to say hello. Helen called them by name, though she might have confused mother for daughter. She lifted her drink in a toast and then asked David who the man at the bar was.

"Danny, love? You know Danny."

"The lad with his elbow on the bar. He's mistaken if he thinks I'll fall for his charms just for sending me this drink."

"Our Chrissy brought the drinks, love."

"Did she? That's all right then. You lasses have a grand time at the ceilidh."

Janet and Tallie assured her they would.

"I'll get the drinks," Tallie said. "What would you like?"

"A half of Selkie's," Janet said, "but I'll come with you." She greeted Danny, and turned and waved to Christine. While Tallie ordered, she surveyed the back of the room for other familiar faces. Rhona and Isla weren't in. It wasn't Pub Scrawl's night to meet, so no Maida. No Rab, unless he was playing darts. Janet continued her survey around the rest of the room, turning as she did, and ending with her elbow on the bar looking toward the "lad," on his elbow, down the other end.

"Did you get a good look at him?" Tallie asked as they carried their drinks to the table.

"If the elbow on the bar's supposed to make him look comfortable, it's not working."

"We were lucky when we started coming here," Tallie said. "We had a sponsor." Then to Christine and Summer she said, "Evening, lasses. Christine, your mum thinks we're here for a ceilidh."

"Get the right music going, she and Dad will dance everyone under the table," Christine said. "So then, how is everyone doing tonight after the morning we had? That's a serious question from your personal social worker."

"Doing all right." Summer drew circles on the table with the bottom of her glass. "I hadn't met Heather, but that never mattered when I covered tragedies for the paper back home. And I heard about her from you guys. So it isn't like losing a friend. More like losing a local celebrity. The losing is the thing."

"Can you be numb and angry at the same time?" Tallie asked. "Tomorrow I might be less numb but probably still angry."

"If it doesn't cloud your thinking, channel it." Christine mimed throwing a dart. "Summer's done that."

"I don't like being angry and my dart game is terrible," Tallie said. "But I won't take my anger out on any of you or our customers."

"You should have heard the clean sheets snapping to attention when she made beds today, though," Summer said.

"What about you, Christine?" Janet asked.

"I once heard Queen Elizabeth say something about going forward with quiet, good-humored resolve. I've made those my watchwords." The queen rustled in those words. "And you, Janet?"

"Earlier this week, which now seems a month long and a blink at the same time, I wanted a path forward. Through the tangles and clutter of what Heather called her process—part of that clutter including William Clark, whose book was in her hand." Janet stopped for a swallow of ale. "I think I have a path now. I made it this afternoon, and I paved it with my regrets for not being able to see what was *going* to happen, and my need for—" She held up a finger and took a longer swallow of ale. "Sorry. I was getting dramatic. I was going to say 'revenge.' That's not what this is. I don't believe in it. But let's do what we can to help Norman, and that will have to be good enough."

"I think we know how she's feeling," Christine said to Tallie and Summer. "She's on fire."

"Hush," Janet said. "The man at the end of the bar. Do you know him?"

"Way to be inconspicuous," Summer said. "We're all staring at him."

"Everyone here would have stared at him at some point since he came in," Christine said. "And I doubt anyone here knows him. And he knows it. What do you reckon? Late thirties? Young forties? Hard to say how tall; he's slouching *and* leaning. Bit of a paunch, but would that disappear if he used the posture his mother would be proud of?"

"Your mother was wondering if he'd sent her the drink you took her," Tallie said.

"*I'm* wondering if he could be our mystery man," said Christine. "Or one of them."

"Congratulations," Janet said. "You jumped to a conclusion faster than I usually do."

"You're the one who pointed him out," Christine said. "Don't tell me that didn't cross your mind."

"But it took me longer," Janet said. "He *might* be the right height and build for the guy at the Murray house."

"Do you want to go chat him up?" Christine asked.

"No, I do not. I don't think you should, either. But he just paid with a credit card."

"And Danny might be game to give us a name. Very good, Janet. I'll go slip that lovely man behind the bar a note with our question. Going for less conspicuous for your benefit, Summer."

Christine wrote the note and took it to the bar. Danny read it and glanced toward the man at the end. Janet imagined Christine's struggle to keep a beleaguered look from her face, for Danny's benefit. She saw the same struggle on Danny's face from time to time. All must be well, though, because Christine came back to the table looking pleased.

"Danny doesn't know him. He can't talk now—he must be worried about the sloucher having the supersonic hearing of a bat. I ordered fried mushrooms. When Danny gets a chance for a break, he'll bring them with our information. It will all look perfectly natural."

"Information." Janet rubbed her hands like a miser with a new chest of gold. "So, now, the path forward. We heard Norman's ground rules for our agreement with him. Do you have any objections to setting our own? I'm thinking about mechanics—how and what we do with questions, discussions, and—"

"Suspects," said Tallie.

"And Norman," said Christine.

Janet looked at Summer. "Anything?"

"Just let's get it going." Summer took out her phone. "I'll record as we go and make a guidelines document in the cloud later. Add other guidelines as you think of them."

"Be careful about discussing any of this in the tearoom or the shop," Janet said. "Or anywhere public." She swirled a finger around, indicating the pub.

"If we identify a suspect, or if we're considering suspects, think about motive and opportunity," Tallie said, "but most of all, remember how dangerous this person is."

"May I suggest we set a limit on how often we check in with Norman?" Christine said. "Say, no more than once a day, unless we have something we think is crucial."

"That's good," Tallie agreed. "There's no point in bugging him, and good reasons not to."

"If you have questions, thoughts, or answers, remember to pop them into the cloud," Summer said. "And create a new document if you need one. I've got a question now, though, about the book she had in her hand. You said you recognized it, Janet, and I believe you. But you also said Russell could be right, that there's more than one."

"I also told him it's unlikely," Janet said. "I read up about the publisher, Bryce and Sons, this afternoon. Not all of the miniatures they made are rare, but this edition, in its metal box, doesn't come up for sale often. When it does, the price is way out of our league. Thousands of pounds."

"Then there's a slew of questions about the book that need to be answered," Summer said. "The police will be—should be—working on those, but it won't hurt for us to put them in the cloud. We can think about them. They might spark other questions or ideas."

"Is the book important to understanding the case?" Janet asked.

"Is it the key?" Christine said.

"How or why did she have it? Did the killer put it in her hand? Did WC give it to her?" Summer rattled off.

"Did she take it from him?" Tallie said. She looked around the table. "Anything else?"

"We should send those questions to Norman," Christine said. "He'll answer what he can and, again, they might spark him to ask more questions—of the specialists or on his own."

"That question about a second book could be our entrée to a chat with WC," Janet said. "That's something I'll look forward to. I wonder what else he has in his collection?"

"Which gives us the perfect opportunity to remember the ground rule about suspects being dangerous," Tallie said.

Christine leaned forward and whispered, "And the perfect opportunity to play a preliminary round of who's your favorite suspect. If we're whispering, will your phone be able to record us, Summer? Or shall we pass notes?"

"Let's just be careful," Summer said. "It's pretty obvious WC is on the list. Who else?"

"The mystery man, or men," Janet said. "And her brother. And person or persons, unknown about whom she wrote. I haven't found anything she's written. But what if she wrote about some other crime, from other angles and perspectives, and shared it privately? What if that became a pattern for her, and that's what she did here?"

"Blackmail?" Summer said. "That's never a safe business model."

"Especially if this is the way she was going about it," Tallie said. "Is this how *you'd* blackmail someone? She's been fairly public."

"Her research methods were unconventional," Janet said. "Maybe her blackmail methods were, too."

"Maybe," Tallie said. "Our investigatory methods are certainly unconventional. At this point, we could put names on a dartboard and let me try to hit someone."

All four looked into their glasses while Patsy Cline sang "I Fall to Pieces" on the jukebox for the fourth time since they'd sat down.

"Did any of you notice the interesting loophole Norman left in his part of the agreement?" Christine finally asked.

Tallie picked up her glass and got to her feet.

"A toast to loopholes?" Christine asked.

"Nope. If you're going to start talking about loopholes, then that's my cue to go humiliate myself at an actual game of darts."

"I'll help you," Summer said. But before following Tallie, she leaned closer to Janet and Christine and said, "I like a good loophole as much as you do, and as a reporter, I took advantage of some doozies. But always remember, a noose is just a fancy loop."

Janet and Christine nodded solemnly until Summer disappeared into the dart room. Then Christine hitched her chair closer to Janet's.

"Norman said we're to let him know if we hear or learn anything pertinent to the investigation. And we will. Goes without saying. But he didn't specify how soon after hearing or learning we should do the letting him know part of that ground rule. It's a clear loophole."

"You don't think it's understood that we'll let him know as soon as possible?" Janet asked. "At what point does a clear loophole become the murky water of withholding evidence?"

"Again, a loophole," Christine said. "*As soon as possible* gives us wiggle room."

"Wiggle room within reason," Janet said.

"Och, well, that also goes without saying."

"The other flaw—"

"Our wiggle room is more of a technicality than a flaw," Christine said. "So this will be *the* flaw, rather than the *other* flaw."

"*This* flaw is that we're amateurs, so we might not be able to distinguish between a clue and a red herring."

"You're right about that," Christine said. "Even if the herring comes up and slaps us with its little red fins. Here comes Danny. Without the mushrooms."

Danny sat down with an apology. "I waited too late. The mushrooms are finished for the night. Sorry, love."

"Och, well," Christine said. "They were just a way to bring you over here."

"I have the name—Owen Nicholson. Means nothing to me. He wasn't much for talk. Said he came because a friend died. He didn't say who, and it's not the sort of question I'm going to ask."

"The name is plenty, Danny," Janet said. "Thank you."

"Another name we're interested in is William Clark," Christine said. "A lawyer who doesn't practice. He, James Haviland, and Ian Atkinson are the trustees named in Gerald Murray's will."

Danny shook his head. "When we were looking for the lass and her kayak, I heard about the other lass, Clark's wife. But that was back before I moved home. If there was talk—and there was bound to be talk—it died down before I bought Nev's. And he's not been in here that I know of."

"Do you know what Rab's up to lately?" Janet asked.

Danny laughed and went back to the bar.

"I wonder if 'disappeared' is an official Police Scotland term," Janet said.

"Are you talking about Rab and Ranger?" Christine asked. "What makes you think they've disappeared? Don't you remember our aha moment this morning? Didn't you hear Danny laugh just now? You know how they come and go, shimmering in and out of the shop without a thought for a schedule or regular work hours."

"I'm not talking about Rab and Ranger. I do want to know where they are and what they're up to, but neither Norman nor Maida is alarmed, so I'll wait to find out. And I *will* find out."

"Then who are you talking about?"

The pub door opened and both women looked to see who'd come in. Not Rab, which would have been like him—to show up as though he'd heard his name and wondered why or what needed doing—but just another Nev's regular.

"I was talking about Heather's brother," Janet said. "And I wonder if his name is Owen Nicholson."

20

Janet yanked at tangled sheets as she made her bed the next morning. A soft rain fell and she would much rather fall back into bed, pull the duvet over her head, and disappear. She'd stayed up too late reading, then fallen into a restless sleep. The cats had tried to ride out the storm of her tossing, but at some point abandoned her. She'd dreamed of falling, woke up with a full-body startle reflex, and fallen again in the next dream.

Now she flipped the duvet back into place and two sleepy cats picked their heads up to blink at her. Butter stood and stretched, tail upright, his whole small body quivering with the effort. Janet scooped him up and held him to her cheek. "This is a tough choice, lads. Do I go back to bed with you or be a drudge and go to work?"

Smirr lifted his nose, and Janet smelled an intermediate choice—coffee and bacon. The three went down to the kitchen, Butter riding in the crook of Janet's arm.

"Don't let the lads fool you," Tallie said without looking up from her phone. "They've had breakfast."

"When did we buy bacon?"

"We didn't. Ian brought it."

"That's—"

"Odd, I know. He hadn't opened it, and I ate a piece half an hour ago, so I think we're safe."

"Safe but confused," Janet said. "This is two mornings in a row he's been up and out of the house. I didn't tell you about yesterday. He drove off before I left, wearing an old pair of jeans."

At that, Tallie put her phone down. "I knew there was something else different about him when he came to the door. Something besides being oddly neighborly at an early hour. He was wearing blue jeans this morning."

"It's good bacon." Janet took a second piece. "A nice treat."

"Not to look gift bacon in the mouth, but I think we should always say, 'beware Ian bearing gifts.'"

"If it's a bribe, it isn't a good one. Unless *you* know why he's bribing us, because I don't. What did he say when he brought it?"

"That he had more than he could use. I told him it freezes well. He backed away, said 'cheers,' and left."

"I know what it is," Janet said. "Research for a new book. And here's the title—it fits the pattern for his series—*Bribed by Bacon.* Maybe he's going out early to shadow a butcher."

"You should be a detective or something."

~

At the morning meeting in the doorway between the shops, the women checked their to-do lists for the upcoming birthday celebration. They expected delivery of the new bags and tea towels at midweek. Members of the ceilidh band providing the live music planned to drop by at the weekend for a sound check.

"How do you feel about the gingerbread?" Christine asked. "Do we go ahead with the stone circle?"

"What do you think, Summer?" Janet asked.

"I'm just the baker. This has to be a joint decision. It might depend on what details come out and how far they go. Stone circles are a hot topic, though. The press might run with the story, and we could end up looking pretty macabre."

"When were you going to start baking?" Tallie asked.

"I planned to do practice runs this week, for real next," Summer said. "We'll have plenty of other food, so don't worry about needing a substitute if we scrap it. And don't worry about *me*. The decision isn't going to keep me up at night. Stone circles aren't the only things that float my boat. I'll move on to the next thing." Her fingers tapped a moving-along song on her thighs. "Shall we move on to the investigation? Have you heard anything back from Norman?"

"Not yet," Janet said. "But here's what *did* keep me up last night."

Summer reached for her phone. Janet stopped her.

"It's not in the cloud yet. It will be," she said. "I've been trying to figure out why I want Owen Nicholson to be Heather's brother and I think I know."

"Who is Owen Nicholson? This is not how we use the cloud. He's not there at all." At the word *who*, Tallie had started shaking her head at her mother. She didn't stop until Christine put a hand on her shoulder.

"That's the name of the man at the bar," Christine explained. "You two were playing darts when Danny told us. He told Danny he came here because a friend died."

"Sorry, I forgot you didn't know," Janet said. "Honestly, though, you don't want me putting every cockamamie idea that runs through my head into the cloud. Owen almost certainly isn't Heather's brother, but if he is, then that means her brother hasn't disappeared off the face of the earth. More specifically, off the edge of the headland."

"You did add questions about her brother to the cloud." Summer had her phone out now. "Did you put these in last night?"

"Or early this morning."

Summer read, "Where is her brother? Has anyone seen him? Was he in on the kayak incident? Was he aware of the search? Was he one of the searchers? Apparently not. No one's seen him. He must have left and missed all of it."

"Heather told Norman her brother was fine, but not here," Janet said.

"Wiggle room," said Christine. "There's no specificity in 'here.'"

"That's what I've been worrying about."

"What else?" Tallie asked.

"What I've already told you. I found the jacket on the headland, near the edge. It was a dark night. What if he went over?"

"No bodies have been found," Summer said.

"They quit looking for one when I told them she was on the ledge. Norman's calling in a favor to find the brother. No word so far. I'll type my notes sometime today."

"One more question," Tallie said. "Is it a coincidence that Owen is here because a friend died, and another one that he drank at Nev's last night?"

"It might not be that odd," Summer said. "Not many strangers wander in, but Nev's is a quiet place away from the tourist buzz. Maybe that's what he was looking for. But here are my questions. If his friend is Heather, who let him know she'd died, and where was he that he got here so fast?"

∽

"Thank goodness for books and people who like them," Janet said as a gust of wind and rain blew another group of tourists through their door. "And thank goodness for the umbrella stands and absorbent doormats."

A couple of women, obviously sisters, stopped at the counter to ask if Janet or Tallie could recommend picture books for three- and five-year-old boys.

"Something really Scottish," one sister said.

"Paperback, too," said the other. "Lighter for packing."

"I have grandsons just about that age," Janet said. "I'll show you some of their favorites."

The first sister pointed at Janet. "American. Midwest." She turned her finger on her sister and herself. "Wisconsin."

"Illinois," Janet said, nodding toward Tallie. "Both of us, and one in the tearoom."

The sisters' eyes widened, and they grabbed each other by the arms. When they started squealing, Janet didn't see any point in tracking who was speaking.

"Do you know what this is?" one said.

"It's one of those bookstores where you can pay to run it for a week and you live upstairs!" said the other.

"It would be like we died and went to heaven!"

Janet thought they might jump up and down. But they calmed, let go of each other, and asked, "How much is it for a week?"

"It actually isn't one of those bookstores," Janet said. "My daughter and I, and our two friends in the tearoom, own the shops and the B&B upstairs."

The Wisconsin sisters gazed at the Marsh women with awe, or as Tallie said in a warning text to Christine and Summer, *Like we're baby pandas or tigers or wombats on display for the first time at the zoo.*

Janet left the sisters to browse the children's picture books and returned to the counter. She slipped bookmarks into the books Tallie rang up, then Tallie slipped bookmarks into the books Janet rang up. Eventually, the sisters came back and put six paperbacks on the counter.

"We aren't going to argue over them," one said. "We'll take all six. Then we'll have tea."

At midmorning, Tallie's phone buzzed with a text from Christine. "She wants to know if I mind switching places for a wee while," she said.

"Do you?"

"Not at all. She sweetened the deal with a scone. It's my lucky two-bribe day."

Christine hadn't left Janet out of the deal. She and Tallie passed each other in the popular fiction aisle, Christine bringing a tray with tea and scones for two.

"Did you read the questions I added to the cloud this morning?" Janet asked.

"I haven't. It's been a zoo in there—wombat and panda watchers included. That made me wonder if we'll rate a visit by Inspector Weasel at some point." Christine sat on the stool with a small *woof*. "I came to see how you're really doing, though it won't hurt to be off my feet for a few minutes, either."

"It wouldn't hurt for you to have a stool behind the register in the tearoom."

"Then I'd have to think of other excuses for popping in here. How are you? Sleepless nights and worries take their toll."

Janet handed her a cup of tea and took a sip of her own. "Daylight hours and friends working together go a long way."

"Being strong and asking for help when you need it go a long way, too. You are the first, and do the second. So, good." Christine did an exaggerated scan of the area. "Let's talk suspects."

"Quietly."

"We should be fairly safe, to begin with, as we haven't any or many names. But I will continuously scan for approaching customers. I've been thinking about the suggestion of blackmail. If a blackmail victim did this, then that means this could be someone who slipped into town, killed her, and slipped out again, never to be traced."

"Except that person knew where and when to find her," Janet said. "Are blackmailers that careless? Was *she* that careless?"

Christine put a finger to her lips then spoke to an approaching customer. "Janet will be right with you. She's finishing her tea break. Lovely scones they have in Cakes and Tales. She can't resist."

Janet wiped her fingers and rang up one of the popular guidebooks and one on Scottish ghost stories. The customer wandered over to the fireplace chairs and opened the ghost stories.

Janet moved closer to Christine. "She riled someone. *Enraged* someone. But she might have thought she remained anonymous and wasn't worried that this person knew how to find her."

"That works if it's someone local *or* from outwith the area."

"She had a car and a bike. I didn't see either one. How did she get there?"

Christine ticked answers on her fingers. "Took herself, willingly accepted a lift, taken against her will."

"Or ran into someone there with no connection to her, was killed, and her car or bike was stolen. Norman will know if they've found either or both of them."

"How often is murder done by a stranger?" Christine asked.

"Murder of a lone woman? I don't know, but we warn our friends and daughters about walking alone at night and accepting rides from strangers. What did Norman say to Rancid Russell about local crimes?"

"They depend on the convergence of possibility and nerve. In my experience, nerve doesn't require brain. I'm thinking of another student, one who admired the one I told you about the other evening—'the showman.' This lad was a problem solver. We found out *after* that he and his father watched those shows where teams build contraptions out of junk."

"After what?" Janet asked.

"After the lad objected to being skipped over for an all-star soccer team, built a trebuchet, and launched a flaming soccer ball onto the field during practice. Eight years old and already a delinquent. Thankfully, no one was hurt."

"Oh my God. But building something like that *did* take brains."

"It wasn't the child who lacked brains," Christine said. "The father. He bought the materials and provided the accelerant. Some of the brawn, as well, I should think."

"Was this in the paper when it happened? Why didn't I hear about it?"

"The dad might not have used the brains he came equipped with, but he made excellent use of the money and connections he was born into. I bring up dad and lad's sad story to illustrate that, although possibility and nerve might converge, the artist does not always think through the consequences. And those consequences might trip him up. Or cost him the price of a new soccer field to hush it up."

"Or make him more dangerous."

"I'll get these next few customers for you." Christine refilled Janet's teacup and handed it to her. "You take the stool and put your brains to work. You definitely have them and know how to use them."

Janet drained the cooled tea and set the cup aside. She went to the office and retrieved her laptop. No one had created a suspects document yet, so she did that and started typing. Then she stopped. She wanted this to look more systematic—make a list with each suspect identified, followed by the reasons they were on the list. Maybe she needed a chart. *No. Start with the list.*

Mystery Man 1
Mystery Man 2
Mystery Man 3

It looked like a game show. She left the list and moved on to reasons for suspecting the man or men.

MM 1 Reasons: We're casting a wide net, eliminating possibilities.
MM 2 Reasons: same
MM 3

She stopped again and listened to Christine and the customer discussing their favorite Ann Cleeves crime novel. The reasons for all three, who might actually be just one, were the same—nothing. Nothing beyond not knowing who they were. They knew more reasons *not* to suspect the mystery men. MM 1 made the urgent call about Heather's location on the headland. MM 2 called with a warning for Lynsey. MM 3 met Heather at the Murray house. *Big whoop,* Janet thought. *He might be an estate agent and she was pretending to be a buyer.* She started again.

Heather's brother
Reasons: same as MMs, plus these questions: Where is he? Who is he? Is he one or more of the mystery men? (Reason he might be MM 1: He and Heather are close enough that she wears his jacket. He'd call to make sure she's safe.)
WC
Reasons:

Christine finished with the customers and came to read over Janet's shoulder. "It doesn't look like much, but I suppose it's a start."

"It makes me realize how little we have to go on. We have a bunch of guesses and feelings. Not even a bunch. Just *some*." Janet hit SAVE and closed the laptop. She moved the stool back from the counter and plopped herself on it, elbows on her knees, chin in her hands.

"We must have more to go on for WC," Christine said. "You've quit already? You barely started. WC could be any or all of the mystery men, for instance."

"We have no proof he is, and even *if* he is, there's nothing about the mystery men that makes them any more suspicious than some guy off the street. And remember to keep your voice down."

"That's your sleepless night talking," Christine said. "About my voice and the proof. We have no proof of anything, but we have questions. You added questions about her brother. We have as many, or more, about WC. Why did he come into the shop with the wee book?"

"He said he brought it for a visit. He was being whimsical."

"Was he? Maybe he also took it for a visit to the stone circle."

"Pure guesswork," said Janet.

"You forget how good we are at that. Maybe he didn't just bring the book for a visit here. Maybe he came to take something away with him, too. He's a collector, aye? Maybe he came to collect fingerprints—yours, or the fingerprints of whoever he found standing at this counter. And then he took the wee book and its new fingerprints to the stone circle, soon to be a crime scene, and left them as big fat clues for that not particularly bright but very *nasty* policeman."

Christine, with her back to the counter, had seemed to swell with each of her statements, becoming almost overwhelming at the words *nasty policeman.* She eclipsed Janet's view of the shop, making Janet feel like a mouse who might want to make a dash for a hole.

When they heard the quiet *ahem* of Constable Hobbs from behind Christine, both women squeaked.

21

Good morning, Mrs. Robertson," Hobbs said. "Ah, and Mrs. Marsh. Forgive me, I didn't see you there. I thought Mrs. Robertson must be practicing lines for a pantomime."

Christine recovered with the ease of someone who had known the local constable since she'd babysat him and had occasion to change his nappies. "Present company excluded, Norman," she said. "That is, if you heard my remarks about a certain policeman."

"How much *did* you hear, Norman?" Janet hopped off the stool to stand beside Christine.

"Enough to be thankful I'm not the policeman in question."

"You got the file I sent?" Janet asked.

"Thank you, yes. I've come to let you know of a complication."

"You aren't having second thoughts about our agreement, are you?" Christine asked.

"A complication about the wee book. It isn't visible in any of the photographs Ms. Jacobs sent to D.C. Shaw."

"Did she send all of them?" Janet asked. "Maybe she held back a few because they were blurry."

"I've just asked her. She sent the lot."

"But you saw the book in her hand," Christine said. "And surely Russell's men took pictures of it."

"Russell is calling the book planted evidence, until it's proven otherwise. *Not*—are you listening, Mrs. Marsh?"

With great effort, Janet blinked twice.

"*Not* that you are his only, or even his number one, suspects," Hobbs continued. "Despite being a nasty policeman, Russell is not entirely dim or unprofessional."

"Bugger," Christine said. "You see that we can't quit now, don't you, Janet? And our watchword?"

"Resolve. Right." Janet nodded. "Notebook out, Norman. Heather took notes. She had a map. She'd done research. She was writing a book—or so she said. But where are her papers or electronic devices? Russell will find out where she was staying and check through what he finds there, but he won't know what's missing. Don't forget she had a bike, and presumably a car. If they aren't at her place, they should be found. Do you know where she was staying?"

Hobbs looked up from his notebook. "Please do not think you can make a search of the place yourselves."

"Would we *ever*?" Christine asked.

Janet admired Christine's affronted tone, but made a mental note to remind her, after Hobbs left, that they would and they had once done that. Legally, with a key, but . . .

"We can trust Russell to look at her family, can't we, Norman?" Janet asked. "But have you found her brother?"

Janet couldn't tell if he hesitated at that question, or if he'd needed another few seconds to make a note about the bike.

"Because we've been busy and might have found him for you," Christine said. "Laid eyes on him, anyway."

"Where did you see him, Mrs. Robertson? And may I ask why you didn't call me?"

"Sorry, Norman," Janet said. "We—"

"There's no need to apologize, Janet," Christine said. "Norman. Be logical. We cannot call you every time we see a stranger."

"She has a point. And sometimes you don't answer when we do call," Janet said. "We saw him in Nev's, and we did get a name, in case your favor hasn't come in yet. Owen Nicholson."

"What brought him to your attention?" Hobbs asked.

"He stood alone, at the end of the bar," Janet said. "No one recognized him. And you could tell he felt uncomfortable." Feeling uncomfortable herself, she turned to Christine. "Right? Sort of down."

"Not quite desolate, but somewhat lost. We do realize it's a leap, but he told Danny he's here because a friend died."

"I wonder how often a stranger would feel comfortable in Nev's?" Hobbs said. "I also came to tell you that the favor I'm owed was repaid. I have a name for Ms. Kilbride's brother. Kilbride is her married name. His is Calum Donnelly. His driving license is lapsed. But the favor only went so far. Last known address was a flat in Fort William."

"You might have told us sooner," Christine said. "Perhaps now you could look at the jacket. I suggest you look through the pockets, as I would have done already."

"Inspector Russell has the jacket. He has more resources to track the brother."

Christine made an exasperated noise.

"This is progress, Christine," Janet said gently, then turned back to the constable. "You said 'track.' Is the brother the main suspect?"

"I'm not able to comment."

Christine made her noise again, and a third time when Tallie came from the tearoom. "Resolve," she said, with an encouraging nod for Janet. She leveled a severe look at Hobbs while she returned teacups, teapot, and scone plates to the tray. Then, bearing the tray before her, she returned to her realm.

"Bad news?" Tallie asked, watching Christine stalk away.

"Did Norman tell you that Summer and I are Inspector Russell's suspects?" Janet asked. "He thinks one or both of us might have put the book in Heather's hand."

"Not just you and Ms. Jacobs, I'm afraid," Hobbs said. "All four of you. He mentioned something about unreliable witnesses offering unreliable roadside directions."

Tallie borrowed Christine's severe look and leveled it toward the tearoom. "How serious is he and how dangerous?"

"I don't trust him or like him," Hobbs said. "But Shaw has never heard of him fitting anyone up."

"He's still planning to retire, though, isn't he?" Tallie asked. "Will he cut corners to tie up a case before he goes? I know *you* can't imagine doing something like that, Norman, but would a weasel like Russell?"

"I would like to say it could not happen."

"Not the resounding answer I wanted," Tallie said.

"It won't happen," Janet said. "That's all there is to it. It won't."

Hobbs scratched his nose.

"Did Mom tell you about the other kayakers?" Tallie asked. "It's a longshot."

"But it's *information*," Janet said, and told Hobbs about the two kayaks she'd seen after the incident at the Beaton Bridge. "Something odd went on with that whole scene at the headland," she concluded. "How she did it, why she did it. If she had help or did it on her own. Maybe the other kayakers saw something. Maybe one of *them* sabotaged her kayak."

"The rental company should know who they were," Tallie said.

"Will they give us that information, though?" Janet asked.

Hobbs didn't answer, but made a note in his notebook. *Not a long note,* Janet thought. *Not long enough to be serious. More like an appeasement.*

"Anything else?" Hobbs put notebook and pen away.

"What happened to your purple pen and notebook?" Tallie asked.

"Russell had an objection or two."

"Prat," Janet said. "Oh, sorry, Norman. If we have developments on our end, we'll send them tonight."

Hobbs took his leave, and Janet waited on the next drizzle of customers. They arrived steadily enough that she and Tallie didn't try to discuss other suspects. Janet did mutter, "Call *us* suspects, will you," as Tallie passed her on the way to the history section. And Tallie whispered, "Our status as suspects is suspect, if you ask me," as Janet re-shelved an illustrated self-help book a child had mistaken for a graphic novel. When the drizzle of customers sputtered to a few drips, Janet went to the office and got her coat.

"Where are you going?" Tallie asked.

"Skye View Sea Kayaks. You saw Norman's lack of response when I asked if they'd give us information about the people in the other kayaks. That was a nonverbal shrug if ever I saw one."

"Shrugs *are* nonverbal."

"But this one said, 'Go ahead and ask, just don't mention my name.'"

"Funny, to me it looked more like, 'I'm not really listening, because I've thought of something else, which I'm not going to tell you about, so that you don't muddy the investigation any further than you already have.' He's probably right, too. But you're going anyway, aren't you?"

"I'll be back before you know it."

"Take your umbrella."

❧

A curtain of rain wrinkled across the harbor as Janet headed down the High Street. Janet popped open her umbrella. She and Tallie had driven to the shop that morning, and the short walk now would do her good. She hadn't willingly walked in the rain back in Illinois. Here, except when it came down in stair rods or blatters—the kind of rain Sheila claimed would drown the rival Pub Scrawlers, who kept their noses so high the air—walking in the rain didn't bother her. *And there's nothing like a* smirr *of misty rain to clear the head after hearing you're a murder suspect,* Janet thought.

Skye View Sea Kayaks occupied a granite block building similar to Yon Bonnie Books and Cakes and Tales. It stood near the corner where Janet would turn to go up the hill toward home. The last time Janet had stepped inside the building, the place had been a video store. Tallie and Allan, teens then, had slunk in with her, chosen their movies, and slunk out again. They'd never been sullen teens, but they'd known how to work the look.

A young couple glanced around when Janet opened the door. The woman waved her in with, "You're the bookshop. Come ben. Bring the brolly with you. We like water."

"Still, let me get some of the rain off." Janet shook the umbrella out the door, and collapsed it before letting the door close behind her. "This is lovely," she said, taking in the poster-size photographs of kayakers and gorgeous destinations on the walls and displays of paddles, wetsuits, goggles, towels, camping supplies, "you have everything."

"Aye, but do we have what *you* want?" the man asked. "You're not after renting a kayak for today, are you?"

"Sorry, they're aye rented," the woman said. "Tomorrow?"

"That's okay. I'm looking for a birthday present for my son. All right if I browse?"

"Brill."

Janet had almost panicked and followed her umbrella back out the door when she'd turned around to shake it outside. The rainy walk was supposed to clear her head so she would know how to ask intrusive questions from people she didn't know about business that certainly wasn't any of hers. The walk and the rain had let her down. She knew she couldn't ask these sinewy people doing yoga poses at their sales desk for confidential customer information. *She* would never breach the privacy of her own customers.

Thank goodness she'd remembered Allan's birthday. Christmas was coming, too. She fingered various camping gadgets—did Allan need a compass? A neoprene wineskin? Did *she* need them for bike trips? *Can I lie about why I want to get in touch with their customers from Tuesday morning?* The grandboys would look adorable in tiny wetsuits—though the suits would be a complete waste of money. *No, I can't lie. I can't even think of a lie that would be convincing.* Oh, but look at the life-size, plush Scottish wildcats! She took two wildcats and two compasses to the counter.

"Two of each? Twins?" the woman asked.

"A compass for my son, a compass for me, and a wildcat each for Wally and Freddy, his little boys."

"No wildcat for you?" the man asked.

"I've two cats at home. It wouldn't do to make them jealous."

"They're a bit dear, but a percentage goes to fund Scottish Wildcat Action," he said. "They're endangered, you ken."

"I do. Wouldn't you love to see one?"

"Have you heard of camera trappers?" the woman asked.

Janet shook her head.

"Volunteers who tend trail cameras in woods, forests, the back of beyond. They do it to track movements and what not. They 'trap' all sorts of animals, but it's the wildcats they're after, to get an idea of the shifting population. I did it last winter."

Janet remembered that Norman thought he might have seen a wildcat Tuesday morning. "Have any been spotted near the Beaton Bridge recently?"

"I dinnae ken," the woman said. "If I did, I wouldnae say. It's to protect the cats. Locations are kept hush-hush."

"That makes sense. I love the photographs on your walls. Do you take them yourselves?"

"Most, not all. I'll show you our newest," the man said.

"No, don't," the woman said, then added to Janet, "I told him we can't hang it. It'll make the customers *feart*."

"An advisory," he said, and brought another large photograph from behind the sales desk. The camera had caught the moment between waves when the water is smooth, and looked beneath that surface to a kayak, wedged between rocks, battered and empty.

"He took that one, as well. Went out with search and rescue," the woman said. "Horrible, aye?"

"That's the kayak Heather Kilbride took out, isn't it?" Janet said. "You must have been frantic when she didn't come back, and shattered when they found it. Thank goodness it turned out the way it did. Oh—and then it didn't. You heard what happened yesterday?"

"Aye. You kent her?" the woman asked.

"I spoke with her a few times."

"We liked her," the man said.

"I did, too. So what happened with the kayak? And what was she doing on the headland? Did she tell you anything that would explain that?"

"Except to say she was mortified, no," the woman said. "She couldnae stop apologizing."

"I hate to think of her alone up there," Janet said. "She didn't have anyone with her when she came in, before or after?"

"No."

"And none of your other kayakers saw anything?"

They shook their heads.

"Well, thank you. I'm sorry to bring things down like this. Thanks very much for the wildcats. And . . . no. Don't hang the picture. Not for a while, anyway."

Janet walked back to Yon Bonnie Books with a bulky package and a furled umbrella. It might yet be a day of scattered sunshine.

She had answers and new questions. No way to contact the other kayakers, but that was probably a dead end anyway, and she'd eliminated a possibility. If Norman thought otherwise, he would work on it.

Up ahead, the old woman with her shopping trolley came toward her. Reflexively, Janet glanced overhead for gulls, and then at the harbor wall for ear-washing cats. *Tcha, I'm a numpty.* She gave the woman a slightly wider berth than she ordinarily would and passed her without speaking. *And now I'm more of a numpty, avoiding her like that. For what reason? What if she's alone in the world?* Janet berated herself for a few yards, then turned to walk back, not knowing what she'd do or say. Too late, the woman was gone.

But the man walking behind her, so close to the building he practically brushed it with his shoulder, abruptly stopped and slued around to face the window. With exaggerated interest, he studied a circular in the window, his nose almost touching the glass. An amateur attempt to follow a mark, if ever she'd seen one. She'd only ever seen them in movies or on television, but that was probably where he'd learned his technique. It was Owen Nicholson.

Janet wrestled the package and the umbrella so that she could reach her phone. She pulled it out, held it up, and said loudly, "I've taken your picture. I know what you're doing. I have 9-9-9 on speed dial. I will use it." She saw his shoulders twitch as her words hit. Satisfied, she hurried back to the bookshop. There, she held the door for an emerging family, too tall and broad to see past, so she couldn't check for further pursuit by Owen Nicholson.

"Cool. Is that an inflatable kayak?" Tallie asked when she saw the package.

"I'll show you later." Janet went back to the door. And saw only a trio of women coming, regulars who stopped for tea once a week. No one else. She took the package to the office and left her coat, then opened recent photos on her phone. *Ha. Got him.*

Tallie had no customers with her when Janet went back to the counter. "Look who I've caught on camera," Janet said, showing Tallie the photo of Owen. "It isn't a great shot, but it stopped him in his tracks. He followed me from Skye View. This is good enough to identify him for the police, and I told him I would."

Tallie looked at the picture, at her mother, and then at the man standing at the end of the nearest book aisle looking back at them. Owen Nicholson.

Into the silence that followed came the businesslike *tickety-tick*ing of claws on the floor—the sound of a terrier arriving for work. A sandy-haired Cairn, carrying a tea towel in his mouth, came down the aisle from the tearoom, passing Owen Nicholson on his way to the fireplace chairs. The dog sniffed each of the four chairs. He might have raised his eyebrows, but then jumped up into the one he usually chose and set about arranging the tea towel. When the arrangement satisfied him, he lifted his nose toward Janet and Tallie.

"Hello, Ranger. It's nice to see you," Janet said. "We've missed you."

"We're a wee bit behind today. Sorry." Rab MacGregor came to a stop behind Owen Nicholson. He wiped his hands on another tea towel and arranged it over his shoulder. "Now then, sir, is there anything I can help you find?"

22

Owen Nicholson swung around to Rab as though grabbing for a life preserver. "Do you have a, uh, er . . . *Kidnapped*? No, no, not that. How about *Treasure Island*? Have you got a copy of that?"

"Aye, this way."

Tallie pointed at Nicholson's retreating back and whispered, "The guy from Nev's last night?"

"Yes, and that wasn't a mistake when he asked for *Kidnapped*, that was a Freudian slip. Possibility and nerve. He had some nerve following me, and it seems very possible he's one of our mystery men."

"You might not be using Norman's concept quite right. But Owen seems to be a bundle of nerves." Tallie looked at her mother. "So do you. Are you sure he was following you?"

"I was positive. Now I'm wavering. Did I just scare the bejesus out of a mild-mannered, recently bereft total stranger? Oh dear."

"Rab will smooth it over. We'll probably find them next door having tea. Rab spreading his *easy-oasy* ways, saving the universe, one nutter at a time."

The bell at the door jingled, bringing in Agnes and Sheila.

"Derek not with you today?" Janet asked. "How's his head?"

"Hard as a rock," Sheila said. "But it's not as easy for him to get away during the day."

"There's a new member waiting for you," Tallie said.

Agnes pulled up short. Sheila peered around her and said, "Must've buggered."

"Tallie means Rab's dog, Ranger," Janet said. "Caveat—he snores."

Sheila went to meet the new member. The new member invited a belly rub.

"Och, Ranger's all right." Agnes stopped in front of the counter. "I was surprised not to see him last week. I hope you understand, though, that we aren't looking for more members. The three of us work well together."

"Completely understood," Tallie said. "Sorry to alarm you."

"And I'm sorry," Agnes said, leaning in, "about Sheila's remark about Derek's head being hard as a rock. You flinched, Janet, and no wonder. I heard that you were the one who found that unfortunate woman yesterday. Sheila doesnae always think before she speaks, but she didn't mean anything by it. How are you holding up?"

"Well enough. Thank you, Agnes."

Janet waited until she saw Agnes's head bent over her writing before motioning Tallie closer. "How does she know I found Heather?"

"It's not *so* unbelievable. Anyone who was out there yesterday could have let it slip. Or said it outright. We didn't say anything about *that* last night at Nev's, did we?"

"No, but you're right, news travels. Another question," Janet said. "About Rab showing up now. Do you think it's a coincidence?"

"Coincident to your feckless follower showing up?"

"Or now that Heather's gone, but either one."

"He runs on the easy-oasy operational system. It's probably as complicated as the Enigma Code."

"You brushed that off like it might not be true," Janet said. "But not everything happening in town is related to Heather. It would be nice if the Heather-related were easier to separate from the non, but it's good to keep that in mind. And it's good to have Rab and Ranger back. It makes things feel more normal."

"*Are* you holding up?" Tallie asked.

"Oh, yeah."

"Keep that going, then. I'll go see if anyone needs help out and about. And I'd like to pin Rab down on the display for the celebration."

"Sure, take your time."

Between customers, Janet tapped notes into the cloud about the dead end at Skye View Sea Kayaks and Owen Nicholson. She read through the notes Christine had scorched into the file about the SCONES being suspects.

When she heard the next customer approaching, Janet looked up to see Nicholson. *Hold it together, one book at a time,* she told herself, and asked him, "Was Rab able to find the book you wanted?"

He put a copy of *The Black Arrow* on the counter.

"A Stevenson fan, are you?" she said. "We see a lot of them in Inversgail. Some of them take selfies with the statue down the street. Were we out of *Treasure Island*?"

"I changed my mind."

They stocked a variety of editions of Stevenson's works, including beautifully illustrated hardbacks. Nicholson had chosen an inexpensive paperback. True, it wasn't the kind of book customers stroked as they lay on the counter, or gazed at lovingly as Janet slipped a bookmark into it. But Janet didn't detect even a spark of interest in Nicholson's eyes. *He's lost a friend, for heaven's sake,* she told herself. *Be decent and give him a break.*

Janet rang him up and offered him a bag. He shook his head, and stood staring at the counter.

"I think I owe you an apology," Janet said.

"Actually, I wondered if you'd come for a meal with me?"

"I'm sorry?"

"The four of you. The four"—he pointed back and forth between the bookshop and the tearoom—"of you?"

"May I ask why?"

"Everyone has to eat, and I'd like to ask you some questions about my girlfriend."

"Your . . ."

"Heather. She told me about you."

Janet texted the others. They agreed to meet over fish suppers at Nev's at six.

⁂

Tallie and Rab brought plans for the Farquhar display to the counter to show Janet. "We're going photographic," Tallie said, "and most of it will be in the tearoom. It has the wall space. But we can have at least a dozen more in here, too. Rab suggested photographs of Morag's other paintings around the watercolor above the mantel. The photos will be black-and-white, to create a cool look-back-in-time and here-we-are-today juxtaposition."

"I love a good juxtaposition," Janet said. "This sounds wonderful. It's good to have you back, Rab. I already told Ranger I missed him. I missed you, too."

"Sorry you didn't get my note."

"He left a note with Ian letting us know he'd be gone," Tallie explained.

"Ah. Perhaps next time you should call us."

"I would have this time, if I'd known he wouldnae deliver the note."

There's no arguing with that logic, Janet thought.

"I see we have resident writers," Rab said.

"Not resident," Tallie said. "Agnes asked if the group could meet here and drop in from time to time. We're having a trial period."

"Aye. Trial." Rab nodded. "That's one of the words goes through my mind when I see Agnes."

"Really?" Janet asked. "Do you think this will be a problem for us?"

From the way Rab's easy-going face worked as he considered his answer, and the seconds that ticked away before he said no, Janet felt compelled to ask, "Are you sure?"

Rab looked over at Agnes and Sheila, heads bent over their writing. "Ranger's not bothered. I'll just go measure the space for the photographs, shall I?" He nodded toward the tearoom, and let the nod carry him there.

"I hope we don't lose Rab over the crime writers," Janet said.

"If you really wonder, ask him. Or approach it from the other direction—talk to Agnes."

"That might be an odd conversation, but I've never let that stop me."

A short time later, the two writers stretched and packed up their materials, and Sheila rushed out.

"She'd rather be writing, but she's running late," Agnes said, stopping at the counter.

"A good session?" Tallie asked.

"Putting words in, taking them out. It's a dance, but I love it. A shame Derek couldnae be here. If Sheila hadn't been in a hurry, I'd stop in the tearoom for that shortbread he likes and take it to him." She looked out the window at the steady rain. "I dinnae mind getting *drookit* myself, but it would be a shame to ruin good shortbread."

"Why don't I give you a ride, Agnes? You don't mind if I do that, do you, Tallie? Rab is here if you're run off your feet, and I'll be back—"

"Before I know it. Sure. Agnes, that's a great idea."

"We'll be a shortbread delivery service," Agnes said. "That's grand. I'll go buy it and be right back."

"I'll bring the car around to the front door," Janet called after her, and to Tallie she said, "I'm a shortbread delivery service and odd conversation specialist. Before I go, do you think we should let Norman know about Owen, or should we invite him to supper, too?"

"Let me think about it. My first inclination is yes, tell him."

"What's your second?"

"He probably already knows and doesn't need us running around in his wake pointing out the obvious. My third is that the guy just lost his partner, he's lonely, and he wants friendly ears to pour his sorrows into."

"When I get back, you can tell me about inclinations four through six."

"And you can add odd notes about odd conversations to the cloud."

❧

"This *is* kind of you," Agnes said as she flapped rain off herself and onto Janet. "You know where the kirk is, aye? Derek will be in his office there. You can wait for me in the car, if you like."

"Or I might come in and say hello to Derek, if you think that's all right?"

"Och, I'm sure he won't make a fuss. He gets along with anyone."

Janet felt like looking around the car to see who Agnes was talking about that might need Derek's charitable brand of friendship. She kept her eyes on the road. "I was glad to hear Derek say, the other day, that he likes Rab. I've known Rab for at least twenty years. Such a genuinely nice person."

"You and Derek, then, peas in a pod," Agnes said.

"What pod would that be?"

"Turn just ahead. The kirk's up the hill."

Janet didn't see any advantage in trying to revive that odd conversation. She followed Agnes's directions for where to park, and when Agnes asked, Janet told her again that she would come in to say hello. They passed beneath scaffolding raised on either side and above the door. When the church secretary sitting in the small reception area told them to go on into Derek's office, Janet took wicked pleasure in getting her hello in before Agnes.

Derek didn't hear either hello. He sat at a broad desk, facing the door, eyes closed, with a pair of wireless earbuds, like miniature drainpipes, in his ears.

Janet turned back to the secretary. "It might be naptime."

"No, it's not." She heaved herself up and came to knock loudly on his door. Derek's eyes opened, indeed looking fully awake. "I've told you," the secretary said. "Don't close your *een*, you look dead."

Derek apologized. He tapped the screen of the cellphone on his desk, pulled the earbuds out, and stood.

"Mind, he couldhae been dead," the secretary said softly. "I worry about him, Agnes. He's not been sleeping well since that crack on the head."

Janet's attention had wandered, as it tended to upon seeing someone's bookshelves for the first time. At first glance, Derek's contained an interesting mix of theology, philosophy, and civil engineering.

At the secretary's remark, Janet's attention snapped back to the man himself, and she recognized the slightly hollow look she'd seen on Curtis's face when they had a newborn in the house. Hobbs hadn't answered any of the questions she'd poured out at the stone circle, including the one about a connection between the attack on Derek and the attack on Heather. Just how lucky had Derek been the other night?

"Is the injury catching up with you?" she asked.

"No, I really am very well. You caught me indulging in my guilty pleasure—podcasts."

"He records them himself. I keep telling him he should call them Godcasts," Agnes tittered. "He has quite a following."

"Then today you find me even guiltier," Derek said. "This wasn't my own, or even work-related. I've been listening to the *Crime is My Calling* series. This one has a pharmacist, called the Poison Lady. She tells you how to do in your victims with common household products. Delightfully entertaining. I appease my conscience by calling it research for my novel. In any case, it's my lunch hour. But how lovely to see you both. Welcome to my inner sanctum, Janet. To what do I owe this honor?"

"Agnes and Sheila were in the shop writing this morning. Agnes mentioned coming to see you. I offered her a ride, because of the rain, and thought I'd say hello, too." Janet glanced at Agnes. Agnes seemed stuck on staring at Derek's phone. "Agnes brought you something from Cakes and Tales."

"His entertaining podcast must be the one *I* mentioned to him," Agnes said.

"No, there's no shifting the blame, I'm afraid," Derek said. "I found this one all on my own. I wanted to give it a listen before recommending it to you and Sheila. Some of the details in the forensics episodes can be quite gruesome. Useful, though."

"Perhaps you should listen to these at home," Agnes said with more of a tut than a titter and looking at Janet rather than Derek. "Others in the congregation might not understand."

Derek laughed. "Point taken. Now, is that wee bag what I hope it is?"

Agnes handed the bag to him. "If you hope it's shortbread, then you're right."

Janet wondered if Agnes really worried about the rest of the congregation catching Derek in the Crime is My Calling act. Had Agnes looked at her expecting backup in her scolding? *Maybe she's afraid I'll think he's malingering,* Janet thought. *But after a conk on the head, anyone deserves a malinger or two.*

"Do you mind if I ask, have the police found out anything else about the attack here Thursday night?" Janet asked.

"Not that I've heard," Derek said.

"They haven't been in touch?" And, if not, Janet wondered, was that good news or bad? With Russell, who knew?

"No. I've my own theory of what happened, though," he said. "Of course, I can't back it up with a clear memory."

"You shouldn't be trying to remember it at all," Agnes said. "You might do damage."

Derek's eyebrows drew together in concern. "That might be an old wives' tale, Nessy," he said mildly. "I think this has upset you more than it has me. I'm quite recovered, though." He looked out the office window. "Good. The rain's stopped. On your way out, I'll show you where I think it happened."

He shepherded them ahead of him, past the secretary, and out the door. Janet listened to his explanation of the repair going on. She tried to ignore the fussing noises Agnes couldn't quite manage to keep under her breath.

The women followed him down the front path then turned to look back at the church. "The scaffolding's the culprit." Derek, head back, hands on hips, gazed upwards. The scaffolding climbed to the top of a granite bell tower. "The work's been necessary for years. The workers—you might ask where they are now—have been leaving tools and materials on the platforms. Rather haphazardly."

"Tapsalteerie?" Janet asked.

"A good word for it." Derek said. "Not quite that bad, but not secure. The scaffolding is meant to be secured, as well, so no one goes up it who shouldn't. Well, if you ask me, unless you do secure it, you've issued an open invitation."

"Not one I would answer," Janet said, "but kids?"

"The foolhardy ones, yes. Foolhardy or *pished*. I was a bit of lad, in my day, so I know what I'm talking about. Either way, I'd say by the time they'd climbed, they'd further lost their sense, or inhibitions. Up there, they found tools. Down here, they saw a door. They made a poor choice and decided to go in that door. And when they came across me, or I came across them, they stopped me in my tracks. Or stopped me identifying them." The dark smudges under his eyes were more pronounced in the natural light.

"It could have happened that way," Janet said. "Have you wondered if this incident is somehow connected to what happened at the stone circle Sunday morning?"

"It sounds nothing like it," Agnes said. "God rest that poor soul."

"It is hard to see how it might," Janet said. "But I hate to think there's more than one person out there wrestling with what they've done."

"What makes you think they're wrestling at all?" Agnes asked.

"Hope," Janet said. "I might be naïve, but I almost always have hope. Derek, you should call Norman."

"I've been praying about it," he said. "I'll phone, too."

"Where *are* the workers?" Agnes asked.

"I'm allowed to say this, Nessy, so you needn't be alarmed. But God only knows where they are. I'll let you go now. Thanks for the shortbread. Write well."

"Tell me where you live, Agnes," Janet said on the way to the car. "I'll drop you at home." She unlocked, then, not seeing Agnes, looked around. "Agnes? Oh."

Agnes was already at the next street and turning the corner.

Janet got in the car muttering, "Sure. Fine. Write well. Whatever."

23

The winds that had swept the rain away that afternoon left a clear sky for Inversgail that evening, bringing a drop in temperature. Janet and Tallie pulled out the hats, mittens, and scarves they hadn't worn since the last spring cold snap back in Illinois. On the way to Nev's for their fish supper with Owen Nicholson, Janet told Tallie about her visit with Agnes at the church.

"Agnes is right that the two attacks aren't that similar," Janet said. "But it wouldn't hurt for her to relax a little. Maybe she can find a meditation podcast to listen to."

"So Rab might have good reasons to think of her as a trial?"

"Oh, sure, but it might just be that they rub each other the wrong way. She seems to get along with Derek and Sheila fine. She did say that Derek gets along with anyone, though she was making a dig at me when she said it. In the end, I don't know if she walked off because she was more annoyed with me or with him. She's an odd one. So I made odd notes in the cloud. The trouble is, with all the odd notes, we end up with a lot of dross to sift through."

"Agnes seems to like being in charge," Tallie said. "She likes to march Derek and Sheila in and out for writing. Maybe that's the key to getting along with her."

"In that case, she and Rab would definitely rub each other wrong. He doesn't like to march for anyone. Except maybe Ranger, but I think that's more of a mutual understanding. I can't see Maida putting up with being marched around, either. James would probably just laugh at her. And I guess I kind of hijacked her visit with Derek."

"You also did a good deed by giving her a ride in the rain," Tallie said. "Two good deeds. You told Derek to call Norman, too."

"When I send our latest notes to Norman, I'll tell him Derek said he'd call. I don't suppose there's any point in asking him if Derek actually did." Half a block from Nev's, Janet put a hand on Tallie's arm. "Do you ever worry that we spend too much time at Nev's?"

"You worried about that the other night, too. What's that about? We don't go there to drink. We go because it's our neighborhood. Nev's is our living room and the regulars are our neighborhood pals, even if we only know them to nod to. An evening at Nev's is a good walk, when we walk. A half pint is a small indulgence. A game of darts is fun for Summer and usually a disaster for me, which is also fun for Summer. It's hard to complain or see anything wrong about spending time with people we like or would like to know better. Besides, Monday is one of our usuals."

"Those were lovely, impassioned closing arguments, dear. Much better than a simple no."

Christine passed them in the Vauxhall and pulled into a parking spot ahead. Tallie texted Summer to let her know they'd arrived. Summer popped out the *Guardian* door as Christine checked a second time that she'd locked the car. The four went in together.

Nicholson sat at the bar, watching the door, an almost empty pint in front of him. He drained the glass and thanked them all for coming.

"I'm Owen, by the way. You're all up for the fish? The barman says it's cracking. And what will you have to drink? You find a table and I'll take care of the rest."

"Four of the Selkie's," Christine said. "Halves."

They took their usual table, pulling a chair over for Owen. Christine insisted they leave it so that he sat between Tallie and Summer.

"Is this supposed to give us a psychological advantage?" Tallie asked.

"It's supposed to give me the advantage of not getting a kink in my neck from turning to look at him all evening," Christine said.

Owen brought the drinks on a heavily loaded tray, setting another pint down in front of himself as he sat. "Cheers," he said, after they'd introduced themselves. "I had a drink here last night." He glanced around with more interest than he'd shown the night before. "It's not a bad place."

"How did you find it?" Tallie asked.

"I stopped in somewhere, asked for a quiet place. Out of the way. Tell you the truth, I wasn't sure you'd show up tonight. Not that I'd have blamed you. I wasn't at all sure I would show up myself."

"We're sorry for your loss," Summer said. "This must be an awfully hard time for you."

"I know what people mean now, when they say they have no words."

"What did Heather tell you that makes you think we can answer your questions?" Tallie asked. "Not that we won't, if we can."

"We don't really know much about her," Christine said.

Owen rubbed his hands over his face and swallowed an inch of his pint. "I think I didnae ken her, either. We've been together for two, three years. I thought we were okay. Then, a fortnight ago, she says she's going on holiday the next week. To Inversgail. I'd never heard of it. She asked would I like to go along. I told her no. I was meant to be tied up at a business conference all week. The conference was a big deal. I couldn't afford to miss it. I honestly could not get away. Then Heather said we'd spend the week sea kayaking and hiking. That made it a definite no. Not my thing. At all."

Janet could see that. Even in Nev's low light, he had the soft look and pallor of an online game enthusiast. "So she came on her own?" she asked.

"Aye. She wasn't best pleased. She phoned one night, from here, and asked again. Said we could do rock climbing. I told her the call was breaking up and disconnected."

"No rock climbing for you, eh?" Christine asked.

"*Never.*"

"What business are you in?" Summer asked.

"I'm an insurance claims adjuster."

Danny brought their fish suppers over, with only a quick, bemused look for Christine.

"Owen, what about her writing?" Janet shook vinegar over her plate and passed the bottle to Christine. "She was working on a book, based on a crime that happened locally. That's why she came here. We'd like to carry some of her work in the shop, but we're having trouble finding where to get it. Do you know any titles? Anything that will help?"

Owen had stopped with his glass either halfway to his mouth or halfway back to the table. It had been motionless for so long, Janet couldn't remember which direction he'd been going with it. *To* the mouth seemed to be the default. He took another long drink and held the glass ready for another.

"She wrote true crime, aye?" Christine said.

Owen took the next swallow. "To say that I am gobsmacked doesnae do justice. She fancied herself a writer. I knew that. Pecking away at her laptop late at night while I tried to sleep. I used to joke about her working on bodice rippers. About how, if she'd hurry and get famous, like J.K. Rowling, I could quit my job. She never would show me what she was working on." He ate a chip, took a drink.

"What did she tell you about us?" Janet asked.

"She met you early on. She liked you." He shrugged, drank. "She said she admired you. I don't know why. We did talk, see. Sometimes that was more her talking and me listening. Tuning out, too. I get that I did that, but I truly am gobsmacked. First she said it was a holiday, then it was a pilgrimage. Then she said her brother liked the area, so she knew she would, too."

"She mentioned her brother," Christine said. "What's his name?"

"Calum."

"That's right," Christine said. "Calum Kilbride."

"What? No, Donnelly," Owen said. "Kilbride's her ex. An alcoholic loser."

"Did they break up over that?" Christine asked.

"He left. Felt more at home in a gutter in Glasgow."

"What do you know about her brother?" Janet asked.

"A sapper—a combat engineer. Royal Engineers. I've heard about that a time or two too many. Kilbride probably did, too. I never met him. Either of them."

"What was Heather taking a holiday from? What work did she do?" Christine asked.

"Not true-crime writing. Secretary for a lawyer."

"And where do you live?" Christine asked.

"Fort William." He ate a chip and picked up another. "You'd think," he said, waving the chip, "after however long it was, she'd have got over it, moved on a bit. He's dead. Now, so's she." He drank the rest of his pint and looked toward the bar.

"He who?" Tallie asked. "Kilbride?"

Owen turned back to them. "Calum. Been dead for years."

"How did he die?" Summer asked.

"No idea."

"Did you tell this to the police?" Janet asked.

"They didn't ask." He turned back to the bar and held up his glass.

Danny, busy with another customer, didn't see Owen's plea. *Or he's ignoring him,* Janet thought.

Owen turned back to the table and picked at a sad flake of the barely touched fish on his plate. He tipped his glass and peered at a disconsolate last dreg of ale. "A bodice ripper I could see," he said. "But true crime? Where did *that* come from?"

From suppressing the urge to kill you, possibly, Janet thought. She would have felt guilty, but from the narrowing eyes and crossing arms around the table, she guessed her view wasn't unique.

"I'm not sure we've helped you at all," Janet said. "We didn't know her well, but we liked her, and we're very sorry she's gone. Is there anything else you want to ask us?"

Owen's gaze shifted to the darts room door. "Aye, does Nev do darts through there?"

"Nev? Och, aye," Tallie said.

Owen stood. He started to pick up his plate, thought better of it, and wandered off to the darts, spirits as low as his hands in his pockets.

"Fancy a game with him and Nev, Summer?" Tallie asked.

"Nev doesn't exist, and even *he* would say no."

Danny came by to collect empties and plates. "Is he coming back for this?" He pointed at Owen's.

"No," Christine said. "He's mourning in his own odd way, but he shouldn't have any more to drink, either. He and Heather, the woman at the stone circle, were a couple."

"In their own odd way, it sounds like," said Summer.

Danny looked toward the bar. A server from the kitchen was there, so he waved and sat down. "You're using your expertise on this?" At a bristle from Christine, he added, "That was said in pure admiration, Chrissy. You'll get no hint of sarcasm from me. I've my own observation on your true-crime writer. Would you like to hear?"

"We would value it highly," Christine said. "Also said in admiration."

Janet watched Christine peer toward Danny's now slightly redder neck, then sit back looking satisfied.

"She never set foot in Nev's," Danny said, and he, too, sat back, looking satisfied.

"And?" Christine asked.

"And, nothing. If she was any kind of a researcher, she would have been in here. Gerald Murray came in here. That was no great secret. If she was stirring all that up again, how did she not know his habits and come in herself to ask questions? Her *in*significant other found us quick enough. That *was* sarcasm, Chrissy."

"It makes you wonder if it's her research methods that were off," Summer said, "or if she wasn't really researching the Murray case. She didn't talk to us about it, either, and we're the ones who solved it."

"I see I've given you something profound to think about, so my work here is done. Also *not* sarcasm, Chrissy."

"Are you sure she didn't come in, Danny?" Janet said. "For lunch a week ago? I saw her at the library. She'd just arrived. She took out a temporary membership, then asked for a place to eat near the *Guardian*. Sharon told her to come here. It sounded like she meant to. In fact, I thought Ian might have followed her here."

"Is that why he sat there looking long-faced for well over an hour?" Danny said. "Barely touching his plate so he could ask her to join him? I thought he'd taken a scunner to the haggis balls. Anything else for you tonight?"

"Thanks, love, but no," Christine said, and when he'd gone, "I take it the next question we have is what or who was she researching?"

"Or more basically," Tallie said, "what was she doing here?"

"There's a lot we need to digest to get at that," Janet said. "Starting with, we've lost one of our candidates for mystery man. How sad that she lost her brother."

"Does his death add a wrinkle?" Tallie asked.

"It adds another rag of fankled web to our cobweb," Christine said. "Does Norman know the brother's dead? Has he been keeping that information from us?"

"No, I don't think so," Janet said. "I'll put it in the updates I send him tonight."

"You'll be typing into the wee hours," Christine said. "The rest of us can read it all first thing in the morning. Crack eggs for breakfast. Crack the case during the morning meeting. Crack the reins and send Russell packing on the first stagecoach before elevenses. Who've we still got on our list of suspects? Can we add anyone new to it?"

"WC and the mystery men. That sounds like a dance band." Janet had her phone out, reading over the suspects page—so little there. She glanced toward the darts room. "I'm going to add Owen to the list." She listened for objections. She didn't hear any, so she tapped in his name.

"I have a new candidate for mystery man," Tallie said. "Ian."

"That's . . . entirely possible," Janet said. "And interesting. Do you remember the advice Reddick said he learned as a new detective? That there's a difference between what might have happened, what's likely to have happened, and what's possible. Ian definitely wasn't the man who met Heather at the Murray house, but he might have been either or both of the callers. I would say it *isn't* likely, but Tallie and I saw him do unlikely things each of the past two mornings." She told Christine and Summer about Ian driving away before she left to pick up Summer the day before. "And this morning, even before I'd gone downstairs, he knocked on the door and handed Tallie a package of bacon."

"It was both delicious and suspicious," Tallie said.

Summer held up her phone. "James is still next door. I asked if he's coming over. He says not tonight. That probably means he's in the middle of losing an online space battle to his brother in Aberdeen. He doesn't like to give up, but how about we go over there and give him a chance to save face? Surely his brother will let him forfeit if he's aiding a murder investigation."

"What are we asking him to do?" Tallie asked.

"Tell us what he knows about WC," Summer said. "And because he likes games, we'll try one of our own—bait and switch. A version of it, anyway."

"Ah," said Janet. "And I know where we can get some tasty bait."

24

The *Inversgail Guardian*'s offices recalled a time when reporters hammered away on typewriters in a haze of tobacco, caffeine, half-eaten meat pies, and a longing for whisky. When Summer let them in with her key, the light spilling from the lone office occupied that night led them to the managing editor's domain. They looked in the office door at James Haviland, hammering away at his games console, large, earmuff-like headphones cocooning him in the angst of the space battle, making dire threats into the voice-activated microphone.

"Derek's podcast made him just as oblivious," Janet whispered.

"Why are you whispering?" Christine asked. She walked in and bent over James. "Hello, James. Are you in there?"

"Does he have a heart condition?" Tallie asked, watching him start. "I guess not."

He did have a bottle of whisky in a bottom drawer. He poured them each a dram and a double for himself. They moved to the larger, open room with a half dozen empty desks, and pulled chairs into a circle.

"You want my take on Heather Kilbride?" he said. "She arrived only, what, a week ago? She stopped by here, early on. We spoke. Not at great length."

"About?" Summer asked. "Please don't make me drag out my skills for working with difficult interviewees. I'm not at my best with whisky on ale. What was your impression of her?"

"Friendly, positive, eager to continue her research on what she called the Murray Case. Short on details, except that she apparently had a new angle. She did much of the talking."

"What did she tell you about her new angle?" Tallie asked.

He shook his head. "I smelled an interesting story there, and I asked. She didn't want to say. I thought she might be worried she'd be scooped." He lifted his nose, like a hound on the scent. It wasn't all for show; Janet saw him eye the bag she'd set on the desk, not quite hidden from his view behind her.

"Heather told me you suggested sharing information about the case," Janet said.

"Not I."

"The way she said it left room for interpretation, I suppose."

"Canny or sloppy in her phrasing, then," James said. "Another impression—she wasn't a terribly brave person when it came to interviewing or speaking one-on-one with someone she'd just met. That might have been inexperience or lack of confidence. She reminded me of a robin in the garden—arrived, had her say with bright eyes and chirps, then off she flew. Before she flew, she apologized for taking up my time. I got the feeling she'd used up her reserve of chutzpah. Or I might have scared her. I'm told I'm intimidating." James, in a woolen sweater with a snag in one sleeve and a hole worn through the opposite elbow, with his hands clasped over his comfortable stomach, was about as intimidating as a favorite uncle.

"Have you read any of her work?" Janet asked.

"I haven't. True crime's not really my cup of tea. How about you?"

"I haven't found any. Anywhere," Janet said. "Zip."

"That's interesting," James said. "Yes, very interesting. That says something, doesn't it?"

"Thank you, James. I think so, too. Not that there was anything wrong with calling herself a writer, if she was writing. She didn't have to be published. But we just came from dinner with her significant other and he didn't know she was calling herself a true-crime writer or that she had any interest in it."

"He didn't know much about her, period," Summer said.

James patted his chest as though feeling for a pen in a pocket under the sweater.

"If you'd like, we can send you our notes from the dinner," Tallie said.

"Appreciate it." His hands found each other on his stomach again. "The secret lives of writers, aye? There might be an article in that for you, Summer."

"How are you and your fellow writers of Pub Scrawl getting on, James?" Christine asked. "Did you know we have a rival writing group meeting at Yon Bonnie? Your lot might want to consider changing venues. We'll happily make room for you at Cakes and Tales."

"We're well-suited to Nev's, thanks."

"You don't think Maida would be more comfortable in a tearoom than a pub?"

"Just the opposite," he said. "The effort that goes into blocking out all the drinking going on around her concentrates her energy wonderfully. Nev's was her suggestion because of that. Besides, Agnes Black thinks we're terribly toffee-nosed. Her pals, too, as far as I know."

"Or she's afraid you and your pals won't let her take charge?" Tallie asked.

James gave a shout of laughter. "You've caught the essence of Nessy—what *is* that lovely smell?" He leaned to the left in an effort to see what Janet was doing with the bag now not quite visible on the desk.

"What? Oh, sorry." Janet put the bag on her lap. "Basant said it's best warm, but I'm not sure . . . I don't think sitting closed up is going to help it." She looked around. "He really gave me too much, and it's probably perfect right now. It's one of those molten chocolate cakes and it has"—she looked in the bag, as if she needed reminding—"a swirl of mascarpone through it and over the top. And a sprinkle of salt flakes. We should probably eat it. All right with you, James?"

"Oh, yes."

He didn't seem to notice that Summer happened to have plates, forks, and napkins with her. Or that Basant had given Janet exactly the right number of pieces for their group.

Janet handed plates to the women first. "I nearly forgot," she said, stopping just short of handing James his plate. "He'd like feedback on the cake. It's a new recipe he's come up with."

"Mmmm. Happy to," Christine moaned around a mouthful.

"And one more favor, James?"

He reached for his plate. "Anything."

Janet waited for him to take a bite. He did and closed his eyes in bliss. "Fill us in on what you know about William Clark. Why do people tiptoe around him? You, Norman, Sharon at the library, Rab, Ian. What kind of power does his wife's death, her memory, or *he* hold over everyone?"

"You're being a bit dramatic, aren't you?" He took another bite.

"Come on. You know how this works," Summer said.

"Entrapment?"

"Digging down deep to develop an accurate report. Help us do that."

"It's for the greater good, but not for broadcast," Christine said. "If we help catch a killer, we'll make the world safe for peaceful people like Basant to create marvels like this."

"Let me finish my marvel first."

They did, and when they'd all set their plates aside, Tallie took out her phone. "Do you mind if I record? For accuracy, not for broadcast."

James flapped a hand. Then he rubbed both hands, as though they were cold. They didn't return to the comfort of his stomach. "You mentioned Norman, Rab, and Sharon. I think you can include Gerald Murray, too. Ian, I don't know about. He arrived after all of this. It's fair to say that we knew William and Fiona in the casual way one does—chatting over the produce at Tesco, after church, a cocktail party, a ceilidh. A pleasant couple, unremarkable. He was an adequate lawyer. If she worked at something, I've forgot. She came from somewhere else.

"Now, her kayak trip *was* remarkable. Recreating that earlier trip by Dunnett. I don't know where she came up with the idea, but there was quite a bit of excitement about it. Then her damaged kayak was found, and there was the agonizing wait while search and rescue teams were out. They found her body. There was the inquest, the funeral. We were all touched by her death. People rallied, as they do. Women from the church taking round food, men being overly hearty and inadequate.

"About a month after she died, Clark went away for a few days. But a body was found and identified as his—he'd died in a climbing accident on Ben Nevis. It was a terrible shock, a tragedy. Then the body was *correctly* identified—not Clark. Nine days later, he showed up again, offering no explanation as to where he'd been. Not that he owed one."

"Like Agatha Christie," Janet said. "She disappeared like that and never said why."

"His disappearance and reappearance were interesting at the time, but only caused a minor ripple."

"And yet you, Norman, and Rab—"

"There's no mystique, Janet. We obviously didn't know him well enough to know how Fiona's death was going to affect him. He disappeared again, not long after the reappearance, but this time without going anywhere. He hasn't been a recluse, but he's made it clear that he wishes to keep to himself. And he has. Life passes him by or glances off. He's rarely seen. When he is, he smiles, shrugs, sidesteps. We respect him enough to respect the wish."

"Respect or fear?" Tallie asked.

James scratched his belly. "Do I look feart?"

"Any idea why Gerald named him a trustee?" Janet asked.

"Gerald left his money in trust to go toward helping veterans," James said. "Clark's a vet. That's the obvious connection. Gerald was a bit of a recluse himself. Perhaps Clark saw more of him in recent years. I wouldn't know."

"Gerald was a sapper, wasn't he?" Christine asked.

"There's another connection for you," James said. "Clark, as well."

"And Heather's dead brother," Christine said.

James patted his chest for the pen under his sweater, again.

"That's all right, James," Tallie said. "I'll send the notes tonight."

∽

The Marsh women sat in their living room, each with a laptop and a warm cat in a kreesal beside her. The wind had picked up, bringing images of struggling waves, tossed birds, hunching shadows.

"Do you mind if I put some music on?" Janet asked. "I'll go instrumental so I don't sing along."

"Listen to whatever you want. I'm checking email, then I'll do summaries of the recordings. But I'll put my earbuds in for that."

Janet pulled up a Ludovico Einaudi album with atmospheric piano and strings. Einaudi wrote in the Alps, but the music suited the Highlands, too. Janet checked her own email, then opened the suspects document. At Nev's, she'd added Owen's name, but nothing else about him. She saw, now, that Summer had added a question under his name: *Mystery man?* She'd added a question under WC, too: *James says they respect WC, that he isn't feart. Should he be?*

Two good questions, Janet thought. *Especially about being afraid. Was Heather afraid of the person she met at the circle?* She added two more questions under Owen's name: *Is he reliable? He said he had questions to ask us, but he spent most of the time answering ours—was that on purpose?* Then she worked on the update for Hobbs.

"Do you know you've got that set to play the same track over and over?" Tallie asked.

"The repetition is meditative. Put your earbuds in and hush."

Janet added three questions to the update that Hobbs might or might not answer: *Who did Heather talk to while she was here? Did she talk to anyone involved in the Murray case? What questions did she ask?'* Janet read it over and hit send.

She relaxed into the back cushion with the piano and viola, and rubbed Butter's head and ears. *Unless that's a cello,* she thought. But thinking a cello might be a viola, or vice versa, brought her upright again. She added three questions for the SCONES: *Why would Heather tell us she was researching one thing when she was researching another? If she wasn't researching the Murray case, how did she choose that as her cover? Is there some part of the Murray case that connects to her real reason for being here?*

"Lemon. Still warm," Summer said at the start of their meeting between the bookshop and tearoom the next morning. She handed each of them a plate with a scone. "I left out the poppy seeds. They get caught in your teeth, and we don't need anything else bugging us while we're working on this case. To answer your question, Janet, about why Owen didn't ask us more questions, it could be he didn't really have many, because he never really gave his partner of two or three years much thought. Or maybe we intimidated him."

"At a guess, I'd say we're more intimidating than James," Christine said. "After reading the updates from last night, do we all agree we've a dearth of suspects? Just WC and Owen."

"We're also short on motives," Tallie said. "A random act is still a possibility. So is domestic violence."

"That would be Owen." Summer bit into her scone.

"We also have pieces of information," Janet said. "Although it isn't clear how many of them are useful."

"The with-it amateur detectives call them clues," Christine said. "Or is it only a clue if we understand it? A question for another day. What do we have?"

Tallie took out her phone. "So far, we have WC's miniature book, Heather's research methods—i.e., getting into people's heads and recreating deaths—the Royal Engineers, her last words—'It's dreich.'"

"Edit the part about her research methods," Janet said. "She didn't put it like that. She said she was developing a connection to Malcolm. Maybe she tried that with the killer, too."

"She might have made a connection she wasn't aware of," Tallie said. "That could be why she went with this person or met them at the circle. Has Norman answered your questions about who she talked to?"

"Not yet."

"What about your bike ride to the bridge?" Christine asked.

"She said she wasn't waiting there for me."

"She was also a peculiar woman, and she might have lied. Humor me," Christine said. "If she knew your habits, knew enough to wait for you there, then she spent time talking to someone. That's logic. We need to find that person. Who do we *know* she talked to?"

"Basant, although he said he didn't really talk to her, because most of the talk came from her," Janet said. "And Ian. Remember, he came to brag about consulting."

"He's coming in to sign books today," Tallie said. "I wonder if I can ask him about the consulting without being insulting? Who else?"

"The only ones who know I ride out there regularly, besides all of you, are Rhona, Isla, and Lynsey," Janet said. "They didn't talk to Heather on Monday. And she had to hear it Monday, because she created that horrible scene Tuesday morning."

"Unless she talked to someone before she came to Inversgail, and that opens a whole new creepy path to follow," said Summer.

"It does," Janet said. "She might have talked to someone before she came, but let's use Reddick's advice and Norman's convergence test. Did sitting out there at the bridge, waiting for me to come along on my bike, take nerve? Yes. And from her headland stunt alone, we know Heather had plenty of nerve. Was there a possibility I'd come along? Sure. So it meets Norman's test. Now Reddick's. Is it really likely she went to all that trouble on the chance that I'd come along that morning? Is it likely she risked hypothermia in the hope I'd stop on the bridge? That I'd look in exactly the right place to see her tattie-bogle? She did risk hypothermia, but she actually told me why—that twaddle about feeling the experience and developing the connection."

"That's better logic than mine," Christine said. "But didn't I throw decent logic at Norman just yesterday?"

"You did. And that's obviously one of the reasons he needs our help with his cases," Janet said. "He's a smidge logic-deficient. *I* didn't get the feeling out there at the bridge that Heather had been waiting for me. Norman suggested it."

"We need a red herring column," Summer said. "The bike ride can be the first entry."

"Her brother's role as a mystery man goes in that column, too," Tallie said.

"He might yet be playing a role, though," said Christine. "We don't know how long ago he died, but he continued to play a role in Heather's mind. She carried his memory—and his jacket."

25

Tallie set the stack of Ian's newly arrived books on the sales counter. He enjoyed being recognized by readers, enjoyed playing to their misconceptions of a writer's life. But as often as he stopped in Yon Bonnie Books, he more often stayed away.

"'For all my faults, my first allegiance is forever to my writing.' Will we hear that line this morning?" Tallie asked. "He repeats it more often than you repeated that song last night."

"It might be like meditation for him, too, dear. What about setting him up in the tearoom and lulling him with Summer's lemon scones?"

"We've lured him there before. He'll see the ambush coming. What are we going to do if we have a rush while he's here and he just signs and gets away?"

The bell at the door jingled—Rab and Ranger arriving for work.

"Good morning, you two," Janet said.

"If you need me to watch the register this morning, give the word," Rab said. "Shall I put those on a table in the inglenook?" He nodded at the stack of books, then toward the fireplace, where Ranger made minute adjustments to his tea towel in his preferred chair.

"*Is* it an inglenook?" Janet asked.

"Near enough," Rab said. "It's an area around a fireplace. I'll"—he nodded in the vague direction of the rest of the shop—"find something needs doing."

"Will Ian be suspicious if we set him up over there?" Janet asked.

Rab's voice came from the gardening section. "Tell Ian he's the first to use the newly christened Inversgail Writers' Inglenook."

"He'll go for that," Tallie said.

A flurry and a half of customers later, Janet stopped Tallie and said quietly, "Covering bases here, we don't think Ian's a suspect, do we? When he took off early Sunday morning, he wasn't on his way to meet her at the circle, was he?"

"There's no reason to think that at all."

"Except for his bragging, his weird trip, and his habit of following people."

"That might mean he was out there spying, but otherwise?" Tallie shook her head. "It would make him a witness, but he wouldn't keep quiet about that. Would he?"

Another flurry later, Ian came through the door, tugging the sleeves of his Harris Tweed jacket. Rab moved in behind the counter, and Janet and Tallie introduced Ian to the Inversgail Writers' Inglenook.

"I say." Ian sat expansively in the chair farthest from Ranger. "The name gives the place a different feel. Well done." He took a pen from his inside pocket and opened a book. "You might think it silly, but this is a thrill every single time. A damn shame Heather will never know it. Sorry, didn't meant to sound insensitive."

"It is a shame, Ian. No need to apologize." Janet handed him another book. "We're glad to know you liked her, too. How did the consulting go? Did you get a sense for what she was working on?"

He paused and tapped his cheek with the pen, leaving ink spots. "Her methods fascinated me, but sad to say, I decided I wasn't interested in being her consultant."

"Why not?" Tallie asked.

He didn't seem interested in answering, instead asking, "Have you met her fiancé?"

"Owen?" Tallie asked.

"Yes. He got in touch with me. I rather thought you might have told him about the consulting relationship."

"No," Janet said, handing him another book.

"I suppose he was telling the truth, then." He signed several more books, eyebrows slightly raised, giving the impression he was waiting for them to ask him to go on.

And we do want him to, Janet thought, so she obliged, though with a shift in direction. "Why did you think he might be lying?"

"That might be putting it too strongly," Ian said. "We all grieve in our own way."

"But he didn't sound terribly broken up?" Tallie asked.

"He didn't. It colors one's opinion, however unfairly. He said Heather told him about our consulting. I wonder what *exactly* she said."

"When did you talk to him?" Janet asked.

"Twice, actually. Sunday evening, and then yesterday morning we bumped into each other on the High Street. To be frank, I wasn't interested in speaking to him again. But I had a brainstorm when I saw you through the window at the kayakers, and told him he could get a decent cuppa in your tearoom."

"Thank you," Janet said, biting back what she would rather say—*thank you for foisting your problems off on us.* "I saw you backing out of your drive Sunday morning."

"Must have been the day I dashed out for milk for my own cuppa. And now—" He clicked the pen with a flourish. "I must dash again."

After he'd dashed, Janet gathered the signed books into a stack. Tallie took them from her. "I'll shelve them. You can go start wondering why Ian decided not to consult with Heather."

"And what she told Owen."

Janet went to the office for her laptop. She typed with it on her knees, while sitting on the stool behind the counter, adding their new questions to the cloud. Rab worked quietly around her, and she thought of another question.

"Did you get the chance to meet or talk to Heather?' she asked.

"No."

She decided not to ask him his thoughts on William Clark. The question might not remind him he needed to be somewhere else, but why take the chance?

Tallie finished shelving and came to look over her mother's shoulder.

"It's beginning to seem like we're all questions and no answers," Janet said.

"'Beginning' being the key word," Tallie said. "This *is* just the beginning. Lay some more questions on me."

"A few about William Clark." Janet held her breath. Rab stayed put at the other end of the counter, demonstrating the folded boxes within boxes of a zhen xian bao for an entranced customer. "Did Heather have her appointment with him? And why was the miniature book in her hand? That detail—I can't get the picture of that out of my mind. So then I wonder how many people have seen the book or know about it."

Rab finished ringing up two of the zhen xian bao for his customer, then tidied the display. "When you phone him," he said, making the sort of minute adjustments to the display Ranger might, "ask if he has photos we can borrow for the Farquhar exhibit." He glanced up. "He's not ex-directory."

"Thank you, Rab," Janet said.

Tallie found the number and, with some trepidation, Janet placed the call. It went to voice mail. She left a message, mentioning the exhibit and the miniature Burns, and asking him to call. She disconnected and sat staring at the phone for several seconds, then shook herself. "All right then. After that, I could use—Thank you, Rab."

He'd set a cup of tea on the counter in front of her.

"He shimmered to the tearoom and back while you left your message," Tallie said.

Sometime that afternoon, Rab and Ranger's workday ended. Neither Janet nor Tallie witnessed that end, but when Janet stepped into the tearoom to ask if Rab might be in the kitchen, Christine gave the helpful answer, "Here one minute, gone, and possibly never to be seen again, the next."

Janet checked to see if Ranger might still be snoozing in his chair. He was not. When the door jingled for the next customer, Janet looked up from placing a book order—and greeted William Clark. "Hello, nice to see you again. Did you get my message?"

Clark didn't have the smudges below his eyes that Janet had seen under Derek's, but they reminded her of the watchful eyes of a bird—curious, careful, ready for flight.

I'm projecting, she thought, but she also noticed that he stood slightly back from the counter.

"I did get your message. You mentioned a Farquhar exhibit. I wasn't clear on what you think I can do to help. At the moment, I can't lend the Burns miniature. But I wouldn't, even if the police didn't still have it."

Janet thought his tone was matter of fact rather than angry or accusatory. But in case she'd misjudged the tone, she took a verbal sidestep. "We were hoping for photographs of Farquhar, if you have any. Rab MacGregor thought you might. He's putting the exhibit together."

"Is he?"

While Clark seemed to be turning that over in his mind, Janet looked for Tallie. She saw her coming from the tearoom with Christine.

"If you don't mind, Mom, I'm going to give Summer a hand for a while."

"And I told Tallie I'd tend books in her place." Christine approached Clark with her hand out. "I don't believe we've met. I'm Christine Robertson. I'm half of the tearoom half of this business." When Clark took her hand, she clasped his with both of hers. "I'm very glad to meet you. Janet's told me so much about your wee book, I feel as though I know you. What can we do for you today?" She leant an elbow on the cash register, and any distrust in Clark's eyes took flight rather than he.

"Norman Hobbs told me you found the victim at the Stuart Stones," Clark said to Janet. "That must have been a horrible experience. He also said you identified the book as mine. Thank you. I'm not certain I would have ever known what happened to it, otherwise. The book is evidence now and the man in charge—Russell—has other priorities."

"Like asking you lots of questions, I'm sure," Janet said. "We've met Russell."

"He's not as kind as Norman," Christine said. "Do you mind if we ask you a *few* questions?"

"About the book?" Clark asked.

To start, Janet thought. "Do you have any idea how the book ended up where it did?"

"None at all."

The door jingled for customers on their way in. "I'll go if they need help," Christine said.

"I heard Heather say she had an appointment with you," Janet said.

"I don't generally take appointments. I've no need to."

"But did she try to set one up?" Janet asked.

"Why do you ask?"

"We liked her," Janet said. "She's gone. We're trying to understand what happened."

"Is that wise?" Clark asked.

Janet thought how best to answer that. She went with simplest. "Yes."

Clark's eyes weren't convinced, but they didn't deride or dismiss. "She phoned," he said. "We spoke. She said I knew her brother. I told her that as far as I recalled, I didn't. He and I may have crossed paths at some point. We were both sappers, but I didn't know the chap."

"Why did she think you did?" Christine asked.

"Small world syndrome?" Clark said. "Rather like meeting someone from the States and saying, oh, I have a cousin in California, perhaps you know him. She mentioned places I might have run into him since getting out. Places I've not been. Suilven, Dalbeg, Stornoway."

"Did you know her brother is dead?" Christine asked.

"She didn't say as much, but I realized she was dropping hints. I recognized the pain behind her questions."

"You knew Gerald Murray?" Christine asked.

"He and I overlapped in service by a few years. We became reacquainted in the last few."

"It was a good thing he did, leaving his money to help veterans," Janet said. "Could he have known Heather's brother?"

"He might. We talked books, not mates."

"I told Russell to be careful with your book," Janet said.

"She told him to treat it like a piece of treasure," Christine said. "There's no telling if Russell listened."

"Thank you for trying."

"When was the last time you saw it?" Janet asked.

"I can't believe I don't know."

Clark stepped aside for customers, and Janet and Christine both became busy. Seeing him fade toward the door, Janet interrupted her transaction to thank him for coming.

"I'll look for photos of Farquhar," he said, "but can't promise anything."

When they finished with their customers, Christine said what Janet had been thinking. "He can't believe he doesn't know when he last saw his treasure. An amazing coincidence, that. I can't believe it, either. And I don't."

⁂

Janet sent another update to Hobbs that evening. Then she tried calling and texting him. He hadn't answered any of their questions.

"I know it's only been three days," she said to Tallie, "and the specialists are busy—"

"Two and a half, actually."

"Thank you. It feels at least like two and three-quarters. Our agreement with Norman is beginning to feel one-sided."

"It might be." At the noise her mother made, Tallie looked up from her laptop. "Through no fault of his own. Remember who's in charge. Norman doesn't necessarily have access to answers. He has to be careful Russell doesn't think he's messing around, screwing up evidence, or undermining the investigation."

"They say the first—how many hours do they say are crucial to solving a murder? It doesn't matter. We're bound to be past them. Norman really does need our help with this, doesn't he?"

"I hope so, because we're giving it to him whether he wants it or not."

~

At their meeting the next morning, Janet reported that again they'd had no answers from Hobbs. "But as Tallie reminded me, we don't know what he's up against with Russell."

"I wonder if I should find Norman and give him a pep talk," Christine said.

"Let's give him more time," Tallie said. "He did stop by Monday. He might be working feverishly in the background."

"Resolutely, I can picture," Christine said. "Feverishly is a stretch. But your point is taken."

"He needs us," Janet said. "And Heather does, too. Anything else to report?"

"I started looking for her brother's obituary last night," Summer said. "Without dates or locations, it takes time. It's something Norman should be able to do. Maybe he is. Me, I fell asleep."

"I looked for Fiona online," Tallie said, "and ended up downloading a copy of the Dunnett book—the one that inspired her trip. I can see the appeal, and the idea of a woman doing it solo doesn't bother me. It makes me wonder why they wouldn't go together, though."

"If they were having problems?" Christine asked. "James didn't suggest any."

"That isn't the kind of information we're likely to find," Janet said.

"But I found a couple of other things," Tallie went on. "Shortly before Fiona died, WC inherited his parents' estate. Fiona had a nice life insurance policy. He inherited *that* money, too. He quit practicing, and, as James said, disappeared without going anywhere."

"What are you thinking about, Janet?" Christine asked.

"So many questions. And when your local constable hasn't replied to your repeated texts or phone messages, then a good place to start looking for answers is your public library. Ours ordered replacement copies of some of Ian's books. Why don't I save them a trip and run them over? And while I'm there, why don't I see if Sharon's in her office and in a chatty mood?"

"And why don't I pack a little something to sweeten your chances?" Summer said.

❧

"Lovely of you to bring them." Sharon Davis, sitting at her desk, smiled at the books and bakery bag in Janet's hands.

"Shortbread is small thanks, but I want you to know how much we appreciate you buying Ian's books through us. I know full well you can get them through your distributors."

"It's part of being a community," Sharon said. "I wish the budget allowed us to do it more often. Sit down, if you like. I've been staring at said budget this morning and could use a break." She picked up one of the books. "Did you know that Ian and that poor woman were going to work together on a book? So he said."

"He mentioned something about consulting."

"*Consulting.* Is that what he calls it? She didn't strike me as the type to fall for his lines, but I saw them having a meal together. He looked thrilled. It's possible she did, too, but the lights were low and I didn't like to stare."

"Good heavens. When was that?"

"It must have been Friday night. Before the boyfriend arrived. They came here Saturday afternoon—she and the boyfriend. Did you not know about him?"

Janet guessed that she looked close to gobsmacked and decided that worked in her favor. "I've met him, but I had no idea they spent her last few days together. That's so sweet and so sad at the same time."

"Tragic. She's become a character in her own true crime. Not the sort of story our writers' group go in for. I hear you've poached them from us."

"Did we?" Janet asked. "I'm so sorry. They came to us—"

"Och, I'm not bothered. Keep a firm hand on Agnes. She's a tiny general. Sheila and Derek are all right. You heard someone attacked him?"

"Shocking. It could've been another tragedy."

"Do you think the two are related?" Sharon asked.

"I have wondered, but it's hard to see a connection."

"Writing and being hit on the head—you're right; it isn't much. I'm not fond of either of their genres—military espionage or true crime. Too gritty. Give me travel essays, biographies, and mysteries set in places I'd like to live. Thanks for stopping in, Janet. Always a pleasure."

Before leaving the library, Janet added two questions to the cloud:

Owen in town Saturday?

Where was he Sunday morning?

Then she sent a text to the SCONES: *Be on guard around Owen. He arrived before she died.*

As she passed the Stevenson statue, her phone buzzed with a text from Christine. *The weasel has landed. He's eating scones and drinking tea.*

26

Tallie, Summer, and Ranger greeted Janet when she returned from the library. Summer and Tallie at the counter with customers, Ranger in his chair with his ears perked.

"News?" Tallie asked, as Janet brushed past her.

"I have the same question. Let me put my things away." Janet dropped her jacket and purse in the office and checked her phone. Nothing from Hobbs. She rejoined the other two.

"Nice to have you here for a change, Summer," she said. "I got Christine's text. Is Russell still there?"

"He gives me the creeps," Summer said. "Rab's in with Christine."

"He gives Ranger the creeps, too, I think," Janet said.

"D.C. Shaw keeps dog treats in his pocket," said Tallie.

"I'll go see what sort of treat the weasel is today," Janet said. "If he turns nasty, I'll insist he move to the office or straight out the door."

The clink and clatter of cups and cutlery sounded like any other day as Janet headed to the tearoom. From the door she saw that about half the tables were full. Christine chatted with a couple exclaiming over the lemon curd. Rab, wearing a tartan apron tied at the waist, put scones in a bag for another couple. Russell sat at a table nearest the window, wasting the lovely harbor view by sitting with his back to it. When he saw Janet, he waved her over.

"D.C. Shaw couldn't stay for tea, Inspector?" Janet asked, eyeing the remains of an indulgent tea for one.

"The D.C. is apparently tying up loose ends," Christine said, coming to stand beside Janet.

Russell dabbed his lips. "I've good news to share. Sit down." They did. "I've cleared you. You're no longer under suspicion."

"*You* did. Not the evidence?" Janet asked.

"Wheesht, Janet," Christine said. "He's brought us good news, indeed. Is this a celebratory tea, then? Are you close to making an arrest?"

Russell smiled, and Janet almost felt sorry for the villain. "Congratulations, Inspector," she said. "Please excuse my snide remark. I'm sure you can imagine how on edge we've all been." She wasn't at all sure he could. "For my own peace of mind, may I ask a couple of questions?"

"I might not answer, but you can ask."

"Did you find any connection between the murder and the attack on Derek Spiers?"

"None."

"When did Owen Nicholson arrive in Inversgail?"

"The boyfriend? Sunday. Late."

"Thank you, Inspector."

"That's it? It's that simple to set your mind at ease? I'll be off, then."

Russell left, and Janet's phone buzzed with a text from Tallie.

"What is it," Christine asked.

"We're plagued by policemen. She says Norman's here."

"I'll tell Rab to text if he needs me."

Hobbs waited for them in the chair next to Ranger's. Ranger, having given up on Shaw returning with another treat, had returned to napping.

"I'll stand," Tallie said, "and be ready to handle customers."

Summer sat on a footstool. Janet and Christine took the remaining chairs.

"I've answers to some of your questions," Hobbs said.

"Another question, first," Christine said. "Were you following Russell? Is that how you arrived so soon after he left?"

"That sounds like a waste of my time." Hobbs opened his notebook. "You asked about her bicycle. Russell believes Ms. Kilbride rode it to the stones, though they found it at the school. You asked about notebooks and electronic devices. They did not find notebooks. Russell has her phone and a laptop belonging to Owen Nicholson. Nicholson says he lent it to her." Hobbs put the notebook away.

"That's it?" Janet asked.

"For now, yes."

"Russell said he cleared us, and that he's ready to make an arrest," Janet said. "But he doesn't know that Owen was here at least as early as Saturday afternoon. What kind of slipshod job is he doing?"

Hobbs took out his notebook again.

"Has Owen left town?" Tallie asked.

"He asked me how long Russell will keep the laptop," Hobbs said. "I told him I would try to get it back and suggested he stay in town, as that might happen any day. He's arranged to stay until the weekend."

"Norman Hobbs," Christine said.

"Yes?"

"I'm very proud of you at this moment."

Hobbs told them he was leery of conducting a formal interview with Nicholson, lest Russell get wind of it. The women suggested they conduct an informal interview, inviting him for supper around the fireplace, as repayment for their fish suppers at Nev's.

"You can come, too, Norman," Christine said. "Lull him into trusting you by wearing one of your jumpers from Nana Bethia."

"Problem," Summer said. "How do we get hold of him?"

"Our constable might be able to help with that," Tallie said.

Hobbs flipped to another page of his notebook.

❧

Hobbs pulled a switch on the women that evening, asking Rab and Ranger to stand in for him. He attended within earshot, but out of sight. He wore his uniform, in case the evening turned official. Rab brought two chairs from the tearoom. He made sure Hobbs had a slice of the pizza Christine brought.

Owen, when he arrived, either had more appetite than he'd had for their previous meal, or preferred the pizza to Nev's fish.

"We're glad you could join us, Owen," Janet said. "How are you liking Inversgail?"

He nodded around a mouthful.

"Isn't the view from the library beautiful? I heard you and your fiancée were there on Saturday."

Summer put her hand to her heart. "You were engaged?"

"Yeah. Somewhat," Owen said.

"It's so nice you got to spend that time together," Tallie said. "When did you get here?"

"Saturday noon. I meant to get here sooner. Slept in a bit."

"I hope the police didn't question you for hours about where you were Sunday morning," Christine said. "They can be brutal."

"I was afraid they might, so I told them I got in Sunday night. I'm not proud of that. But it wasn't going to hurt her. She's gone. Hell of a way for her to break up with me. Is anyone having that last piece?"

Rab passed it to him. "Was she going to break up with you, then?"

"She talked about it. She talked a lot. Got so I had to tune her out a lot of the time, you ken? At the conference last week I lined up a new job. In Edinburgh. I came down to tell her."

"So you were dumping *her*," Summer said.

"Not really. I took holiday time. Thought I'd surprise her by spending the whole week. Wait for next weekend to tell her about the job."

"But if you came for the week," Janet said, "how come the police didn't know you were here before Sunday night?"

"I left soon after she did, Sunday morning. I only pretended to be asleep, when she got up, to keep her from havering on about relocating.

Buying a house here. I'd had enough and I cleared out. But I stopped for breakfast and had a coffee by the harbor. That cleared my head, so I went back to her rental. When I got there, I saw the police. I didnae want to get involved, so I went on by. But it's nice here. I can see why she liked it."

"When you were pretending you were asleep, did you hear anything?" Tallie asked. "A phone call? A hello? Any sound that might have been someone besides Heather?"

He shook his head. "If I had, do you think it would have been the killer?"

"Possibly."

"I dodged that one, then."

When Owen stood to go, Rab let him out the front door and relocked it behind him. Then he and Hobbs sat in the tearoom chairs. Ranger surprised Summer by sitting in the chair next to her.

"He's sorry for the failings of his fellow men," Rab told her.

"What do we think?" Christine asked. "Is Owen a suspect?"

"Motive?" Hobbs asked.

"Avoiding things," Janet said. "That's a sad way to go through life."

"I kind of wish it were him," Tallie said. "But he seems too indifferent to have wanted to kill her. Did Russell figure that out, even though he didn't figure out Owen spent the weekend here?"

"He's nasty, but not dim," Hobbs said.

"Have you heard anything about an imminent arrest?" Christine asked.

"No, but I doubt I will before it happens."

"Then while we have you," Janet said, "and as long as we've fed you and conducted your interview for you—"

Hobbs took out his notebook.

"The bike, Norman. Why not leave it at the scene, and why take *it* and not the body?"

"I can only guess," Hobbs said. "But it's easier to move and dispose of a bike. It might have been sheer panic. It could indicate lack of premeditation."

"Or someone who doesn't keep the supplies for carrying or disposing of a body in the boot," Rab said. When they all stared at him, he added, "They'd be the same tools you keep for weather emergencies—blanket, bungee cords, shovel."

"It would be easier to put a body than a bike in the back of a Mini," Janet said.

"The killer might have been clever," Hobbs said, "trying to confuse the issue by leaving the bike at the school."

"Or kids found the bike at the stones, but not Heather, and took it for a joyride," Tallie said. "Or they found it wherever it was dumped and moved it."

"Has anyone found out what she was doing at the stones?" Summer asked.

"Not that I've heard," Hobbs said.

"We wondered if she was recreating another death," Janet said. "She did Malcolm's and Fiona Clark's."

Hobbs shook his head. "I'm not sure that was Fiona's, and I'm not aware of a death associated with the Stuart Stones." He looked at Rab, who also shook his head.

"The book, then," Janet said. "And we'll let you go."

"How or why did she have it?" Hobbs asked.

"And how did someone get it away from William Clark?"

"I don't know."

"When Janet and I asked William that, he had a similar answer," Christine said, "but yours was more convincing. While he *said*, 'I can't believe I don't know,' something about his eyes suggested he'd thought of something, or maybe someone."

Hobbs made a note.

"Before you put your book away." Rab tapped and swiped his phone, then handed it to Hobbs. The women crowded behind him to peer at it. "The lad wanted a walk. We passed by the kirk. They don't keep office hours Wednesday afternoons. With odd things going on, I thought it worth a video."

"Is that Agnes?" Tallie asked. "It is."

They watched Agnes try to open the church office door, then walk around the scaffold.

"She isn't going to climb it, is she?" Janet asked. "No. She's too short. Thank goodness. But play it again, Norman. There, where Rab panned the parking spots. I thought you said they don't keep office hours on Wednesday afternoons, Rab."

"Not official hours."

"Then which odd thing did you want us to see?" Janet asked. "Agnes or the green Mini?"

⁂

Later that evening, during the night, or early Thursday morning, each of the women opened the cloud file and added a thought or question. Christine added Agnes and Derek to the suspect list. Next to their names, Tallie typed *Motive?* Christine countered with, *Not enough information. That's the same as no idea. Puts a more positive spin on it.* Summer underlined Owen's name on the list and added, *Not satisfied he's clear.* Janet wrote, *Re: conversations with Sharon and Ian. Did he decide not to consult with Heather because he felt threatened by Owen?*

"As much as I'd like to find it funny," Tallie said at their doorway meeting that morning, "I don't like the idea of Owen threatening Ian."

"That's been *our* role," Christine said. "Not to threaten, per se, but to keep him in line."

"I've actually done some threatening, too," Tallie admitted.

"Threats," Janet said. "And fear. James told us he wasn't afraid of WC. What if *WC* is afraid of somebody? What if the book was a message to him? To keep *him* in line?"

"As messages go, a dead woman is more obvious," Summer said.

"Not if WC wasn't going to make the connection," Janet said. "The book personalized the message and added the threat of being charged with the murder."

"Who's he afraid of, then?" Christine asked. "Are you thinking Derek, the minister? Or was WC there yesterday looking for sanctuary? That's not a joke, Janet. This might put us back with blackmail as the motive. But how do you propose we follow up on this idea?"

"That's the hard part, isn't it?"

"Then let's follow up on Owen threatening Ian," Christine said. "Anyone up for another spot of genteel interrogation? Shall we say eight this evening? The Marsh residence."

That evening, Ian took a glass of sherry from Janet and thanked her. "Your invitation gave me an excuse to leave a library committee meeting early. My motto is, 'Just say no and go.'" He sat on the couch next to Summer, setting his messenger bag to the side. "I am onto you, though. I recognize one of your fact-finding sessions when I see it. This one looks more serious than our fireplace chat of the other day, which I also recognized, but I'm happy to help."

"Thank you, Ian," Christine said. "Good to see you're in a chatty mood."

"Keep the sherry and the questions coming."

"Did Owen, either overtly or by implication, threaten you?" Summer asked.

"So he's your number-one suspect, is he?"

"We'll put it another way," Tallie said. "Did you change your mind about consulting with Heather because Owen showed up?"

"No, actually. We parted amicably. She was thrilled I took an interest in her project. She was keen that I write the fictional version of her story. If I do, I'll have to make changes to make it less mundane."

"Not to protect the innocent?" Tallie asked.

"The innocent won't recognize themselves when I'm finished. My protag can't be stuck in a dreary lawyer's office typing Gerald Murray's will. But it shouldn't be too hard to switch things around. She gave me a file of her notes."

Janet coughed, trying not to aspirate her sherry. "You have her notes?"

Ian glanced at his messenger bag. "I say, perhaps I should have read them. Do you think they'd be useful for the case? This might answer your question about threats, as well. She asked me to keep the file over the weekend because she didn't want Owen looking through it."

"Did you tell the police this?" Janet asked.

Ian put his hands together and rested his chin on them. "I'm a bit of a fool, aren't I?"

"Wheesht, Ian," Tallie said. "We can fix that. May I?" She pointed to the messenger bag. He handed it to her. "Feel free to chat amongst yourselves. I'll make copies. One for us, one for Ian, and we'll give the originals to Norman."

"This calls for another round of sherry," Christine said.

"Thank you, Christine," Janet said. "Ian, did Heather work for Gerald's lawyer?"

"Indeed, and she had a writer's instinct. She saw the possibilities in the Murray story. May I make a further contribution to your detections? You might have noticed my slight agita the other day, when you brought up the name William Clark."

"We did," Janet said.

"Well. See if this doesn't describe him. Leads a quiet life. No obvious source of income. Takes 'trips.' And you've heard the story about his 'walkabout' after his wife's death, haven't you? A body was involved that time, too, and I wonder if that wasn't his first. I've caught your attention, haven't I? It's my theory that Clark is a hit man."

"That's far-fetched, isn't it?" Summer asked. "Nothing at all points to Heather's death being a contract killing."

"The mark of a good hit man," Ian said.

"Or the lack of one," Janet said. "Do hit men operate on their own turf? Are they so crude? It *is* far-fetched, Ian. Think about it. Would this scenario work in one of your books?"

"Is that a serious question?" Ian asked. "Because I can make anything work. That's what fiction is."

27

After thanking Ian and sending him home with his copy of Heather's notes, Tallie gave one to each of the others. "Seemed like a good idea," she said.

Summer and Christine had started to put on their coats, but set them aside. Janet made a pot of herbal tea. Tallie, who had already read the first page, watched as her mother did.

"A pen name. I knew it was a possibility," Janet said, "but it's rare for one to be such a well-kept secret. Calum Donnelly."

"Shh," Christine said. "We're reading."

Heather, writing under her brother's name, had sold a handful of articles to crime-related magazines. Her notes—some handwritten, some typed, a few on scraps of paper—loosely outlined the research she'd been carrying out in Inversgail.

"The Murray case *wasn't* a cover story," Janet said.

"It was, though." Summer separated the handwritten from the typed pages. "I mean—you're right, she really was researching the Murray case, and probably hoped to get at least an article out of it. But these handwritten notes are a different line of research."

"Calum Donnelly's murder," Tallie said.

"But where?" Christine flipped through the handwritten notes. "She substituted 'xxx' for any useful detail. There are no names but Calum's."

"No dates, no locations," Janet said. "The closest she comes is when she wonders about the death of 'xxx's wife.' That could be WC, but what was she wondering? If *that* was murder? That *he* killed her? That someone else did? That it was suicide? She says she'll prove 'xxx killed Calum,' but you can't tell if she knew who 'xxx' is."

"Remember, these are notes," Summer said. "Her real work is probably on the laptop."

"But there are clues here," Tallie said. "She mentions a change of career. That might eliminate Owen, but not our other suspects. WC quit his career, and you could argue that the writers are working at another career."

"We've been using our own version of 'xxx' when we talk about WC," Christine said. "And we know why *she* did it. She was smart and she was feart."

"You're right," Janet said. "Her notes tell us a couple of other things, too. *Listen between the lines*, she says on this scrap. That's what we'll need to do, because this is where we need a plan to set things in motion. And I've got one."

At Janet's invitation, Agnes, Derek, and Sheila came to Yon Bonnie Books the next morning at ten. She'd told them about the new Inversgail Writers' Inglenook and suggested they come for an inaugural inglenook tea. They'd been delighted, Derek saying he'd carve time out of his morning office hours to attend.

Summer brought a tray from the tearoom when they arrived. "Tea, scones, clotted cream, lemon curd, and strawberry jam," she said. "I didn't know which you'd prefer. While I'm here, may I tell you a couple of the questions I'll ask for the local color piece? That way I won't be putting you on the spot, and you can have time to think."

The writers sat with pens poised.

"What kind of interesting backgrounds do you bring to your writing? Jobs, travels, that kind of thing. And, because you're crime writers, do you have any personal connection or real-life experience with crime that informs your stories?"

"Skeletons in the closet?" Sheila asked.

"That would make it a cliché in the closet," Derek said.

"I'll stop back later to see if you need more tea," Summer said.

Janet had called Hobbs the night before. He'd listened and agreed to pick up Heather's notes at the shop at half-ten. He'd then tantalized her by saying he had information to share.

"But if I wait to tell you, it will have greater impact," he said.

Christine found a reason to be behind the bookshop counter when Janet handed Hobbs the notes. "These are two sets of notes, actually," Christine said. "Notes for her book on the Murray case and another set outlining her research into her brother's death, which we've heard nothing about."

"I have new information on that," Hobbs said.

"*Do* you," Janet said. She saw Tallie and Christine's reactions and caught Hobbs's sidelong look at the writers and a pleased constabulary smile.

"He drowned while swimming unaccompanied," Hobbs said.

"Not murder?" Summer asked.

"There was some question over whether he made a habit of swimming alone, but an inquest returned a finding of accidental death."

"I wish I'd known," Janet said. "She loved him and that would be so hard to live with."

"Where?" Christine asked.

"Western Isles," Hobbs said. "Lewis. Thank you for the notes. If you hear anything more, let me know. And . . . I'm sorry about her brother."

Janet nodded, then went into the office and closed the door.

"Give her a minute," Christine said when Tallie turned with surprise to the door. "It's not Calum's death. It's the accumulation of tragedies.

They affect your mother's heart. Me, I get angry." Glowering, she went back to the tearoom.

Tallie waited five minutes, then knocked and opened the office door.

Janet sat at the computer, a wad of tissues next to the keyboard. "Sorry. I didn't expect the waterworks," she said.

"It's okay. Can I do anything for you?"

"No. I'll be out in a minute."

"Are you looking for the obit or the inquest?"

Janet blotted her eyes again. "Watching kitten videos."

When Janet left the office, Summer was checking with the writers to see if they wanted another pot of tea. They thanked her, but said no. Not long after, they packed up for the day.

"We loved our tea and the idea of the Writers' Inglenook," Sheila said. "That's twice you've treated us, but we won't expect it every time. Cheers."

Janet waited for the door to close behind them. "That might not have done anything," she said then, "but it went well. Summer was great. Now let's hope Norman can be as convincing with WC and Owen."

"Christine was good, too," Tallie said. "She didn't lie and say we didn't read the notes, but it sounded clear to me—we don't have a clue."

"Even so, if we've really set something in motion, we should fall back on our rule of traveling only in pairs."

"I'll let the others know," Tallie said. "If we're lucky, this was all for nothing, because Russell will make his arrest."

That afternoon, as if in response to her words, Inspector Russell and D.C. Shaw marched into Yon Bonnie Books.

"Back for another celebratory tea?" Janet asked.

If Russell had been a real weasel, he would have taken the question by its neck and crunched its bones. "I am here to inform you," he announced, "that although you've been cleared of planting evidence and meddling with a crime scene, it has come to my attention that you've been withholding evidence, and I will see you charged."

"The case isn't going well?" Tallie asked.

"Thanks to meddlers, *eejits*, and meddling, eejit constables."

"It seems we cannae get oot o' the bit," Shaw said.

"Stop talking like your eejit granny," Russell barked, and marched for the door.

"*Your* granny?" Janet asked Shaw.

"His, maybe," Shaw said. "Mine's a dear, wee thing. Suffice to say, not only are we not making progress, we seem to be going backward."

"*Shaw!*" Russell barked.

∽

For the rest of the afternoon, the women spent what time they could, between books and teapots, reading over Heather's notes again. As they did, they added notes of their own, followed by their initials, to a new document in the cloud.

> *Does WC have an alibi for Fiona's death? Heather's? Calum's? SJ*
> *At the inquest, who said Calum never swam alone. Heather? JM*
> *Where in Lewis did it happen? TM*
> *She asked WC if he'd been to Stornoway, Suilven, or Dalbeg. Stornoway and Dalbeg are in Lewis. CR*
> *What made her think it was murder? Maybe she was wrong. SJ*
> *Then how to explain her death? TM*
> *The threat of being torn apart in court, the press, on social media might = motive. JM*
> *On that scrap, "listen between the lines." What lines? JM*
> *There are more holes in these notes than there are* xxxs. *CR*

Hobbs knocked on the bookshop's locked door as Janet and Tallie settled the register at closing that evening. Janet called to Christine and Summer. Tallie let Hobbs in.

"What is it, Norman?" Christine asked.

"Agnes Black confessed to Russell. He's taken her into custody."

"Let's go sit down," Janet said.

Hobbs followed the women to the inglenook, letting them take the chairs, until Christine objected. "You can't stand at the fireplace like an Inversgailian Holmes," she said.

Tallie gave him her chair and moved to the footstool.

"Why did Agnes do it?" Janet asked. "We had her on our list of suspects, but didn't have a motive. So why?"

"I had this from Shaw. He stepped out of bounds in telling me. Agnes told them she knew Ms. Kilbride was going out to the Stuart Stones. She heard her say so here, in the bookshop. Agnes went there to confront her, away from prying eyes."

"Agnes always gets a lift," Janet said. "How did she get out there?"

"She owns a car," said Hobbs. "She doesn't like to waste petrol."

"But she'll kill?" Janet asked.

"Hush," said Tallie. "Let him tell us."

"She confronted Heather and asked her to stop digging into the Murray case—for the sake of everyone already hurt in that tragedy. Heather laughed at her. Called her a wee general, trying to order her around. She said she had proof that Malcolm was not the good man everyone thought, that he had blackness in his soul. Agnes said she saw blackness in Heather's soul. Then she picked up a rock. When it was done, she threw the rock in the pool. She left the book as a red herring. She took the bike, but couldn't remember where she left it, by then being in shock. Since that morning, she's been listening to an inspirational podcast. Reading between the lines, she came to the realization she must confess."

"That's . . . plausible," said Tallie.

"But it's full of holes," Summer said. "Shaw stepped out of bounds to tell you all this. Does that mean he questions the arrest?"

"He didn't step that far. Russell expects to get more details over the next few days."

"Like how she knew *when* Heather was going to the stones and how she got the book from William?" asked Janet.

"And how large the rock was and where exactly she hit her?" said Hobbs.

"In a rage, she might not know," Summer said.

"What about Rab's video?" Christine asked. "What was Agnes doing snooping around the church? Looking for higher inspiration up that scaffold? This is all very unsatisfactory."

The rest agreed. Hobbs, having nothing more to add, said goodnight. The others agreed with that, too, and went home. Along the way, Janet and Tallie stopped at Basant's.

"Good evening, Mrs. Janet. Tallie, so good to see you." Basant marked his place in his book and set it aside. "How may I help?"

"Something easy for supper," Janet said.

"Curried sweet potato pasties in whole meal short-crust," Basant said. "Fresh in my case and to die for—do please forgive me. I see that was not an appropriate sentiment."

"We've just had shocking news," Janet said.

Tallie put her hand on Janet's shoulder. "We can't give details, beyond saying that Agnes Black confessed to killing Heather Kilbride, and she's being charged."

Janet put her hand on Tallie's. "We're finding it hard to believe."

"I, too, find that hard to believe." Basant stood still, silent, calm, waiting.

After a few moments, Janet thanked him. "You're a good friend. We'll take two of the pasties, please. They sound perfect."

Basant put two of the hand-size pastries in a bag, then turned to the jars of old-fashioned sweets on the shelves behind him. He looked them over, finally taking one down. Without comment, he took a half a dozen of the candies and put them in another bag. He rang up their purchase and handed them the bags. "You two have good heads and good memories, so I know you will remember that the truths we tell ourselves are often not true, and the best lies come closest to the truth. As well, lies and truth often get into a right fankle."

"*Resolve*," Janet said. "That's our watchword."

"Then I've no doubt all will be well."

"What did you put in our wee bag?" Tallie asked.

"One of my chocolate favorites. Chelsea Whoppers."

Hobbs knocked on the bookshop door again the next morning.

"I'll go." Christine stalked to the door and unlocked it. Before moving aside to let him in, she demanded, "Well? What fresh misery have you brought us today?"

"An update. May I come in, Mrs. Robertson?"

Hobbs followed her to where the others stood in the doorway to the tearoom.

"Our morning meeting," Janet said. "A good time for an update. What have you heard?"

"Her confession fell apart."

"Because of the holes?" Tallie asked.

"One rather large hole. She has an alibi. Ian Atkinson saw her at the beach at Sgaildearg."

"Ian?" Janet said. "That seems so unlikely. What was he doing there?"

"Went for a walk, he says. He found her car poorly parked in the layby. Being Ian, he took a photo. He also felt the bonnet, which was cold to the touch, and he took photos of her doing tai chi. The photos are time-stamped. He spent quite a bit of time there not actually walking."

"So why did she confess?" Summer asked.

"That remains to be seen, but not by Russell. He's being replaced."

"Good Lord," Janet said.

"Good riddance," Christine said. "Why?"

"Shaw assumes mishandling of this case and possibly others."

"What happens next?" Tallie asked.

"The new man will be in touch, perhaps as early as this afternoon."

"I hope he's an improvement over the weasel," Christine said.

"Inspector Reddick will be glad to know your standards remain high, Mrs. Robertson."

⁂

Early that afternoon, Rab paused in showing Janet and Tallie the photographs he'd matted for the Farquhar celebration. "Reddick's just driven past," he said, "Parking round the back, I should think. I'll tell the others."

Christine and Summer came from the tearoom as the door jingled and their favorite detective inspector walked in.

"Afternoon, all," Reddick said. "I wish the circumstances were better, but it's nice to see you, just the same. Quantum is well and wishes he were here sipping whisky with Ranger."

Janet thought Quantum, Reddick's high-achiever Collie, would look right at home in a smoking jacket. "It's nice to see you, too, Inspector. You're looking—"

"Tired," Reddick cut in. "Never lie to a cop. I spent the night catching up on the case. Shaw's been kind and let me catch naps in the car."

"She was going to say you look like someone refreshingly competent," Christine said. "But carry on. We're clear of customers for the moment."

"Thank you, on all counts. I won't keep you long. Hobbs told me he brought you several updates. I have another. Mrs. Black explained her false confession. She says she was very fond of Fiona Clark, that she was shielding William Clark in Fiona's memory. She says Clark killed Ms. Kilbride because she had proof he was responsible for the drowning death of her brother in Lewis. That he failed to render aid, standing by as her brother drowned. She says now that wickedness is too much to bear."

"'Failed to render aid'?" Summer asked.

"Her words."

"This is more plausible than her first confession," Tallie said.

"How is she?" Janet asked. "That was a lot to carry around for almost a week."

"Shaken, but determined and convinced," Reddick said. "And wrong. Calum Donnelly died in Lewis the day Clark attended his wife's funeral here in Inversgail. An unassailable alibi. We are, however, taking Clark in for Ms. Kilbride's death."

"I hope you'll pardon our wary looks," Christine said. "The last twenty-four hours—*less* than twenty-four—have given us whiplash."

"Understandable. I'm sure you know that I can't go into details, but I don't doubt that you'll be learning more. I encourage your efforts, and I'll see you again, rather soon, I hope."

Christine motioned the other women closer after Reddick left. "Tell me if I'm wrong, but 'taking him in' isn't the same as charging him, is it? Not for a carefully worded man like Reddick. And all of that 'you'll be learning more' and 'I encourage your efforts' sound like we're to carry on. The real villain is feeling safe and secure right about now. What do you say we pull the rug out from underneath?"

"One small problem," Summer said. "Who is it?"

"If Christine's right about feeling safe and secure," Janet said, "we have time to do our jobs and catch a comfortable killer, too."

28

The women spent the afternoon taking turns at the office computer, with laptops by the fireplace, rereading Heather's notes, and exchanging ideas in twos and threes. Rab moved back and forth between tearoom and bookshop as needed. Ranger accepted compliments as they came. Janet and Tallie shared Basant's thoughts on truth and lies.

"We really only have two suspects left," Tallie said when she, Janet, and Christine were together. "Owen and Derek."

"The mystery men, too," Janet said. "But they remain a mystery. I'll contact Rhona and see if she's found out or remembered who hers is."

"If WC is out, because of Fiona's funeral, so is Derek," Christine said. "Minister of the church." She returned to the tearoom to let Summer know her instincts about Owen looked better and better.

Summer joined them, briefly, to say, "Can we believe Owen about when he got to town? Can we believe he had no idea what she's been writing the whole time they've been together? I wonder if he's got an ex somewhere." Then she went to sit opposite Ranger and puzzle over the many *xxx*s in the notes.

"Owen's in the insurance business," Tallie said. "Maybe he's sticking around to make sure he's safe and secure. That way, if things get wonky, he can tweak them."

"Agnes is a godsend, then," Janet said. "And WC. I wonder if Owen's even still in town." She texted Hobbs, then went to help Rab ring up a small herd of tourists buying postcards, guidebooks, and *Outlander*-inspired calendars.

"That video," Rab said, after the tourists moved on. "Agnes might have seen the Mini and been snooping round the church, working on her theory and looking for Clark. She might think he cracked Derek on the head, as well."

"Odd behavior," Janet said. "So is confessing to murder in someone's memory, no matter how fond one is of that person. Did you go to Fiona's funeral?"

"Aye. Mr. Brockie's last service before retiring. No dry eyes for both reasons."

"Was Derek his assistant then?"

"He came after. He's been good for the church. His stories brought some of the older lads back."

"Bible stories?"

"Same part of the world, but more recent, and more explosions. He worked in civil engineering." Rab gave a soft whistle. Ranger hopped from his chair, collected his tea towel, and trotted for the door.

"Leaving?" Janet asked. "Good heavens. It's time to close."

"Take care."

The women went through their closing procedures then looked at each other.

"Derek changed his career, did he?" Christine said. "So have we. But I need to get home to my old dears before they start calling me the odd lodger. If our villain is feeling safe and secure, we can have a night off."

"And I really do want to start on the local color piece," Summer said. "But call if anything comes up."

They said their goodnights. Tallie took Janet's arm and they walked home talking about odd behavior and what they might have for supper.

Tallie made up their minds to pasta with sautéed vegetables and pesto, and Janet wondered if Agnes had really confessed to shield Clark.

"That's the least believable part of her confession or re-confession," she said. "I can almost make myself believe WC killed Heather, but that Agnes confessed because she cherishes Fiona's memory? Uh-uh."

"The other parts of her story had details from the crime scene."

"Making the story more believable. But if she made up the Fiona part, does that mean she has some other reason for covering up for WC? Or was she covering up for someone else in the first confession and shifted the blame to WC and hasn't quite carried it off?"

"We've reached the 'right fankle' stage of Basant's wisdom about truth and lies," Tallie said, "but we still have some of his Chelsea Whoppers waiting for us. Supper first, Whoppers after, and while we cook and eat, we'll have light entertainment. I want to know what podcast Agnes listened to and listen between the lines."

"*She* said she read between the lines."

"But Heather's note put it better. She said listen. We don't know what Heather was listening to, but we know she and Agnes both found something useful."

"Agnes likes Derek's podcasts," Janet said. "She calls them Godcasts. But here's more of her odd behavior. The rainy day I gave her a ride to the church, Derek was listening to a crime-writing podcast. She had a problem with that—either the topic or because he was listening to it at the church. She didn't like it when I asked him about the attack, either. If we didn't know she has an alibi, I'd say that was guilty behavior."

Tallie had her phone out. "It isn't hard at all to find Derek's podcasts."

"Podcast and pesto pasta. Oh, goody."

The cats weren't interested in Derek's voice taking up space in their kitchen while Tallie sautéed onions, peppers, and mushrooms. After Janet fed them, they removed themselves. While she set the table, a text from Hobbs came in.

"He says Owen's in town through tomorrow," she told Tallie. "That gives us some urgency. I'll ask if he knows whether Owen has a late or ex-wife."

"Derek speaks in parables," Tallie said when she brought plates of pasta to the table.

"Hm?" Janet had tuned out while reading email.

"There's meaning between the lines in parables," Tallie said. "They instruct. They coach toward a desired behavior. He's telling stories in that vein."

"He's in the right line of work, then. You are, too. The pasta's delicious."

Rhona called after they'd finished, while Janet did the dishes.

"Sorry about the background chatter," Rhona said. "I'm at Nev's. I thought you might come in, or I'd have phoned sooner. I heard him."

"Heard who?"

"The man from the phone call. You asked had I heard him again. I did."

Janet heard Isla laughing in the background and Rhona telling her to wheesht. "I was listening to a podcast from the kirk. It's Derek. He's the one who called. He's a kind man."

"Thanks, Rhona. See you soon." She disconnected and called to Tallie in the living room. "That was Rhona calling from Nev's. She says it's Derek."

"It was clear when we came home," Tallie said.

Janet went to the door, "Not dreich. I said it's Derek. He—" Janet put her hand up. To forestall Tallie. To say it again. "It's Derek. It's dreich. Is that what Heather said? Not 'it's dreich,' 'it's *Derek*'?"

"They're close-*ish*, but it's not a great likeness."

"But Heather was dying, and I have American ears that might have been panicking."

Janet's phone rang. She still had one hand up and the phone in the other. She looked at both, looked at Tallie, and connected. "Hello. This is Janet."

"Agnes Black, here." Agnes's voice stretched thin, like the high string of a violin going even higher. "It's—I need your help. It's Derek."

"Tell me what you need, Agnes." Janet saw that Tallie had her phone at the ready.

"He's going to jump. He's at the headland. *We're* at the headland. He says he's almost out of hope, and he'll jump if the police come, but he'll talk to you so *please get here soon.*"

"I'm on my way, Agnes. Do you want to stay on the line? Agnes?" Janet slipped her phone in her pocket. "I need your phone," she said to Tallie, "and I need you to drive. You'll hear everything on the way."

"Where to?"

"The headland."

Janet called 9-9-9 with Tallie's phone as they ran for the car. She passed the details on to the call handler, stressing the need for caution, then apologized for having to disconnect. Agnes hadn't called back on her own phone. She used Tallie's again to try Hobbs. He didn't answer. Then she called Christine, and she did.

"I'll come," Christine said.

Janet disconnected and soon they were pulling into the library carpark. "Wait here for me," she said. "Wait for Christine and the police. Don't let anyone do anything reckless."

"Mom?"

"I'm not being reckless. I can do this."

Beyond the library, a stick figure of a man stood silhouetted against the sky, arms out as though he thought he had wings. Janet got out of the car and walked toward him, listening to the low, long *shoosh* of waves far below. She concentrated on the slap of cold air against her cheeks and nose with each step through wet grass.

A shape huddled near where Janet had debated retrieving the jacket so many days ago. When she drew closer, she saw it was Agnes in a rocking, silent heap. The forlorn posture pulled at Janet, but the unknown situation stopped her at a safe distance.

"Agnes, I'm here. It's Janet. Are you hurt?" Janet kept an eye on Derek and thought Agnes hadn't answered. Then she saw Agnes shaking her head as she continued rocking. "It's all right, Agnes. I'm going to talk to Derek. It's going to be all right." She knew she was probably encouraging herself more than reassuring Agnes.

Stars above. Solid rock below. Safety behind. Derek ahead at the edge.

He'd heard her and turned, making her believe for a terrible second that the turn would take him and her leaping heart over. "I did nothing," he said.

"Has anyone said you did?" Janet's feet slowed. She had to will each step forward.

"She did. She said I killed her brother."

"Did you?" Janet asked.

"I did nothing. Don't you see? It isn't yes or no. It's both. I stood back and did *nothing.* He was drowning and I didn't try to save him. I left. Went back to my house. But to save myself, to save my reputation, I told the simple truth, which was also a lie—that he died alone. And Heather was right. I can no longer live with that. I'm drowning."

"Will you leave me with that burden then? Standing here, unable to help or offer hope? Because I *can't* take another step to bring you away from that edge." Janet watched her hand reach toward him. "Will you come with me?"

29

Eight made a crowd around the fireplace at Yon Bonnie Books the next evening. Hobbs and Reddick carried four chairs from the tearoom. Christine and Summer brought tea, coffee, and shortbread.

"Decompression, decaf, and dessert," Christine said, handing around plates and cups.

Tallie and Summer sat in two of the tearoom chairs. Hobbs and Reddick took the other two. Janet, Christine, Agnes, and William sat in the more comfortable chairs, William in Ranger's favorite.

"Derek Spiers tells us he's an empathizer," Reddick said. "He sees that as a plus for his ministry and his writing. That's why he phoned the warning to Rhona McNeish for Lynsey Maclennan. He said he knew how upsetting Heather's research into the Murray case would be."

"He phoned me after the kayak incident," Clark said. "In case old devils reared their heads, as he put it. He asked to come round. I went to the church, instead. I showed him the Burns miniature. He said he knew about loss, and told a story about a sapper he knew, who visited him in Callanish. How there'd been an accident and the man drowned. That he could have helped, but he'd panicked. It was the kind of sympathy that wasn't sympathy. More about him seeking forgiveness. He didn't ask for it, but I could have—well, whatever I could have done, I didn't. I suppose

I panicked, too, and having left in a bit of a state I didn't remember leaving the book."

"Spiers said he meant to return it," Reddick said.

"There were never two attacks," Hobbs said. "In the first instance, he tripped on debris left by the stoneworkers, and hit his head. He now claims no memory of the incident."

"We might not be able to make it stick," Reddick said, "but his original story suggests premeditation. He set up a scenario of random attacks."

"When you asked Derek about the attack, Norman, you seemed skeptical," Agnes said. "That's when I became suspicious. I looked around myself, to see if I could find any evidence one way or the other. I had no idea what I was looking for, though, and gave up."

"How did he know Calum?" Janet asked.

"He was a civilian civil engineer involved in the same part of the Middle East as the sappers," Hobbs said. "He didn't know William or Gerald, but he met Calum."

"Last Sunday morning, he met Ms. Kilbride at the stone circle," Reddick said. "She suggested it. She told him her brother had gone to Lewis to see the Callanish Stones. That he'd told her he felt them deeper than his heart. Spiers remembers him as being somewhat spiritual, and said he felt safe meeting her at the circle because he thought she believed Clark witnessed the drowning. She apparently felt safe, too. She told him she was setting a trap. But if she meant to trap him, she failed. He 'reacted'—his word—then panicked. He had the book in his pocket. He left it to confuse the issue. He called it a plot point."

"His plots always do need help," Agnes said.

"Was leaving the book *also* premeditation?" Tallie asked.

"He says not," said Reddick.

"I knew I had to do something when you asked those questions for your article Friday morning," Agnes said to Summer. "And then you came into the shop for Heather's notes, Norman. So I hatched my plot. Sadly, my plots need help, as well."

"Why did you confess?" Summer asked.

"I never planned to sacrifice myself. He came to see me the night after you gave me the ride, Janet. He stays away from alcohol. He's a good man that way. But that night he'd been drinking, and he told a thinly veiled story about Heather's brother drowning, and the horrible scene at the Stuart Stones. It wasn't exactly a confession and not precisely a request, but he was obviously distraught, as well the worse for drink. I told him I understood. I thought if *I* confessed, it would prompt him to do the right thing. When my confession fell apart, he came round and pointed out where I'd read between the lines of his drunken story all wrong. That he'd been telling me about William. I told him I would set things right. William, I am sorry for the trouble I caused. I will admit, though, I was gae pleased when I thought you were the villain, and not Derek."

"I'm glad I made you happy, Agnes."

"What will happen now?" Christine asked.

"Tidy up," Reddick said. "Loose ends and stray chairs."

Chairs and dishes went back to the tearoom, and guests said goodnight and departed. Agnes, looking unbowed and unconcerned, was the last.

"You don't seem angry with Derek," Janet said as she unlocked the door to let Agnes out. "But he let you confess."

"He must have known they wouldn't believe me. It shows I didn't tell the best story I could have."

"He let you *confess*," Janet repeated, wanted to shout. "He let them arrest William."

"We're all frail," Agnes said. "Why would a man who professes to be of God be any different? Mind you, who was it said, 'Fool me once, shame on me. Fool me twice, watch your back'?" Agnes twiddled her fingers and walked away.

❧

The birthday celebration for Stuart Farquhar built throughout the afternoon at Yon Bonnie Books and Cakes and Tales Tearoom. Fiddles jigged in the inglenook. The lucky first twenty-five people through the door made those who followed jealous of their complementary celebration tea towels and book bags. Janet and Tallie stayed busy at the register assuaging that jealousy by selling towels and bags to all takers. Christine and Summer kept the refreshment table full. They'd decided against a gingerbread stone circle and instead served Basant's chocolate cake.

William Clark surprised them by dressing like Farquhar in one of the photographs Rab mounted for the exhibit. He looked quite dashing in plus fours and argyle socks. Ranger wore an argyle collar for the day, and the two graciously accepted when people asked for photos with them.

Summer stopped briefly at the sales counter as she zipped around collecting empty cups. "I finally got an answer from James," she said. "Remember when I thought he said Rab was following Heather? He wasn't talking *about* Rab. He was talking *to* him. Rab's writing an article for the paper about camera-trapping wildcats, and he was telling James about following one through the heather. That's why we didn't see Rab for a few days. He was filling in for one of the volunteer camera-trappers."

Hobbs, Reddick, and Shaw dropped in, Reddick with a book for Janet. "Found in the pocket of Ms. Kilbride's brother's jacket," he said and handed her an advance reading copy of *On Waiting: Short Meditations on a Lengthy Subject* by Calum Donnelly.

"By Calum, or by Heather writing as Calum?" Janet asked.

"You'll have to put on your literary detective hat and let us know," Reddick said.

"I look forward to it," Janet said. "Norman, we've heard what Rab was up to: camera-trapping wildcats. So at the Beaton Bridge that day, did you really think you saw one?"

"No," Hobbs said. "I saw Rab, and hoped *he'd* seen one."

Ian surprised Janet by passing up a piece of Basant's decadent cake. "It turns out I'm not getting any younger," he said. "Shocking news, isn't it? The medico suggested I start walking and clean up my diet."

"No more bacon?" Tallie asked.

Ian put a hand to his chest. "My broken heart became your bounty. By the way, Janet, I heard what you did for Derek. Talking him down from the ledge, as it were. Bravo. It's a tragic story, though. I liked Heather. She had some cracking good research methods. A flair for the dangerous. Good Lord, did you see *her* on the headland? Oh, yes, of course you did. We spoke."

"That was you? You were breaking up. I didn't recognize your voice. Where were you?"

"Doing my bit. Joined a search and rescue team." Ian's tweed chest expanded.

"Then why did you call me?" Janet asked. "Why didn't you tell your team you saw her?"

"It got quite tense out there on the water. They needed to concentrate with no distractions. The best way for me to help was to sit well out of the way and observe in silence. I had my binocs with me, and I saw her there. I tried to get word to the man nearest me, but his concentration was total, and he didn't hear me. So I gave you a call. I knew you'd get the message where it needed to go."

"Why didn't you call Norman?" Tallie asked.

"I did. Perhaps he thought it was a prank call."

Agnes and Sheila stopped by to say they'd like to continue meeting in the shop. "We've chosen our name," Sheila said. "We're the Inglenook Inkers."

Toward the end of the day, Janet and Christine had a moment to catch up.

"As fine as any garden party the queen puts on at Holyrood," Christine said.

"It is. Christine, I've been meaning to ask, do you purposely channel an inner Queen Elizabeth? Do you know how much you resemble her when she's needed? When *you're* needed."

"Is that meant to be a compliment?" Christine asked. "The queen is ancient."

"Not in looks, you ninny. In attitude. As though you assume ermine-edged robes. It's a lovely thing to witness. I makes me proud to know you."

"Havers, Janet. Pure havers."

ACKNOWLEDGMENTS

Two of my favorite words are *thank* and *you*. Together, they do their job exactly right. This book wouldn't be what it is without these kind people, so to them I say thank you.

For lending their names and letting me put words in their mouth—Sharon Davis, James Haviland, and Arati, Basant, and Puja Paudel.

For illumination on whether one is *in* or *on* a Scottish island—Caroline Wickham-Jones.

For consultation on the word *kreesal*—Ann Campbell and Cammy MacRae.

For sharing photographs of their miniature books—James Haviland and Debbie Mandel.

For lending their dogs—Marthalee Wyatt Beckington and Tim and Dana Thompson.

For the careful reading and comments that helped me stop hyperventilating and start digging deeper to improve this book—Pegasus editor Katie McGuire.

For every single book—my agent Cynthia Manson.

For poetry, camaraderie, commas, tea, and everything about our lovely MABs—Janice N. Harrington and Betsy Hearne.

For always—Mike Thompson.